He had he[...]ant fingers with [...]ed, as if he didn[...]spend all his time sitting behind a desk analyzing people. And when he slipped them over the curve of her ear, Tess shivered....

He leaned closer, using a cotton swab to gently clean her cut. "What were you thinking out there in the pool—right before you started to go under?"

His breath was warm against her cheek. Tess shook her head. Concentrating on his words, not on what he was doing to her body. "I don't know. I can't remember. It's all a blur. Just a big blur."

As she spoke, Tess was conscious of how close he was. His mouth was only inches from hers. It would be so simple to lift her head and quickly brush her lips across his, to run her tongue along the swell of his bottom lip and then carefully, slowly suck it in.

She tightened her fingers on the edge of the sheet. What was she thinking? Please don't let me make a total fool out of myself, she thought. The stakes are much too high.

"Do you trust me enough to let me help you, Tess?"

Dear Harlequin Intrigue Reader,

We have another month of spine-tingling romantic thrillers lined up for you—starting with the much anticipated second book in Joanna Wayne's tantalizing miniseries duo, HIDDEN PASSIONS: FULL MOON MADNESS. In *Just Before Dawn,* a reclusive mountain man vows to get to the bottom of a single mother's terrifying nightmares before darkness closes in.

Award-winning author Leigh Riker makes an exciting debut in the Harlequin Intrigue line this May with *Double Take.* Next, pulses race out of control in *Mask of a Hunter* by Sylvie Kurtz—the second installment in THE SEEKERS—when a tough operative's cover story as doting lover to a pretty librarian threatens to blow up.

Be there from the beginning of our brand-new in-line continuity, SHOTGUN SALLYS! In this exciting trilogy, three young women friends uncover a scandal in the town of Mustang Valley, Texas, that puts their lives—and the lives of the men they love—on the line. Don't miss *Out for Justice* by Susan Kearney.

To wrap up a month of can't-miss romantic suspense, Doreen Roberts debuts in the Harlequin Intrigue line with *Official Duty,* the next title in our COWBOY COPS thematic promotion. It's a double-murder investigation that forces a woman out of hiding to face her perilous past…and her pent-up feelings for the sexy sheriff who still has her heart in custody. Last but certainly not least, *Emergency Contact* by Susan Peterson—part of our DEAD BOLT promotion—is an edgy psychological thriller about a traumatized amnesiac who may have been brainwashed to do the unthinkable….

Enjoy all our selections this month!

Sincerely,

Denise O'Sullivan
Senior Editor,
Harlequin Intrigue

EMERGENCY CONTACT
SUSAN PETERSON

HARLEQUIN®

TORONTO • NEW YORK • LONDON
AMSTERDAM • PARIS • SYDNEY • HAMBURG
STOCKHOLM • ATHENS • TOKYO • MILAN • MADRID
PRAGUE • WARSAW • BUDAPEST • AUCKLAND

ISBN 0-373-22776-0

EMERGENCY CONTACT

Copyright © 2004 by Susan Peterson

This edition published by arrangement with Harlequin Books S.A.

® and TM are trademarks of the publisher. Trademarks indicated with ® are registered in the United States Patent and Trademark Office, the Canadian Trade Marks Office and in other countries.

www.eHarlequin.com

Printed in U.S.A.

ABOUT THE AUTHOR

A devoted *Star Trek* fan, Susan Peterson wrote her first science-fiction novel at the age of thirteen. But unlike other *Star Trek* fan writers, in Susan's novel she made sure that Mr. Spock fell in love. Unfortunately, what she didn't take into consideration was the fact that falling in love and pursuing a life of total logic didn't exactly go hand in hand. In any case, it was then that she realized that she was a hopeless romantic, a person who needed the happily-ever-after ending. But it wasn't until later in life, after pursuing careers in intensive care nursing and school psychology, that Susan finally found the time to pursue a career in writing. An ardent fan of psychological thrillers and suspense, Susan combined her love of romance and suspense into several manuscripts targeted to the Harlequin Intrigue line. Getting the go-ahead to write for this line was a dream come true for her.

Susan lives in a small town in northern New York with her son, Kevin, her nutball dog, Ozzie, Phoenix the cat and Lex the six-toed menace (a new kitten). Susan loves to hear from readers. E-mail her at SusanPetersonHI@aol.com or visit her Web site at susanpeterson.net.

Books by Susan Peterson

HARLEQUIN INTRIGUE
751—CONCEALED WEAPON
776—EMERGENCY CONTACT

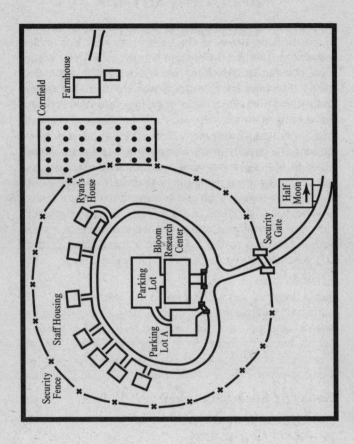

Cornfield

Farmhouse

Ryan's House

Staff Housing

Security Fence

Bloom Research Center

Parking Lot

Parking Lot A

Security Gate

Half Moon

CAST OF CHARACTERS

Tess Doe (Ross)—Although unaware of her own identity, Tess knows that she can trust no one, including gentle but probing psychiatrist Ryan Donovan, called in to treat her. Instinct tells her that her enemies are closing in and she must escape before time runs out.

Ryan Donovan, M.D.—Disillusioned with clinical work, he returns to his hometown, determined to bury himself in research. But he quickly finds himself intriguingly involved with the beautiful but perplexing amnesiac who walked out of a local cornfield.

Gen. Thomas Flynn—A member of the ultraconservative organization The Patriot's Foundation of Family Values, Flynn is a decisive, arrogant man who decides to change the political course of a country by whatever means possible.

Sidney Bloom, M.D.—A brilliant scientist who vehemently believes in the old adage The End Justifies the Means.

Ian McCaffery—A human machine bent on making sure his superior's plans for change come to fruition.

For you, Dad.
I know we haven't always seen eye to eye, but your
deep love, warm support and total belief in my talent
have always made me feel appreciated. I love being
one of your four daughters.

Thanks to my critique partners Chris Wenger,
Linda Bleser & Tracy Rysavy. You made this all possible.

A special thanks to Patricia Otto, R.N. and Eric Lemza
for their wonderful medical insights. Any medical errors
are totally my fault and were done in order
to make this work of fiction possible.

Chapter One

The morning Tess Doe walked naked out of the Half Moon, Iowa, cornfield, psychiatrist Ryan Donovan was three miles away, wolfing down one of Sally Todd's homemade sugar doughnuts and sipping some of her fresh-brewed coffee.

"You want a dozen of them to go, Doc?" Sally asked, backing out of the kitchen and balancing a huge metal tray of iced apple turnovers in one hand. She set the tray onto the counter and wiped her flour-smudged hands on her apron.

"Alice will kill me if I bring any of that stuff into the office," Ryan said, using the corner of a paper napkin to swipe at his mouth.

Shortly after meeting him, his new secretary had lamented to every other secretary on their floor that her new boss could eat like a horse and never gain an ounce. Ryan had taken it as fair warning not to bring in the usual office goodies.

"Pish-posh, the girl just needs to accept the fact that she comes from good farm stock. She needs to celebrate her largeness."

Ryan didn't have a response to that one. Sometimes Sally's hometown philosophy wasn't debatable. He had a feeling this was one of those times.

Sally grabbed a white baker's bag off the shelf and snapped it open. Before he could stop her, she'd shoved a dozen sugar and bavarian-cream doughnuts inside and set it on the counter in front of him.

"Did you hear those helicopters overhead last night?" she asked.

"Heard something hovering overhead, but I didn't have time to go look." Ryan took a sip of coffee. If there was anything Sally Todd liked better than baking, it was exchanging a bit of gossip.

"When I stopped for gas this morning, Gary said he thought he saw an explosion over by the Carson farm," Sally said. "But by the time he got there it was too dark to see anything."

"Wonderful," Ryan said dryly. "Now we'll have Gary telling everyone that aliens have landed in Half Moon."

"Don't be making fun of poor Gary. People are a tad spooked with that research center being here."

Ryan laughed. "Talk about small town paranoia. All we're doing is boring pharmaceutical research."

Before Sally could comment, her phone rang and she reached around to answer it. Ryan pulled a ten-dollar bill out of his wallet, set it on the counter, and picked up the bag of doughnuts. He nodded to Sally, prepared to head out to work. But she waved at him, signaling for him to wait.

A few seconds later, she hung up the phone. "That was the police dispatcher. She said the Chief is looking for you. Wants you to meet him out at the Carson farm."

Ryan frowned. "Chief Cole wants to see me?"

"Yep, right away."

Puzzled, Ryan shrugged. "Okay, I'll head out there."

He waved and strolled out onto the main street of Half Moon. A few cars and pickup trucks were parked along Station Street, the main drag through town. Most belonged to the store owners that occupied the not-so-bustling shopping strip that made up downtown Half Moon. No large malls or superstores in this tiny town. But Ryan figured he'd adjust. He'd have to.

Two months ago, weary from battling traffic and short-tempered city folks, he had quit his staff position at Boston's Neuropsychiatric Hospital and returned home to Half Moon, a tiny, rural farming community. It was only luck that his old mentor, Dr. Sidney Bloom, had a position open for him at the Half Moon Research Center, a small, private facility dedicated to neuropsychiatric research.

Ryan shook his head. Who was he kidding? Crowds, traffic and a busy schedule hadn't prompted his decision to leave. Failure had forced him to leave. There wasn't much room for a psychiatrist who didn't know how to function better than a first-year medical student. A psychiatrist who failed his patients.

He breathed deep, tasting the sweet warmth of summer, and raked a restless hand through his hair. Time to quit analyzing everything. Some things were better left alone. Research, not clinical work, was where he needed to concentrate his talents.

He climbed into his dusty BMW and took off out of town. Fifteen minutes later, he pulled up the winding dirt driveway leading to the Carson farm.

On the front lawn, next to one of Betty Carson's carefully tended flower beds, stood Half Moon's Chief of Police Ted Cole and Bud Carson. Bud's expression was worried enough to send a jolt of concern through Ryan. Not much rattled Bud. Not even the night a private patient had left the research facility and climbed through the downstairs window of his house and started cooking scrambled eggs in the Carsons' kitchen.

Ryan pulled up behind Cole's truck and jumped out. "Morning, gentlemen. What's the big emergency?"

Chief Cole scowled. "Another nutcase has escaped from the center and landed in Bud's cornfield."

"Chief, people don't *escape* from the Half Moon Research Center," Ryan said patiently. "Sometimes people leave the center without signing out or letting anyone know where they're going, but they're at the center of their own free will."

Chief Cole snorted. "Still means they're going over the wall, if you ask me." He nodded his head in Bud Carson's direction. "The nut job scared the stuffing out of poor Bud here."

Ryan smiled at the elderly farmer. "You do look a little rattled, Bud."

Bud ran a gnarled hand through his thinning gray hair. "I have good reason to, Doc. I was out back, taking a look at the corn when I heard something rustling. I looked up and out steps this woman. Damn near dropped my teeth."

Cole shot a sly sideways grin at his friend and then elbowed him in the side. "She got old Bud's pulse aracing, too."

Ryan raised a questioning eyebrow in the farmer's direction.

"She was buck naked, Doc," Bud explained. A twinge of red pinked the tip of the man's ears. "Not a stitch on. Good thing Betty brought me some of that new denture adhesive. Otherwise I might 'ave lost 'em for sure."

Ryan glanced at the Chief. "I haven't heard anything about anyone leaving the center without permission. Did you call Dr. Bloom?"

The Chief nodded. "He was too busy to talk to me. I just got some flunky of his. I figured you'd be easier to deal with."

"I'll help in any way I can," Ryan said.

After nodding to the two men, Ryan took the wooden porch steps two at a time. As he pulled open the screen door and stepped into the cheery farm kitchen, Betty Carson greeted him. "I'm glad they found you, Ryan. She's in the living room. Go easy on her. Poor thing is as scared as a newborn baby rabbit.''

Ryan gave Betty a reassuring smile. ''I'll be gentle.''

He stepped around her and walked into the dimly lit living room. Like a lot of farm folks, Betty Carson kept the main part of the house cool by drawing heavy curtains to block the hot morning sun. The front room was dark, the furniture sitting amidst a heavy gloom.

In spite of the poor light, Ryan spotted the woman immediately. She sat in the cushioned easy chair occupying the far corner of the room. She was covered from neck to feet with a hand-stitched quilt—one of Betty's legendary homemade quilts, no doubt. Her legs were drawn up beneath the blanket, and her chin, small with a slight indentation in it, rested on her knees.

She watched him from beneath a fringe of dark lashes. Lashes so dark they were startling when contrasted with the fall of white-blond hair spread out like a shawl across her slender shoulders.

But it was the wide, iridescent green eyes beneath the straight line of bangs that caught and held his attention, sending a deep and intense awareness shooting through him. He couldn't help but be struck by her stunning beauty.

''Good morning,'' he said softly. ''My name is Donovan. Ryan Donovan. I'm a doctor.''

At the word *doctor,* she stiffened a bit, her expression less friendly. ''I didn't ask for a doctor,'' she said. ''And I don't need one.''

He smiled. ''Good, because I'm in the mood to just talk. Is that all right with you?''

She stared at him in silence, her gaze penetrating, almost haunting in its directness. It seemed to sear him with a heat that was more piercing than twin lasers. But she didn't lift her head off her knees or make any other move to indicate she was opposed to his suggestion.

Ryan crossed the room, moving slowly, so as not to crowd or frighten her. She followed his progress with her eyes, their color radiating an unblinking brilliance in the dimness of the room. She didn't seem tense or skittish, simply wary, as if prepared for anything.

He pointed to the couch directly across from her. "Do you mind if I sit down?"

She shrugged. "Do what you like. This isn't my house."

Ryan leaned forward to catch her words, the sound so soft and light it was like a breeze brushing past his ear. The effect startled him and he struggled to regain his composure, feeling oddly off balance.

What the hell was going on? He was never rattled when meeting a patient. He was the man always in control, always ready to handle the situation. The interns in the E.R. used to love it when he was the attending on-call and showed up to consult on a case. No matter how off-the-wall the E.R. walk-ins got, the interns knew that Ryan Donovan could handle them without breaking a sweat.

He sat down and crossed one leg over the other, taking a moment to get a feel for the situation. As he slid an arm along the back of the couch, he tried to impart an air of calm he didn't feel. But the last thing he wanted to do was spook her.

"The Carsons asked me to come because they were concerned that you might be injured." Ryan waited, but when she didn't respond, he continued. "They thought you might have been in an accident."

She shook her head and the perfect cut of bangs ruffled a bit with the movement of her head. They parted to reveal a small cut on her forehead, but it wasn't bleeding and didn't appear very deep.

"I don't think I was in an accident."

She spoke each word clearly, but there was a slight hesitation, as if she was struggling to form the words before saying them. Perhaps the pause indicated some kind of head trauma, he thought. She seemed oblivious to the cut on her head.

"May I ask your name?"

"Tess." The small frown was back between her brows, and she looked as though she might have searched for the name, dug it up from somewhere deep inside. "My name is Tess," she said slowly.

Ryan waited a beat and then asked, "No last name?"

Beneath the quilt, her hands moved, tightening around her knees. "Just Tess." Her shoulders braced as if anticipating his next question.

Ryan attempted to inject some lightness into the tenseness that hovered between them. "I don't know too many people who go by only one name."

She lifted her eyes, her gaze slightly mocking. "Cher. Batman. Garfield."

He had to laugh. "Okay, you've got me there. A famous celebrity and two equally well-known cartoon characters. Are you telling me you're someone famous?"

She shook her head and the hair shimmered in the soft light. Her chin settled back on top of her knees. "No, I'm not famous."

"Can you tell me how you got into the Carsons' cornfield?"

"I walked."

"Yes, but where were you before you walked into the field?"

"Somewhere else."

Ryan tried another tack. "I haven't seen you around here before. Do you live close by?"

For the first time, she smiled, a slight trembling stretch of her lips, as if she were afraid of him but wanted to come across as compliant. Cooperative. As if she hoped that if she kept things on an even keel, everything would be all right and he'd leave her alone.

"No. I don't live close by. I'm visiting."

"Who did you come to visit? Perhaps we could contact them and tell them you're here."

She shook her head. "There's no need. Betty and Bud are out in the kitchen. They know I'm here."

"You're here visiting the Carsons?" Try as he might, Ryan couldn't keep the confusion out of his voice.

"Yes, this is their house." She sat forward, the tiny frown popping up between two delicately arched eyebrows again. "You didn't know this was the Carsons' house? Are you lost?"

Ryan rubbed the side of his jaw. It wasn't often that patients were able to get around him so easily. "No. I'm not lost. I thought you might be the one who was lost or confused."

She settled back again and smiled with relief. "No, I'm not lost, either."

Ryan decided that he needed to get a bit more direct. Otherwise they were going to talk in circles all morning. "You said you were visiting the Carsons. But the Carsons don't seem to know you. Why would you visit people you don't know?"

Tess smiled serenely. "New friends are important. Bud and Betty are my new friends."

Ryan tried to keep his exasperation from showing. "Where specifically were you before you came to Half Moon," he asked.

"I told you, I was somewhere else."

Ryan swallowed hard. This was going nowhere. Maybe his ex-boss's assessment of his clinical skills were right. Perhaps he had lost his touch. "I noticed you have a small cut on your forehead. Did that happen last night?"

Tess stared at him, her emerald-green eyes seeming to cut

right through him. "Yes. I tripped and fell in the dark. It's nothing. A small scratch."

"I'd like to examine it, if you'll let me."

She sighed, a tiny puff of air passing between lush, slightly parted lips. Ryan waited. The corner clock clicked off the minutes as she considered his offer.

Finally she nodded, her gaze still wary. "I guess it would be all right."

Ryan stood up and moved over next to her. Tess tilted her head back, giving him access to her forehead. He brushed aside her silky bangs, his fingers sliding over her soft skin. Air hissed between her teeth as he touched the edges of the cut.

"I'm sorry. I didn't mean to hurt you."

"It—it's all right. Stings a bit, but you have a very gentle touch."

Ryan leaned across her. "I'm going to turn on the light so I can see it better."

She slid an arm out from beneath the blanket and touched him, her fingers resting lightly on his forearm. A shiver shot up his arm and Ryan paused, glancing down into the clear green of her eyes.

"Please, the light hurts my eyes," she said.

Ryan laid his hand over hers. "It's important that I check your pupils, Tess. The fall might have given you a concussion."

She nodded her understanding and slipped her hand from beneath his. Ryan tried to ignore the twinge of regret when she pulled away.

He reached into his pocket and pulled out a penlight. A quick check of both pupils told him that in spite of the light hurting, her pupil reaction was fine.

Perhaps a mild concussion. It didn't exactly explain her extreme mental confusion, unless she'd been in an accident and couldn't remember the details.

He crouched down in front of her. "Do you know what today's date is?"

"Of course."

He waited.

She tilted her head to the side. "I'm sorry. Have *you* forgotten the date?"

Ryan bit back a grin. "No, Tess. I'm checking to see if you remember. You might have a head injury. I'm checking your memory."

The frown popped up between her brows again. "But I just told you that I know the date. Don't you believe me?"

Ryan paused. He didn't want to anger her or shut her down so that she refused to cooperate. He tried a lighter approach. "Any chance you'd humor me and just tell me the date?"

"July tenth."

"Good. Now, can you tell me the capital of Rhode Island?"

A slight twinkle of humor entered those exquisite eyes. "You're not going to start asking math questions next, are you? Because I'm really lousy at math."

Whatever had happened to her, Tess had managed to maintain her sense of humor. He held up a hand in mock Scout's honor. "I promise, no math questions."

From across the room, Betty interrupted. "Isn't that enough questions, Doc?"

Ryan glanced over one shoulder. "It's okay, Betty. I'm not hurting her."

"I know that. But you're scaring her. I can tell." Betty walked into the room, her dark eyes watching the young girl with motherly compassion. "The poor child must be exhausted. This is no way to treat a person who's been through what she's been through."

"But that's what I'm trying to determine—what she's been through." Ryan didn't bother to hide the hint of irritation. Unlike most interviews he conducted, he definitely wasn't in control of this one. But then it wasn't every day that he had to conduct an initial assessment in the living room of one of his neighbor's houses.

"Providence," Tess said softly.

They both turned to look at her. "Providence is the capital of Rhode Island. And I feel fine—just a little hungry."

The hard-nosed farm wife shot a triumphant look in Ryan's direction. "Of course you are, dear. I'm going to make you a nice stack of buttermilk pancakes." She glared at Ryan. "And if you're done asking silly questions, you're welcome to have some, too."

Tess stood, the huge quilt draped around her like a tent. As she walked toward the archway leading to the kitchen, the quilt caught on the end of the couch, slid off her shoulders and fell to the floor. Seemingly unaware of her naked condition, Tess continued on toward the kitchen, her bare feet padding softly on the hardwood floor.

Ryan blinked and swallowed hard. Lord, give me strength, he muttered. A true goddess walked among them. A goddess with legs that went on forever and a body so magnificently flawless that his tongue stuck to the roof of his mouth.

He tried not to stare, but he had a perfect view of her firm buttocks as she walked away. Muscle dimpled one firm cheek as she moved, and Ryan forced himself to breathe.

She turned to glance at him and Ryan struggled to keep his mouth from falling open. Her breasts were high and firm, and as her hair swung forward, each strand reflected an almost blinding sheen of white in the faint light. The fall of white gold fell over her slender shoulders and onto her chest, brushing the dark, taut nipples that peeped through the silky strands.

The fact that she seemed totally unaware of her nakedness

wasn't lost on Ryan. It was an unusual reaction and one he tucked away for later consideration.

"Are you coming, Doctor?" she asked innocently before turning and continuing on into the kitchen.

Ryan stumbled, getting to his feet, raising a hand to stop her, but he couldn't get any words out. Damn. He had expected beauty, but this went way beyond even that. Way beyond.

A shaft of heat shot through him and settled deep in the pit of his belly. Sweat dampened his hands. He sucked hot air.

"Oh, my," Betty blurted out as Tess brushed past.

A string of startled curses and the sound of chairs scraping frantically across the linoleum told Ryan he wasn't the only male getting an eyeful.

He bent down and picked up the quilt. "If I were you, Betty, I'd find Tess something a little more permanent than a blanket. Otherwise, none of us are going to be able to concentrate on your good cooking."

Betty snatched the quilt out of his hand and marched through the archway into the kitchen. "Close your eyes, all of you!" she ordered in the crisp tones of a drill sergeant.

Ryan followed, concern replacing his amusement. Tess might be beautiful, but her confused mental state and the hesitation in her speech worried him. If she was from the center, it would be a relatively easy task to get her back there.

But he couldn't deny the small tug of regret that pulled at him. He didn't like the possibility of her being a patient at the center. Patients came to the center because they had a long history of not responding to the more traditional medications and treatments. Most of their families had given up hope of them ever living normal, productive lives, and the patients came because they were desperate to try some of the more experimental, riskier treatments.

The thought of Tess, a vibrant, beautiful young woman, being one of those desperate individuals, unresponsive to other treatments, saddened Ryan.

If there was anything he'd learned over years of practice, it was that the results of experimental treatments benefited future generations, not the people who subjected themselves to it in the here and now. Tess might be a pioneer, but if she was from the center, her prognosis was most likely poor.

Washington, D.C.

"CALL FOR YOU, General Flynn. Line two, sir."

General Thomas Flynn swallowed his irritation at the interruption and swung his desk chair away from his office window. He reached out and stabbed the intercom key. "I'm busy, Lieutenant. Take a message please."

"It's a Dr. Sidney Bloom, sir," Lieutenant Sanders said, her soft feminine tones drifting musically through the intercom. "He's somewhat insistent that he speak with you immediately, sir."

General Flynn ran an impatient hand through the close-cropped iron-gray hair. It never ceased to annoy him that someone in personnel had taken it upon himself to assign him a female aide.

Not that Flynn advertised his prejudice against women in the military. No siree. He wasn't a fool. He knew what the twenty-first-century army was all about—a dumbing down of the troops and a lowering of standards.

"I'll take the call, Lieutenant." Flynn punched the button for line two and picked up the receiver. "Why are you calling me here?" He didn't bother to keep the anger from seeping into his voice.

"You asked to be kept informed of anything having to do with the project. I didn't want to wait any longer." Dr. Sidney Bloom's cool tones conveyed his lack of intimidation.

Flynn reached down and flicked a switch on the side of the phone, the one that scrambled anything and everything that came through the phone. "What's the problem? I'd prefer to keep any specifics out of this conversation."

"My sentiments exactly, General."

Flynn could hear the bristle of indignation in Bloom's voice. From his dealings with him, Flynn knew that the doctor wasn't used to being treated as a flunky. It brought a smile to Flynn's lips. He couldn't deny that he took a certain amount of pleasure in doing exactly that. He waited for the doctor to continue.

"Our subject took off last night. She knocked out a guard and escaped the grounds." Before Flynn could react, Bloom rushed to add, "But we were able to locate her fairly quickly. Unfortunately, we haven't been able to get her back here to the center."

Flynn's hand tightened so hard on the receiver that his fingers ached. "What do you mean she took off? I thought you had a handle on things down there. She's supposed to begin her assignment in a week."

"I realize that, General. Why do you think I insisted on talking to you instead of being put off by your trained seal in the front office."

Flynn didn't mind his own bias against his aide, but he didn't appreciate anyone else making comments. "Lieutenant Sanders was only following my instructions. Why isn't the subject back at the facility? Has she spoken to anyone?"

"Slow down, General. One question at a time," Bloom said softly.

Flynn shifted the phone to his other ear and took a deep breath. "Don't ever tell me what to do, Bloom. We're paying the bills for your little research facility out there in God's country. Without us, you're just another egghead looking for funding." He paused for a moment to savor the shocked silence on the other end of the phone. Nothing worked better than threatening a greedy research scientist with cutting off his funding. "Now that we've got that straight, why don't you tell me what happened and keep it short."

"Apparently her accomplice had a car waiting for them. When my men gave chase, they crashed through the perimeter fence."

"Let me guess—you're calling because your men screwed things up?"

Silence hummed on the line, but Flynn waited, his impatience building.

"My men were concerned they'd get away," Bloom said, his voice rising a bit as he tried to explain. "They were forced to shoot the accomplice."

"He's dead?"

"Yes."

Flynn sighed. "I hope you're calling to tell me that they were able to take our subject back into custody."

Bloom sucked air. "Unfortunately not. She took off across the field, and in the dark my men were unable to find her."

"Then at least reassure me that your men were able to sanitize the crash scene before the local authorities arrived."

Another long pause.

"Well, they had time to wipe the car down," Bloom said. "But a local farmer must have heard the commotion and came to investigate. They were forced to leave before removing the body."

A searing heat churned in Flynn's stomach. "Wonderful. And where is the test subject? Has she been found yet?"

"We know *where* she is, we just haven't been able to take her back into custody yet. My men tell me that she's inside the farmer's house. Uh, the chief of police is there, too."

"How cozy. Do we know if she's been connected to the body or the car?"

"Not yet." Bloom paused again. "We do, however, have a more serious problem."

Flynn closed his eyes and rubbed the bridge of his nose. Of course there was a more serious problem. He couldn't expect anything less. "Please, enlighten me."

"Reports indicate that the subject doesn't remember who she is."

Flynn came up out of his seat, his fist hitting the center of his thick green desk blotter. "What's that supposed to mean?" He glanced toward the door, concerned his roar might have drifted out through the steel door into the outer office. There was no knock on the door.

"She has amnesia—no memory of who she is or why she's there. My man says that she has a small cut on her forehead. She might have fallen or hit the dashboard of the car. It's possible the recent drugs and programming have added to make the injury a little more than a mild concussion."

"It's possible? What the hell am I paying you for if it's not to give me answers, Doctor?" Flynn forced himself to take a deep, cleansing breath. Anger ripped through his veins, heating his face and neck. If he didn't calm down, he'd have a coronary right here in the office and never live to see the changes he'd worked so hard to bring about.

"Are you still there, General?"

"Of course I'm still here, you idiot," Flynn snapped. "Where is she now?"

"One of my new doctors—someone not connected to the project—is out at the farmhouse talking to her right now."

"Are you insane?"

Silence met Flynn's question.

"Get the unauthorized physician off the case immediately. Tell him you're taking over. And while we're on the subject, why the hell do you have someone not connected to the project working at the facility?''

"Ryan Donovan is an old student of mine. A brilliant researcher and clinician. He finally took me up on my offer to leave Boston and come help me with some of my research.''

"I don't care if he's the Albert Einstein of medical research. It's too risky having him involved.''

"But Donovan has done some interesting research that dovetails perfectly with mine. There are no plans for him to be directly involved in the project. He'll continue his research without any knowledge of what we're doing.''

Flynn rubbed the side of his jaw, unable to quiet the rumblings of concern from shooting acid into his already aching stomach. "I don't like this, Bloom. I don't like it one bit. Get her back under lock and key, and then call me. I don't plan on losing this window of opportunity because you can't arrange for the proper amount of security.''

"I'll get back to you in an hour or so. Everything is under control.''

Flynn snorted his disbelief. "If everything was under control she'd be in her room, and you'd be finishing up the final touches on her programming.'' He slammed the phone down.

Less than a week to go before the *test subject* was scheduled to perform her duty and she'd taken off like a jackrabbit on speed.

Flynn sighed and got to his feet. Walking over to the window, he stared down at the river and clasped his hands behind his back. Things were starting to unravel.

Perhaps he needed to make a trip to Half Moon. To really check on his investment and see if there was still time to carry out his plans. After all, the decision to control the destiny of United States politics demanded one's full and undivided attention.

Chapter Two

Tess lifted her fork and bit into the syrup-soaked pancake. Sweetness burst across her tongue, and she sat back to savor it. She hadn't realized until that moment how truly hungry she was.

As she chewed, she tried hard to remember the last time she'd eaten. Nothing came. No memory of food or any other interesting tidbit about her life floated to the surface. What she felt was a total void.

She shifted slightly on the hardwood chair, thankful that Betty had found some clothes for her. Strange, but until the moment Betty had put an arm around her and ushered her into the tiny laundry room off the kitchen, Tess had no idea she was naked. It was if her mind had lost its ability to register anything about herself. As if she'd suddenly become this clean slate, aware of nothing.

The jeans Betty had given her were too big, and none of the belts Betty offered had fit her small waist. So, she'd been reduced to using a piece of clothesline to keep them from falling down around her knees.

The T-shirt, one with a logo of a giant combine and *Mid-State Farm Equipment* lettered across the pocket was long enough and boxy enough to serve as a dress. One side kept sliding down, baring one shoulder, and she had to keep hitching it up. But the clothes were soft, smelled freshly laundered and rested smooth as silk against her skin.

She took another bite and then glanced around, surprised to find everyone's attention focused directly on her. Four pairs of eyes held the same questioning look, but Tess knew she didn't have any of the answers.

Heck, she couldn't even answer her own questions, and things didn't get much scarier than that. She was totally lost. No matter how hard she tried, she couldn't remember anything other than her first name.

And even then, she wasn't sure that was her name. It was simply the one that had popped into her head when Donovan had asked her for a name. But that sure didn't mean it was the right one. She'd realized fairly quickly that no amount of trying to force the memories was going to help.

Even now, as she tried to pull something—anything—out of the confusion swirling around in her brain, a stab of pain shot through the center of her head. The harder she tried, the more it hurt. It was as if someone had done a nasty root canal on her without the required Novocain.

She squeezed her eyes shut.

"Tess, are you all right?"

She recognized the voice immediately. Ryan Donovan. The handsome doctor's voice. She cringed inwardly. She'd barely met him and already she was thinking of him in terms of looks.

But what bothered her even more was the fact that he seemed to hold some kind of power over her—at least his voice seemed to possess that kind of power. The sound of it soothed her jitteriness. She wasn't sure why but it unsettled her.

She kept her eyes shut, determined not to respond to those deep raspy tones with the velvet undertone to it. Something told her that if she looked at him, she'd be giving in, submitting to him in some way. And as crazy as that sounded, Tess wasn't about to let it happen.

But as soon as the thought flashed into her consciousness, she questioned it. Why in God's name would she think that a doctor, a man who insisted he only wanted to help her, was out to hurt her? He was a healer, held to a higher oath. Dedicated to helping people. Wasn't he?

Finally, Tess looked up, steeling herself to meet his gaze, and she immediately found herself drowning in a sea of Caribbean blue. She bit her bottom lip, trying to keep her focus. His eyes were so stunningly blue that she found it hard to breathe. Hard to look away. He smiled at her and she felt as though she might melt.

It wasn't a particularly beautiful face. Rather, it was a tough face, one that was in direct contrast to the velvety tones of his hypnotic voice. A face shadowed with lines of fatigue beneath beautiful light-colored eyes. A face with interesting angles and deep grooves in lean cheeks. The grooves deepened with his smile, telling her that things hadn't always been easy for Ryan Donovan.

He leaned forward, his muscular arms coming to rest on the table, and his broad shoulders shifted effortlessly beneath the somber-colored cloth of his suit. His movements were graceful for such a big man.

His hair was black, thick and meticulously styled. An expensive haircut. One that spoke of a man who took care of himself and liked looking good. But in spite of the precision cut, several strands had escaped and fanned out over his forehead, giving him a slightly unruly appearance. A few shots of gray highlighted the sides. Not much, but enough to make things interesting.

Tess wanted to respond to the smile but she didn't. Couldn't. She recognized Ryan Donovan for what he was— danger. Someone to be avoided. The sooner she got herself outside his range of charm and potent masculinity, the better off she'd be.

She broke eye contact and rubbed the bridge of her nose, trying to concentrate, trying to understand why her mind was screaming for her to back off. To be cautious.

"Are you in pain, Tess?"

Apparently Donovan wasn't in the mood to back off, because instead of picking up on her unwillingness to engage in any type of verbal exchange, he was going to use that deep, whiskey-smooth voice until she couldn't ignore him for one more minute.

She looked up again, and her chest tightened. She forced a smile. "I've got a slight headache, that's all."

"We need to get—"

Before he could finish, the phone rang. Betty reached over and picked up the receiver, cradling it between her shoulder and ear as she flipped the remaining cakes on the grill. "Hello?"

"Just a moment, please." She turned and extended the phone toward Chief Cole. "It's for you, Chief."

The big man grunted and stood up, pulling the napkin out of the neck of his shirt. He grabbed the phone. "Cole here."

Tess shifted restlessly, trying not to stare. For some reason, the beefy cop made her nervous, created an anxious flutter in the pit of her stomach. Whenever he moved, the gold bars on his collar glittered, sending off a blinding flash of light. She squinted, trying to hear what he was saying on the phone.

But she couldn't make it out. The Chief talked low, darting covert glances in her direction every few seconds. Suddenly he straightened up, his dark eyes meeting hers across the length of the room.

He nodded. "All right. We'll be right there. Don't let anyone touch anything." He hung up the phone hard, the receiver rattling in its cradle. He hit her with his best cop stare.

"What?" she asked.

He didn't answer.

Tess swallowed against the lump of pancake that caught in the back of her throat. She fumbled for the glass of orange juice, trying to wash it down. It tasted like grit.

"Something wrong, Chief?" Donovan asked, his coffee cup halfway to his lips.

Chief Cole's gaze moved over to Donovan. "Seems that this was a night for strange happenings. There's been an accident out on the Plank Road. A car plowed into Bill Johnson's cornfield—the one that borders Bud's and is backed up against the research center's fence." He moistened his thick upper lip with the tip of his tongue. "The driver's dead."

From beneath lowered lashes, Tess watched Donovan stand up, towering over the table. Damn, he was tall and powerfully built. Concern etched deeper lines around those magnificent eyes. "Anyone else hurt?"

The Chief folded his arms, the leather of his holster creaking loudly. "No." He turned, his cop stare back on her. "No one else in the car. Just the driver." He moved over to stand next to Tess, his frame seeming to loom over her, his bloated belly inches from her face. "You wouldn't know anything about that car in the cornfield, now would you, miss?"

Tess shook her head and took another bite of pancake. She didn't know anything about the car, but her stomach was clenched up tighter than a fist. It took all her concentration to get the small bite down.

"I think it's time you told us your full name," Cole said, pulling a notebook out of his hip pocket.

"I—I'd love to." Tess laid her fork alongside her plate. "Unfortunately, I seem to have forgotten it."

Donovan moved to the other side of her, and he reached out to lightly touch her shoulder in a protective gesture. She could almost feel his concern, his compassion, radiate down through his long, masculine fingers. Welcome warmth saturated her shoulder. She shot him a grateful look.

"Don't push so hard, Cole," Donovan warned.

The Chief snorted. "Look, you two, I ain't playing games here. I want her name, address and an explanation of what the hell she's doing here in Half Moon."

"You seem to think I'm trying to be uncooperative." Tess paused, pressing the tips of her fingers to her forehead. Her head ached. "But I—I can't tell you anything that I have no memory of."

Ryan held up his other hand. "Back off, Chief. She isn't yanking your chain. She really doesn't remember."

"Yeah, right. And I'm the freakin' Pope. Give me a break, Doc. She's playing you—playing all of us. That little nudie show was to keep us all interested."

Anger surged through her, and Tess stood up, pushing her chair back so quickly it crashed to the floor. "I don't have to take any of this."

She started for the door, but Cole stepped in front of her, grabbing her upper arm. Tess struggled, but he had a good grip on her.

"You aren't going anywhere, missy," he said. "I want answers and I want them now."

Tess stopped struggling and stepped in close. So close she could smell the heavy stench of old coffee and bacon on his thick breath. Her stomach recoiled in protest.

But she didn't back down. "I don't need this kind of harassment from you or anyone else."

Cole matched her toe-to-toe. "Don't sass me, little lady, I'll—"

Donovan stepped between them. "That's enough," he ordered. "You," he said to Tess, "sit back down." When she hesitated, he gently spun her around and pointed to the chair. "Now."

He waited until she was actually seated before turning back to the police chief. "And you need to back off. You're not going to get anywhere with that tone of voice. If Tess knew her name, she'd tell you. She isn't trying to hide anything, and you trying to force her to answer questions obviously isn't working."

Tess watched as skepticism fought for dominance on the cop's ruddy features. No big surprise there, she thought. All cops and military types held that take-no-prisoners attitude. It was second nature to them.

She paused, her fingers tightening on the arm of the chair. There it was again, another thought that seemed to trigger a value statement out of nowhere. Did it mean that she normally distrusted cops and other people of authority?

"Maybe if she comes with me and takes a look at the crash site, she'll remember something." Cole grabbed his cap off the sideboard and slapped it on his head. "Let's go, miss. We'll take a drive out to Plank Road and see if you experience a sudden memory flash." The last sentence dripped with sarcasm.

Donovan shook his head, signaling she shouldn't get up. "She's not going anywhere. She needs medical attention, Cole. Not the third degree."

"I wasn't about to whip out the rubber hose, Doc." Irritation flickered across the Chief's face. "You have to go by the crash site to get to Doc Reed's. You can come along for the ride. That way you can make sure I don't abuse the little lady."

"I'm taking her out to the center. The facilities are better there," Donovan stated.

Cole threw up his big hands. "Take her wherever the hell you want. But first let her see the car. It might jog her memory. Okay?"

Donovan finally relented and Cole stomped out the door.

Tess stood up, carefully setting her napkin next to her unfinished breakfast. She smiled at the Carsons. "Thanks for the clothes and the delicious meal. It was very gracious of you."

Betty clucked her tongue and glanced out the window. Her glare of disapproval directed at the Chief's back spoke volumes. "Ted Cole can be a bully sometimes. Don't you let him push you around." She shifted her attention to Donovan. "You make sure to watch out for her, Ryan."

Donovan nodded and then stepped aside to let Tess go first. A pang of regret shot through Tess. She missed the feel of his hand on her shoulder, the warmth and comfort of those long fingers against her skin. Somehow his touch seemed to reach down and fill a cold, empty place deep in her chest.

And that spot seemed to get bigger and wider with each passing moment, especially when she imagined seeing a car in the middle of a cornfield. A car with a dead man inside it. She hid a shudder as she climbed into the police chief's cruiser. Something told her she didn't want to go anywhere near that car.

RAW TRACKS CUT THROUGH the freshly mowed grass leading up to the edge of the cornfield and then continued on into the heart of the field. The ground leading to the crash site was uneven, and Tess stumbled a bit as she skirted the broken stalks.

"Easy, Tess," Donovan said, reaching out to steady her. "There's no rush to get there."

The corn on either side of them seemed to rise up and close in around them, creating a green chute. The raw earth smelled pungent, and a light breeze slipped through the rows, making a soft rustling sound.

"Are you sure you're up to this?" he asked, his big body

so close a whiff of his aftershave, something tangy and enticing, swept up her nose. She tried to ignore its effect.

"I'll do whatever he wants. Just as long as he gets off my back."

The car was about twenty or thirty yards in. A sleek gold Intrepid. It looked as if the driver had simply lost his way, plowed through a high fence on the end of the field and driven directly into the corn. Broken stalks were caught in the door handles and under the wipers. All the doors were open, and a uniformed policeman was rummaging around in the back seat. He ignored her.

For the first time, Tess realized the car hadn't left the road and plowed into the field. The tracks they'd followed in had been made by a farm tractor, the farmer's attempt to make it easier for the police to get to the site.

The car had crashed through the fence straight ahead. It had a huge gaping hole in it. Tess couldn't help but wonder what all that lethal-looking metal fencing surrounded. Was it meant to keep something in or out?

Guards—private security guards from the looks of them—stood on the opposite side of the hole, watching the local cops conduct their investigation. One of them was speaking into a cell phone.

"Does the car look familiar?" Cole asked.

Tess shook her head. "No. But it's a nice-looking car." She glanced at the cop. "If you're asking me if it's mine— I have no idea."

"Does anything about it look familiar?" Cole pressed.

"No."

"Pretty convenient response," Cole said, his expression sour.

"A fairly typical response for someone who has amnesia," Donovan said. He glanced in Tess's direction, and she could tell without him saying anything that he was assessing how she was holding up.

His concerned expression bothered her for some reason. She didn't want him hovering over her, worried if she could handle things. She wasn't some shrinking violet that needed a caretaker, especially not this sexy-as-sin doctor.

She turned away. She didn't need him or anyone else. Trust was not something that came easy. Wait a minute. She paused and rewound what she'd just thought. Interesting. She wasn't supposed to even know her name, yet suddenly she knew she was fiercely independent.

She smiled inwardly, savoring the knowledge.

"I want you to take a look at the body," Cole said. "Tell me if it's anyone you recognize."

Tension gnawed at the pit of her stomach. "If I'm having trouble remembering my own name, what makes you think I'd remember some guy who is sitting in a car I've never seen before?"

"Humor me." Cole pushed her up toward the driver's side of the car.

The driver lay slumped over on his side, his head resting in a pool of blood, his eyes wide and staring. Tess's fingers tightened into fists, her nails digging raggedly into the palms of her hands. Oh God, please don't let me know this person, she prayed.

The coppery stench of blood seemed to fill the air trapped in the car and for a moment, she thought she might lose her breakfast. But she breathed shallowly, determined not to give Cole the reaction she knew he was looking for.

Cole reached around her and tipped the man's face up so she could see better. Tess sucked in a relieved mouthful of air. The face didn't strike any chord of recognition in her.

"Anything?" Donovan asked.

She shook her head. "Sorry. Nothing."

"Any feelings of remorse? Guilt perhaps," Cole drawled.

Tess met his gaze head-on. "I don't feel anything, Chief. Zip. Zero. Nada." She yawned. "Are we done yet?"

Out of the corner of her eye, she tried to gauge Donovan's reaction to her staged attitude of callousness. She'd decided early on that it was better not to let any of them know what she was feeling. But with the exception of one dark eyebrow quirking upward, he didn't appear anywhere near as appalled as she might have thought.

In fact, if she wasn't mistaken, one corner of those magnificent lips twitched upward a touch, as if he knew she was doing her best to yank the persistent police chief's pompous chain.

And for a brief moment, Tess found herself wondering what those lips would taste like, especially the full bottom one. The one with the small crease in the center that bowed out just a little, bordering on being almost too full. Too ripe. Not fitting with the overall toughness of the rest of his face.

She'd give anything for one small taste, and the thought almost made her burst out laughing. Whoever she was, amnesia obviously didn't seem to put much of a damper on her libido.

"All right, I think we need to go down to the station and talk this out," Cole said.

"She's not going anywhere, Chief," Donovan said. "We agreed to stop here on the way to the center. Your questions will have to wait until after I'm done conducting a few tests."

Cole scowled. "Just make sure you don't leave town before checking in with me." He turned away, throwing one final threat over his shoulder. "I'll have more to go on after the forensics people finish up with the evidence gathered from the car."

Tess watched him walk off, unable to deny the tiny twist of fear that coiled in her belly. What if she really did have something to do with this accident? What if it wasn't an accident but a murder? Would the Chief's men find something to connect her to the man's death?

"You can tie yourself in knots over this, Tess. Or you can let it go for now." Ryan moved up to stand next to her. "Let the Chief and his men figure out what happened and then we'll deal with whatever they find. Until then, let's you and I focus on finding out more about you."

"Sure, that sounds reasonable," she agreed, deciding that agreeable was the tack to take at the moment. But she wasn't foolish enough not to listen to the warning in her gut that no matter how honorable Ryan Donovan seemed at this moment, when things heated up, he would throw her to the wolves.

IMPATIENT, RYAN SHOVED the CT scan onto the view box and studied it. No big surprises. Her brain was uniform and the ventricles were normal, no sign of a bleed.

Not that he'd expected the scan to show anything significant, but he'd insisted Tess have the head CT anyway. He believed in covering all the bases.

He glanced at the screen showing a camera view of Tess lying on the table waiting for them to tell her she could get up. Her eyes were closed, her lips, pink and lush and lightly parted as if she were sleeping. There was no panic in her relaxed limbs.

The technician turned in his chair to check and make sure Ryan didn't have any last-minute instructions before he told Tess that the examination was complete. Ryan shook his head and headed for the door leading to the examination room.

Inside, he hit the light switch and Tess turned her head.

"Everything looks good," Ryan reassured her.

Tess nodded and jumped gracefully off the table. As she bent down to scoop up the striped cotton robe lying across the back of a chair, a section of her gown parted and allowed him to see the smooth glide of her skin and the line of her backbone. He'd never thought of a cotton hospital gown as particularly sexy, but somehow Tess had made it seem that way.

He jerked his thoughts off that particular track. Better to keep focused on Tess's mind, not her body. Anything else would lead to trouble. The kind of trouble he didn't need now or anytime in the future.

"So, no idea why I can't remember anything?" she asked as she shrugged into her robe.

Ryan shook his head, trying to ignore the twinge of regret as she cinched the robe around her slender waist. "Not a clue. Sorry. But then I wasn't really expecting to find one. I ordered the scan as a precaution only."

"I take it that's a good sign."

"It is." Ryan motioned toward the door. "Why don't you go get dressed and have a seat in the waiting room. I'm going to go over the scan with the neurologist on call. At this point, I'm going with the diagnosis of a mild concussion. We'll see what he has to say."

Tess didn't move. "Then why can't I remember who I am? I've had a concussion before and didn't lose my memory."

"When was that exactly?" Ryan probed.

Tess tilted her head, those exquisitely clear eyes unfocusing slightly as she accessed the memory. "I was rock climbing and my rope slipped. I fell about ten feet and hit my head on the rock face. Got a nasty bump and a real shiner." She stopped, and her green eyes cleared. She locked gazes with him. "How did you do that—get me to remember like that?"

Ryan smiled. "Your memories are still all intact. Something is just blocking you from getting to them."

Her shoulders tensed, as if she was ready to rev up for some kind of unforeseen battle. "So how do I unblock them?"

"You don't." Ryan reached out and touched her shoulder, trying to impart some comfort. A zing of awareness shot through him, but he kept his face carefully neutral. "The more you try to force your way through the wall, the stronger it gets. You and I are just going to have to find a way around it."

Frustration flickered in her eyes, and her fingers tightened into fists at her sides. "Why can I remember the fall but not my name?"

"Relax, Tess. You're trying too hard. Let the memories come back on their own. You haven't lost them—they're all still there."

She yanked on the belt of her robe, cinching it tighter. The tops of her knuckles turned white. Her agitation was clear. "That's easy for you to say. You're not the one who can't remember if you like cream in your coffee or mustard on your hot dog."

Ryan laughed. "Food jokes. Something tells me that you're hungry again." He pulled two doughnuts wrapped in a napkin out of his jacket pocket and offered them to her. "I happen to have these. I thought you might get hungry later. Want one?"

Tess accepted the doughnuts and slipped them into the pocket of her robe. "Not at the moment, but I'll be keeping a close eye on them." She glanced toward the technician's booth. "What now?"

"Why don't you go get dressed. When I'm done talking to the neurologist, we'll go to my office and talk for a while?"

"Oh, so now you get me on the couch."

"No, just a comfortable chair." He flashed her an easy grin.

"I already told you I'm not in the market for a shrink."

"Fair enough. We're only going to talk. Decide on what you want to do next, okay?"

She nodded and then headed for the small dressing cubicle across the hall. After she was out of his sight, Ryan leaned down to pick up the sheet that had fallen to the floor.

"Where is she?"

The voice broke into Ryan's thoughts. He glanced up to see Sidney Bloom, his boss, standing in the doorway. The light from the brightly lit hall silhouetted his stubby figure.

In spite of being a few inches short of five feet seven inches and on the plump side, Sidney never had to work to gain anyone's attention. When he walked into a room, people sat up and took notice.

"I assume you mean the young woman I brought in a little while ago?" Ryan said, draping the sheet over the back of the chair.

Sidney nodded, his bald dome catching the light. He didn't appear happy. In fact, he looked downright peeved. Ryan sighed inwardly. Only on the job a few weeks and he already had his boss breathing down his neck for some perceived infraction. Sad fact was, it made him feel right at home. Breaking infractions seemed to be his lot in life lately.

"She's across the hall dressing." Ryan cocked his head. "Who mentioned to you that she was here?"

Sidney smiled. "This is my facility, Ryan. I know everything that goes on here—especially when patients are admitted without my approval."

"She sustained a mild concussion, Sid. She needed to be checked out. The closest medical center is over two hours away."

The door behind them opened and a petite redhead poked her head in. "Someone in here request a consult from the neurologist on call?"

Before Ryan could answer, Bloom angrily waved the woman off. She shot a quick glance of sympathy in Ryan's direction before closing the door again.

"I requested a consult with Dr. Adams."

"You don't have time to waste treating patients, Ryan. That isn't why I hired you."

"I thought you told me you were working on fostering good relationships between the center and the townspeople?"

Bloom's lips tightened. "Chief Cole tells me this woman isn't from Half Moon and isn't cooperating with his investigation. How exactly is that helping the relationship between the center and the town?"

Ryan didn't have an answer for that, but the fact that Cole had already gotten to Bloom told him that most of his avenues of defense were cut off anyway.

"I'll take over the treatment of this patient," Bloom said with an air of authority. "I want you to focus on the reason I brought you here in the first place—your research."

The demand angered Ryan. He wasn't about to ditch Tess right now. She was just beginning to trust him, and he had a strong feeling that trust was a major issue with this woman. Abandoning her now was more than therapeutically dangerous; it was downright unethical.

ACROSS THE HALL, Tess stepped tentatively into the small waiting area. The receptionist glanced up and gave her a chilly smile before resuming typing at her keyboard.

Hoping she wasn't in for a long wait, Tess plopped down on the couch and grabbed a news magazine off the pile sitting on the coffee table. She restlessly started leafing through the magazine and stopped at a page. A picture of a grisly-faced man with tattooed arms stared out at the camera from between heavy bars. "Waiting For Clemency" was the title.

A quick skim of the opening paragraph told Tess that it was an article about a man on death row. Wonderful. Nothing like a little light reading to calm her already-jangled nerves.

She flipped the page and came face-to-face with a picture of the death chamber—a stark white room with a stretcher in the middle. Padded straps crisscrossed the thin mattress, ready to clamp some death-row inmate to the table.

Tess's fingers tightened on the edges of the slick paper. The pages of the magazine started to shake, and a jolt of terror shot through her. A strange, searing flush blazed across the surface of her skin, and the page ripped beneath her suddenly sweaty hand.

Her head dropped back, bumping the wall. Her vision seemed to darken along the edges. Suddenly, it was as if *she* was strapped to the table and pain coursed through her body. The straps seemed to tighten over her bare limbs and she strained against them, fighting them. Her back arched off the table as the leather cut into her flesh.

She opened her mouth to scream, but nothing came out. The magazine dropped from her nerveless fingers and her entire body shook violently.

"Miss!" A voice cut through the pain of the nightmare. "Are you all right, miss?"

Numbers, the color of shiny brass flashed in front of her eyes—5-6-8-7. They drifted and floated as if carried on a current of air. Hovering over her, Tess could see the outline of a small ghostly figure. Then, from somewhere far away, she could hear the roar of a crowd.

She frowned, straining to hear. She was seeing people. People cheering someone. Calling his name. She strained harder, trying to make out the name. But the cheering died away, and the corner of the dream folded and disappeared.

Tess opened her eyes to find the receptionist standing over her, an expression of concern on her tight, narrow face. "Are you okay, miss?"

Tess leaned forward and wiped the palms of her sweaty hands along the sides of her legs, trying to hide the fact that they were trembling. Her hair fell over her shoulders and hid her face. "I—I'm fine," she said, her voice raspy and uneven to her own ears.

"I thought you were having a seizure," the woman said.

Tess swallowed. Her mouth had become so dry that her tongue stuck to the roof of her mouth. Speech was near impossible.

What had happened? Sucking in a mouthful of oxygen, Tess peeked through the curtain of hair falling over her face. She watched as the woman bent down and snatched the magazine up off the floor.

"I'll have to throw this out. The entire article has been destroyed," she said.

Tess grabbed the arm of the couch and levered herself up off the cushions. Her knees quivered, and she almost fell over backward. But she locked her knees and straightened up. Sweat broke out between her shoulder blades and ran down the column of her spine, pooling in the small of her back.

"I'm sorry. I guess I got a little dizzy." She reached up and wiped a line of sweat off her forehead. "Please tell Dr. Donovan that I had to leave."

Concern flickered across the secretary's pinched face. Tess was pretty sure it had nothing to do with the fact that her face was probably the color of rice paper. More than likely the woman was simply worried she'd be somehow blamed for Tess's sudden departure.

The receptionist touched Tess's elbow with her perfectly manicured nails. The hard tips skittered across her skin, giving her goose bumps. "Why don't you sit back down, dear. I'm sure Dr. Donovan will be finished very soon and you can tell him yourself that you'd like to leave."

"Tell Dr. Donovan I got tired of waiting," Tess said, trying to tamp down her rising hysteria. She had to get out of there.

The woman protested further but Tess ignored her, concentrating on putting one foot in front of the other. Her breath came in short pants. By the time she reached the door leading to the hallway, her shirt was plastered to her body with a fine sheen of perspiration. Amazing how quickly a person's body went into hyperdrive.

She yanked open the door and stepped out into the empty corridor. She could barely breathe, hot air catching in the back of her throat. She ran the palm of her hand along the cool wall, attempting to steady herself.

Seeing the scowling secretary standing in the doorway Tess took off. Rushing for the front door, she felt her legs grow steadier with each stride. She hit the release bar of the door with an urgent smack and the door swung open. A slight tickle at the back of her neck made Tess glance over her right shoulder.

The receptionist was still framed in the office doorway, but now two men in dark suits flanked her. In spite of the fact that they were inside, both men wore mirrored sunglasses, their facial features frozen, unreadable. The woman whispered something to the one on her right, and he nodded, his head never moving from staring straight at her.

Tess tried to ignore the chill that swept through her as she turned and walked out into the warm afternoon.

Chapter Three

Ryan was more than frustrated, he was royally ticked off. Not only was Sidney Bloom telling him that he wasn't permitted to treat Tess, he was outright ordering him to turn her case over to him.

It had been a long time since Ryan had felt the need to acquiesce to Sidney Bloom. He might respect the man as a teacher and benevolent mentor, but sometimes one had to step out of the shadow of the teacher. Ryan was sure now was that time.

But before he could speak, the door behind them swung open. Mrs. Mackie—the waiting-room receptionist—stood in the doorway, her face the picture of frosty disapproval. "I thought you should know that the young woman you brought in just left."

"What you mean she left?" Ryan said.

"Just what I said. She got up and walked out."

Bloom scowled. "Well, where did she go?"

Mrs. Mackie glanced in Ryan's direction, an accusatory expression on her narrow face. Obviously, she didn't appreciate her boss's irritation and blamed Ryan.

"She wasn't exactly forthcoming about her plans. When I tried to convince her to stay until you were done talking, she got quite rude."

"Did she seem upset? Confused?" Ryan asked.

Mrs. Mackie stiffened. "I have no idea, Doctor. She was reading a magazine and then, all of a sudden, she started to shake and tremble so violently I thought she might be having a seizure."

Concern ripped through Ryan. "And you let her just leave?" he demanded. "What's the matter with you?"

Mrs. Mackie stiffened, her lips tightening. "I resent your tone, Doctor. She was angry, and I didn't feel it was my place to wrestle with her. I notified the front gate as soon as she left. I knew they'd make sure she didn't leave without prior authorization from Dr. Bloom." She sniffed. "Besides, she's *your* responsibility, not mine."

"Damn right she's my responsibility," Ryan said, starting for the door. He glanced over his shoulder at Bloom. "If there was any question up to this point of who would be taking care of Tess's case, I hope this settles it. It'll be me!"

Bloom shook his head. "You're losing your objectivity, Ryan. I can hear it in your voice. You can't save every young woman who walks through the door as a way of making up for the mess in Boston."

Ryan clenched his hands and fought against the swell of anger rising in the back of his throat. "My desire to help Tess has nothing to do with Boston."

"Go ahead and tell yourself that," Bloom said, "but you and I both know that you're still battling intense feelings of guilt."

Ryan pushed aside a twinge of self-doubt. "I don't have time to argue. I'm going after her."

He left, ignoring Bloom's parting shot, "Don't get in over your head, Ryan. I've already thrown you one lifeline. There aren't any more left."

LESS THAN A MILE down the road, Ryan spotted Tess. She was running. A wild, full-out run of pure, unadulterated fear.

Her legs pumped madly, and her calf muscles stood out in sculpted relief, eating up the road with a long, graceful stride.

Slowing down, Ryan pulled up beside her, the passenger-side window down. "You always leave a place in such an all-out rush?"

She slowed and then stopped abruptly, her feet skidding in the loose gravel. He had to slam on the brakes to keep from sailing past her.

She bent over to catch her breath, thick strands of finely spun gold strands sliding over her shoulders to shield her face from him. She flipped it back and then turned her head sideways to glance at him. Tiny beads of sweat peppered her forehead and damped her hair along the sides of her face.

"Along with hating doctors, I'm not real partial to hospitals," she said, her breath already calming. Ryan realized that she might not have any memory of who she was, but she was in phenomenal physical shape. A marathon runner, with perfect breath control and recovery.

"So pretend I'm a friend and I stopped to pick you up." He reached across and opened the door. "Get in. I'll drive you wherever you need to go. No need to hoof it."

She didn't move. The late-afternoon light hit the green of her eyes, making them sparkle and creating an odd tightening in Ryan's chest. Damn but she was beautiful. Breathtakingly beautiful. The kind of beauty that took a man's heart, squeezed it so tight it pounded in protest and never allowed it to return to normal. He felt as though she'd done that to him with a single glance.

Perhaps Bloom was right. Perhaps he was involved for no other reason than that he was attracted to her.

"I have no intention of going back there."

Ryan sighed. "I'm not stupid, Tess. I definitely get the message that you don't like hospitals. Personally, I think you're making a mistake. But no one, least of all me, will force you to do anything you don't want to do.''

A tiny shimmer of relief flickered in the depth of her eyes, but it was gone almost before he'd noticed it. She worked hard to hide what she felt.

''Come on, get in. My place isn't too far from here. We'll go get something to eat,'' Ryan urged. ''We'll talk. Figure things out.''

A small smile curled the corner of her mouth. ''I'd like that. I'm starved.'' She climbed into the car, folding long legs beneath the dash and snapping her seat belt on.

''I'm beginning to think you're always hungry.'' He put the car in First and hit the gas, making a quick U-turn.

She immediately stiffened beside him, her hand reaching down to unsnap her belt. Her other hand clamped onto the door handle. ''I thought you said you wouldn't force me to go back there.''

''Relax,'' Ryan said as her shoulder went up against the door. He knew that she was two seconds away from throwing herself out of the car. He reached across and touched her arm, trying unsuccessfully to ignore the rush of heat that soaked through his finger and extended up the length of his arm.

''I said I wouldn't take you back to the center. And I won't.''

She shook his hand off, her eyes flashing distrust. ''Then why the hell are we heading back in the same direction I just came?''

She shifted her body away from his and shoved the door open. Pavement rushed past. Ryan slammed on the brakes and the car screeched to a stop.

''Dammit, Tess, will you relax! I live on the same grounds as the center. I'm simply taking you to my house.'' He leaned across, his shoulder accidentally brushing up against her breasts. He slammed the door, trying not to think about the fact that she was naked beneath the thin shirt and her breast had been pressed against his upper arm. He pulled back quickly. "When I said we were going to my house for something to eat, that's all I intended. Wherever you go after that is totally up to you."

Tess studied him, her expression wary. "You live here on the center's grounds?"

Ryan nodded and eased his foot off the brake. He drove past the entrance to the center and headed for the row of houses farther down the road. "A lot of the staff lives here on the grounds. Dr. Bloom likes his people within easy reach." He grinned, trying to put her at ease. "That way he can call us at any time of the day or night and he's assured that we'll be in our labs within minutes of his call. I was lucky enough to get one of the small cottages on the far side of the grounds."

Tess was silent beside him, apparently willing to wait the ride out before deciding whether or not to trust him. Ryan noticed that she kept her hand on the door handle, her frame tense and her eyes watchful. He stepped on the gas, heading up the steep hill leading to his house.

WHEN RYAN CLICKED on his turn signal, Tess craned her neck and peered out the window, trying to catch a glimpse of where they were going. A sloping lawn led up to a neat Cape Cod–style house situated between two large oaks.

She glanced around. The only other house in view was another similarly styled cottage about a half mile down the road, screened from view by a stand of trees.

Ryan gunned the car up the driveway and rolled to a stop in front of the garage door. He turned off the engine. A single row of weed-infested petunias lined a small path leading to the front door.

He sighed. "I confess I'm not much of a gardener. But the lawn is mowed, and I promise that you won't find any dirty laundry hanging on the furniture.'' He opened the door and the car rocked slightly as he leveraged his muscular frame out. When she didn't move, he poked his head back in. ''If you sit out here in the sun all day you're going to roast.''

Without waiting for her answer, he straightened up, nudged the door closed and started up the walkway. With a gesture of unconcern, he flipped his keys in the air and caught them in the palm of his hand. She wasn't sure, but she thought she heard him whistle a bit before disappearing inside. He left the front door slightly ajar.

Tess gnawed on the corner of her lip, ignoring the building heat in the car. Where was her fear coming from? On one level, she wanted to trust him, but on another, the alarm bells were wailing so loudly her head ached from the sound of them.

She ran a finger along the warm metal of the door handle. Was she afraid he'd wait behind the front door, jump her and wrestle her into a straitjacket? She moaned softly and leaned forward to rest her forehead on her knees. What to do, what to do?

If she was so afraid of him, why had she gotten in his car in the first place? She could have kept running, headed off into one of the fields where the car couldn't go. She knew she was fast. She could have outrun him easy.

Tess shook her head and sat up. Who was she kidding? She might be fast, but something told her that Ryan Donovan was faster. When she'd brushed up against him in the cornfield, she hadn't missed the hardness of his body, the glide of smooth, well-conditioned muscles beneath the suit coat. It was a body built for speed and endurance. If Ryan wanted, Tess had a feeling he could run her to the ground.

Grabbing the door handle, she climbed out. A warm breeze cut across the field and ruffled her hair. She could take off now and he'd never know. Instead, she hit the door with her hip, and, as it swung shut, she headed up the path to the house.

When she stepped inside, the coolness of the interior hit her hot skin and she almost whimpered with appreciation. She hadn't realized how hot and irritable she'd gotten.

She couldn't see Ryan, but she could hear him upstairs walking around. She jumped when something cold and wet pressed against her hand. Glancing down, she stared into a pair of warm brown eyes. A chocolate Lab, his body wiggling with delight nosed her again.

"Hey, boy." She ran a hand gently over his broad head, stroking the silky ears. "What's your name?"

"That's Jung," Ryan's called from upstairs. "He's friendly. In fact, he'd probably open the door for strangers and invite them in if he knew how."

Tess froze in the doorway, her cautiousness returning. But Ryan didn't reappear at the top of the stairs. Instead, he continued to rummage around upstairs.

She edged her way into the living room, Jung close on her heels. It was a cozy and surprisingly neat room for a bachelor. An oversize stuffed couch that looked brand-new and two equally new-looking easy chairs occupied most of the floor space.

An ancient-looking cuckoo clock with an elaborate wood-carved design sat in one corner and a battered lounger was strategically located in front of the TV. Apparently, Ryan hadn't been able to ditch all his belongings from his previous home.

"Contrary to the worn-out look of the La-Z-Boy, I swear I'm not the type who comes home from work every night and collapses in front of mindless TV sitcoms."

Startled, Tess whipped around to find Ryan standing at the bottom of the stairs, a few inches away. His ability to get down the stairs and within inches of her without her hearing him surprised her. Something told her that her reflexes were slower than usual.

He had changed out of the well-cut, carefully tailored suit and into a pair of soft, faded jeans and shirt. In the narrow hall, his size was slightly intimidating. He towered over her, his muscular body pressing in on her, making her consciously aware of his size and strength. No weak academic-type body here. This man was built like a fighter.

He smiled and jerked his head toward the back of the house.

"Let me fire up the grill, and then I'll show you around."

Tess nodded silently, following him out through a small kitchen to the glass patio doors. The surprise was the presence of an in-ground pool. Invitingly clear water lapped the edges of the blue tiles lining the sides and bottom of the pool.

Ryan must have seen the gleam in her eyes because he asked, "How about a swim? You can cool off while I cook us some dinner."

Tess shook her head. "No, that's okay. I'll help make dinner." But her eyes lingered on the gentle ripple of turquoise water.

Ryan laughed and slid open the patio door. He walked over to the fence where a row of beach towels and bathing suits hung in the sun.

He grabbed a fire-engine-red suit and a fluffy beach towel off the fence and walked back over. "Here. It's my sister's suit. It should fit. She and her kids were over last weekend testing out the pool and making general pests of themselves. You can change in the bathroom—down the hall and to the right."

Without waiting for an answer, he went into the kitchen and started rummaging around in the refrigerator.

Tess stood in the doorway and watched him pull a steak out of the meat drawer. He slapped it on a platter and then grabbed a pepper grinder and efficiently ground out a healthy amount of pepper on top of the red meat. He opened a drawer and removed a pair of grill tongs.

When he glanced in her direction, he raised an eyebrow. "Still here? I thought you'd be changed by now."

"Your sister lives nearby?"

Ryan nodded. "She lives in town, across the street from my mom." He turned around and scooped up a box of kitchen matches off a tiny shelf over the stove. "She used to live in Des Moines. But she got a divorce about a year ago and moved home to be nearer the family."

"Have you always been close?"

Ryan nodded, a small smile tugging at the corner of his mouth. "We fought like crazy when we were little, but we were always close." He reached into another drawer and pulled out a paring knife. "Does your family live near you?"

Tess shook her head. "My dad's dead. He died when I was twelve. I don't have any sisters or brothers."

She watched as Ryan took a clove of garlic out of a basket and started peeling it. "Your mom still alive?" Ryan asked.

Tess shook her head no, mesmerized by the flashing of the knife blade as he chopped the garlic with cheflike speed. "She died five years ago, shortly after I graduated from college." She swallowed against the dryness in her throat, unable to tear her gaze away from the shine of the knife. "My dad, he would have been proud of me graduating from college."

"Where did you go to school?" Ryan asked, his voice casual. He used one finger to sweep the tiny buds of garlic clinging to the blade onto the cutting board.

"I went to—"

The cuckoo clock in the living room crowed and Tess jumped. Startled, she stared up into the intense blue of

Ryan's eyes. He knew exactly what he was doing all the time.

"You did it again, didn't you?" she whispered. "You got me to remember without me even realizing it."

He shrugged those big shoulders. "No real trick to it, Tess. You were simply ready to tell me those things. You weren't even aware you were saying them, and that made all the difference in the world. In your head, you were simply sharing a normal, everyday conversation with me."

Tess leaned against the counter and watched as he drizzled a few drops of olive oil on top of the steak. He sprinkled the minced garlic over the meat and rubbed it all in. She liked watching his quick, self-assured movements. Somehow they infused her with a feeling of warmth and comfort.

"I still don't understand," she said.

"The ease with which you accessed the information is a good sign. It means your memories are intact, that they're simply waiting for you to recover them."

"Then why can't I simply recover them?"

He smiled gently. "It isn't as easy as all that. You have to give your brain time to recover—to mend itself. The memories will come when they're ready."

He reached over and turned on the hot water, and she watched as he washed his hands. Hands that had manipulated the knife just as brilliantly as his sharp mind had manipulated her brain. Wetting her suddenly dry lips, she watched him lather on the soap and then quickly rinse it off. Intriguing man, this Dr. Ryan Donovan.

He shut off the water and picked up the steak platter. "Now go change and take your swim. I'll put the steak on in about five minutes. Dinner in twenty."

Before Tess could answer, the phone rang.

Ryan picked it up. "Hello…? Hello?"

He frowned and checked the cord. "Hello, is anyone there?"

He leaned in and checked the caller ID screen. "That's funny, they hung up. The caller ID says the call originated from the center."

Tess wasn't sure why, but the hair on the back of her neck shifted and stood on end.

Ryan shrugged and replaced the receiver. "Whatever it was, they'll call back." He gave her a reassuring nod. "Go change. I'll get started on dinner."

Tess nodded numbly and backed out of the kitchen as if going to change. But instead, she made her way down the short hall to the front of the house.

At the living-room window, she opened the curtain a crack and peered out. The late-afternoon sun drenched the front lawn, drying the already-brown blades and heating up the driveway macadam. Cicadas droned rhythmically and a deep heaviness seemed to hang in the air. Nothing out of sync. Maybe she was getting spooked.

She took a calming breath and allowed the curtain to fall back. But then, right when she was about to turn away, the soft purr of a car engine caught her attention. Her fingers, trembling slightly, parted the curtain again. A black sedan, its grillwork flashing silver in the sunlight, motored past. The passenger's side window was down and a man in a dark suit sat with one arm hooked on the ledge.

He turned his head, and, despite the mirror lenses of his sunglasses, Tess knew he was staring directly up at her. She dropped the curtain and stepped away from the window. She knew without question it was one of the men who had watched her leave the center earlier.

Her heart thudded against her breastbone and she wiped her sweat-soaked palms down the sides of her pants. She didn't believe in coincidences.

A FEW MINUTES LATER, Ryan looked up to see Tess slip through the open screen door and step out onto the patio. She had gathered all that luxurious hair into a knot at the top of her head, and even though she'd pulled it tight, silvery strands shimmering in the late-afternoon light had escaped to dance around her face, highlighting her exquisite features.

He fiddled with the lid of the grill, trying not to stare. The suit, a little too big in the hips and bust, should have done nothing for her figure. Instead, her graceful, streamlined body, with its smooth glide of finely toned muscles, caused a tightening in his groin. The kind of tightening that told him his body was going places it shouldn't.

Tess tugged at the top of the suit and smiled self-consciously. "It's a little big." She held up a string. "I took the lace out of my sneaker. Do you mind tying the straps together. Otherwise I'm afraid I'll swim right out of it."

Ryan managed a nod. The thought of her streaking naked through the turquoise water of his pool was almost more than he could handle.

She turned around, flipping the string over one shoulder. It lay against her smooth satiny skin, the end trailing along the upper edge of her shoulder blade.

Ryan had never noticed that his sister's suit had such a low back, cut just above the sweet curve of Tess's backside. His gaze lingered for a moment on the smooth, rounded curve of her behind and then along the straight column of her spine, up to the graceful sweep of her neck.

He slipped the lace beneath the straps of the suit and tied them, his fingers lightly brushing the soft skin between her shoulder blades. Her skin was smooth, like fine satin.

Beneath the tips of his fingers, Tess shivered slightly, and her head dropped forward, revealing the soft downy spot at the nape of her neck. Until that moment, Ryan realized he'd never truly recognized the beauty in a woman's neck. How inviting it was. How erotic. How deliciously vulnerable. His mouth went dry and he felt a sudden tightness in his groin.

He shook his head, trying to break the unsettling mood that had captured him. Man, he needed to get out more. This was ridiculous. The woman wanted him to tie the straps of her suit and he was getting hot, obsessing about her neck. Get a grip.

"Do people from the center drive out this way much?" she asked.

"No, this house and the one just down the road from me are the farthest ones out. Even though the road circles around back to the main gate, no one drives the long way around. So, it's pretty quiet out here." He looped the shoestring into a bow while trying desperately to concentrate on the act of tying it and not the feel of Tess's skin beneath his fingers. He wasn't too successful.

"Who lives in the house just beyond yours?"

"No one. Bloom keeps it for guests—big shots he's courting to finance pet projects."

"Is anyone staying out there right now?"

Ryan paused and then pulled the ends of the string into a perfect bow. He gently turned Tess around. "Okay, I can tell you're worried about something? Want to tell me what it is?"

Her lashes dipped down to shield her eyes for a moment, as if she was considering how much she wanted to tell him.

Her caution worried him. How was he going to work successfully with her if she fought him at every junction? If she couldn't trust him enough to tell him the truth?

But finally she glanced up again. "I know this is going to sound paranoid and a little crazy, but a few minutes ago, I saw one of the men from the center drive by the house."

"And that worries you because…?"

"Because I don't like the thought of anyone checking up on me."

Simply cautious or slightly paranoid? He wasn't sure. She'd been through a lot and that could put a person on edge. "What makes you think he was checking up on you?" he asked.

Frustration tightened the corners of her mouth. "You told me no one was staying in the other house. Why would he drive by a few minutes after you and I get here? The car slowed down and he looked right up here at the house." He saw a flicker of doubt cross her face as what she was saying registered in her own brain. "You got a hang-up call from the center and then this guy drives by. Don't you think that's too much of a coincidence?"

"Not really." He put a hand on her shoulder, trying to ease the tension. "But if you're feeling concerned about this, I understand. You've been through a lot these past few hours."

A flush crept up the sides of her cheeks and she roughly shrugged off his hand. "Don't humor me, Ryan. I hate when people play shrink like that."

"Has that happened to you before—someone playing shrink with your head?"

Rage flashed in her eyes. "More than you'd know. They're always trying to play around with my brain. Force me to—" She paused. Her head tilted slightly as if she were trying to remember something.

"Force you to what?" he coaxed.

She shook her head as if coming out of a trance. "I don't know. I don't want to think about it." She walked over to the steps of the pool. "I'm taking that swim now."

"Don't overdo it," he warned. Flames shot up around the metal grill. "Dinner will be ready before you know it."

Tess nodded and hit the water with a sleek, shallow dive, the water bursting over her head and driving the air from her lungs. She glided to the surface and gulped air, and then lowered her head and struck out for the opposite end of the pool with a powerful crawl.

Her muscles stretched and contracted, and her body hummed with satisfaction. No paddling around in the low end of the pool for her. Somehow she knew that, even though she didn't remember her last name or where she came from, she was a person who loved using her body and pushing it to its limit.

The mind-numbing repetition of doing lap after lap lulled her, giving her a sense of deep relaxation. Her brain seemed to stop fighting her, seemed to forget that she was trying to remember who she was and why she'd been walking in a cornfield.

She dug deeper into the water, the palms of her hands scooping the water backward and propelling her forward. The bubbles whispered past her ears.

When she reached the opposite end, she ducked beneath the surface and executed a perfect flip turn. The soles of her feet hit the wall and she pushed off and headed for the opposite end.

The crampiness in her calf muscles eased and she kicked harder, forcing her arms deeper into the water and reveling in the pull of the water against her shoulder muscles. As she tilted her head for air, she caught a glimpse of Ryan. He had moved closer to the edge of the pool to watch. His stance was relaxed, his expression contemplative.

Tess lapped the pool again, and this time she noticed that he'd moved to sit in the shade, sipping a drink. His steady gaze, with those exquisite blue eyes, was still trained on her. Her stomach growled, but she ignored it, determined to tire herself out before she indulged in food or anything else.

She swam on, numbing her body and mind with the re-petitiveness and fierceness of her workout. At lap twenty, something started to niggle at the edge of her awareness—a tiny ripple of discomfort.

She swam harder, dug deeper into the water and ignored the voice, trying to drown it out. She executed another perfect flip turn and headed back toward the deep end, determined to regain the numb feeling she'd obtained at the start of her swim.

But she failed.

From out of nowhere, scraps of pictures flashed across her consciousness, all clamoring for attention. Disembodied voices filled her head. Frantic, Tess tried to push them away. She dug deeper still, drawing on untapped strength. But the images and voices persisted, beating away at her defenses and forcing her to listen. To see.

A fuzzy image of herself strapped to a table.

Pain ripped through her muscles. She floundered and, when she gasped for air, water rushed into her mouth. Chlorine scorched the back of her throat, and she reared up out of the water, trying to breathe. Trying to escape.

But she was blinded by the rush of water and wet clinging strands of her hair. Her arms slapped the surface helplessly, and she urgently tried to find the bottom.

No bottom. She was in the deep end.

She tried kicking, but her arms and legs had turned to lead. The water around her churned and roiled. One last try to reach the low end. But her body failed her, refusing to respond. She started to sink.

As water rushed her mouth, Tess thought how funny it was that she was drowning. An Olympic-caliber swimmer, and she was drowning in a backyard pool.

An odd sense of peace settled over her, cushioning and cradling her. Maybe this was the solution. Maybe she was supposed to simply let go and allow herself to be pulled under.

She stopped struggling.

Water closed over her head, and she sank to the bottom.

Chapter Four

Ryan jumped to his feet and ran for the deep end.

One minute, Tess had been swimming along effortlessly and the next, she'd slipped beneath the surface. He could see her stretched out on the bottom, her body shockingly white against the blue tiles. She wasn't moving.

He dived, cutting the surface of the water, and swam to the bottom. Two seconds later, he reached her, slipped both hands under her arms and shot to the surface. When their heads broke the surface, Tess's body slumped against his, deadweight. He swam for the low end, towing her next to him. She didn't struggle, didn't move.

When he could touch the bottom, Ryan slipped his arms under her legs and carried her up the steps. Bending down, he gently laid her on the cool patio tiles. A quick check told him she wasn't breathing. He pressed two fingers to the side of her neck. A faint pulse whispered beneath his fingertips.

He rolled her onto her side. A steam of water dribbled from her mouth. He rolled her back, tilted her head up and fastened his mouth over hers. He gave her two quick breaths.

Her breasts rose and fell with each breath, and he continued, until a few seconds later, she took a great, shuddering gulp of air and coughed. Her body spasmed.

He watched as her thick lashes fluttered against the crest

of her cheeks. Reaching up, he grabbed two towels off the back of one of the chairs, tucked one under her head and covered her with the other. He didn't want to move her until he was sure she was going to be all right.

"It's okay, Tess," he reassured her as she gasped and coughed.

He touched the tips of his fingers to her neck again. Her pulse was strong. Steady. For all her appearance of fragility, she wasn't what he'd call a shrinking violet. More like tempered steel.

She turned her head, the brilliant green of her eyes clouded as she tried to focus on him. "Wh-what happened?"

"You didn't listen. I told you to paddle around a little and you decided to do your own iron-man swim in my backyard pool."

She tried to smile, but her bottom lip trembled a bit and he noticed she was shivering beneath the towel. The cut over her eye had opened again and a small trickle of blood darkened her pale skin.

He reached down and briskly rubbed her arms and then her legs, trying to get the circulation going.

"We're not taking any more chances. I'm calling the hospital and taking you in."

"No!" She struggled to sit up, but then fell back. She looked as if she'd lost all strength in her limbs. But then, she rallied enough to reach up and grab the front of his shirt, her fingers clutching it in a death grip. "You promised that you wouldn't force me. You can't go back on your word now."

"I also didn't think you'd almost drown in my pool." He gently disengaged his shirt from her fingers. "Your body is telling you that something's not right, and we need to find out what. I wouldn't be doing my job, Tess, unless I insisted you go."

She shook her head, anger exploding in her eyes. "I know you think I'm crazy, but I know in my heart that something bad is going to happen to me if I go back to that place. I can't go!"

Ryan didn't want to break the news to her that she sounded more than a little crazy. She sounded downright paranoid. "Look, if the center freaks you out, we'll drive over to Kendall. They have a small community hospital. We can have you checked out there and you won't even need to stay overnight unless they feel it's absolutely necessary."

Her reaction was immediate. "How can I make you understand—*no hospitals.* Do whatever tests you need to do, but do them here."

Ryan sighed. "I'm not equipped to do tests here. Besides, I'm a psychiatrist, Tess, not a neurologist."

"Then forget the tests." The finality in her voice and the stubborn jut to her jaw told Ryan that it didn't matter what he said, she wasn't going to change her mind. "I told you before, I don't need a doctor."

He shrugged. "All right. If I promise no hospitals and no tests, will you at least agree to rest?"

Her narrow shoulders seemed to melt back against the wet tiles and a grateful sigh pulled at the corners of her mouth. She nodded. She'd gotten what she wanted.

Crazy or paranoid, she was the most infuriatingly beautiful woman he'd ever met. Ryan was beginning to realize that with a few words and a single glance from those exquisite jade eyes she could wreak havoc on all rational thought.

"I'll rest." She smiled. "As long as I can do it right here."

But in spite of the smile, Ryan didn't feel any sense of relief. Instead, he felt stuck. Stuck with a promise he didn't agree with. A promise that meant not getting Tess the medical attention he felt she needed, and that went against everything he believed in professionally.

But Ryan also knew that if he went back on his word, Tess would simply walk away, disappear. He'd lose the only chance he had to help her, and that was a risk he wasn't willing to take.

He stood and then reached down, offering her a hand to get up. "Come on, let's get you upstairs and into bed."

Tess nodded, but when she tried to stand, her legs buckled beneath her. He caught her before she fell.

"I—I guess I'm not as steady as I thought."

Ryan quickly scooped her up, lifting her with one hand beneath her legs and the other cradling her slender back. She seemed weightless in his arms.

He shouldered the screen door back along the track and stepped into the house, and as they entered the house, a shiver shot through Tess. A part of her wanted to blame the goose bumps pebbling her arms and legs on the air-conditioning, but she knew the real reason was Ryan's close proximity.

Her reaction troubled her. She didn't want to be vulnerable. In her head, vulnerability equalled danger. It meant her survival was questionable.

A tiny doubt niggled at the back of her brain. Where were these feelings coming from? Was she crazy? Paranoid? Or was she simply ready for anything.

She dropped her head back.

Ready for what?

She closed her eyes, trying desperately to pull at the root of that single disturbing thought. But it wouldn't cooperate. The more she tried to capture the thought, the more it seemed to drift beyond her reach.

Frustrated, she opened her eyes. They were in the hall, headed for the stairs. She tried to hide the fact that her teeth were chattering, but Ryan noticed and pulled her closer, shifting her body so that she was pressed tight against him, as if he could infuse her with his own body heat.

He glanced down at her, a shadow of concern touching his Caribbean blue eyes.

His hand was tucked in under her arm, directly beneath the swell of her right breast, and the warmth of his fingers sent a delicious thrill through her chilled skin. His touch warmed her even more than his eyes.

The feelings confused her and sent her brain into a spin. She'd been ready to assert herself, willing to do anything to get what she wanted. And then, she found herself defenseless and helpless in his arms.

She shifted closer to him, realizing that she felt the sudden increase in her heart rate, and with the side of her head pressed against his chest, she could hear the steady beat of his own heart accelerate to match her own. Apparently he was feeling this every bit as much as she was.

He climbed the stairs with ease and entered a bedroom done in a bright yellow. Bending down, he deposited her on the edge of the bed and stepped back.

His shirt was soaked, plastered to his chest and stomach. She could see the stark outline of his abdominal muscles. She swallowed hard, conscious of the hungry urge to reach out and trace the line of those firm, sculpted muscles.

She tore her gaze away. "I'm wet. I'm going to get the bed soaked."

"It's okay, you're on the bedspread. Stay put and I'll get something for you to change into."

He headed for the door, and she started to get up. She wasn't an inch off the bed when he stopped her. "Sit. Don't even *think* about getting up. For once, listen."

She sat back down and folded her hands in her lap. "I'm sitting already. I wasn't going anywhere."

"Of course you weren't," he said meaningfully before he disappeared.

Tess levered herself up and, on shaky legs, walked into the adjoining bathroom. She grabbed a bath towel off the rack and dried her shoulders and arms. When waves of dizziness hit a few times, she steadied herself on the edge of the sink.

Reaching up, she stripped the suit down over her shoulders and hips, and then stepped out of it. She wrapped a towel around herself and tucked the end between her breasts.

"You really do have a problem following directions."

Startled, she glanced up to see Ryan standing in the doorway, a pair of flannel pants and a sweatshirt slung over one arm. She wondered how long he'd been standing there. If it was long, he'd gotten an eyeful. "I figured it made more sense to get the wet suit off." He tossed her the clothes and she caught them, nodding her thanks. "You want to turn around for a minute?"

He nodded, but she noticed he didn't step out or close the door. She shrugged off the towel and quickly donned the dry clothes. Their softness and warmth felt wonderful against her clammy skin, and the fact that they were too big didn't bother her a bit.

She tied the drawstring of the pants around her waist once before tying it in a secure knot. Ryan's smell, the soap he used for his laundry, engulfed her as the sweatshirt slid over her head. She inhaled it, liking the clean scent.

"Okay, I'm decent."

He turned around and their gazes met. Tess pulled up the sagging neck of the shirt.

"Barely decent." A slightly teasing grin touched his lips.

Tess sucked in a deep breath. Okay, the fact that a man's smile turned her knees to Jell-O wasn't what she had expected. Had the bump on her head scrambled more than just her memories?

He motioned toward the bed. "Why don't you get into

bed, and I'll take a look at the cut. It reopened when you were in the pool. Then I'll check your vitals again.''

''I thought we went through this drill at the hospital,'' Tess grumbled. She didn't miss the fact that his unexpected effect on her was making her more than a little irritable.

''Be a sport and humor me,'' Ryan said. ''Like all doctors, I have an intense need to be needed.''

Tess ducked her head. Oh, yeah, he was needed all right, just not in the way he was thinking. She sighed inwardly. Great, now she was getting giddy. He was right, she really did need to get some rest. She slid into bed and tilted her head back so he could get at the cut.

He reached out and swept several strands of her hair back behind her ear. He had a healer's hands, long elegant fingers with a gentle touch, and as he slid the tips of them over the curve of her ear, Tess shivered.

A sharp stab of need shot through her belly, surprising her, and she shifted her feet beneath the covers, trying to hide her reaction. Perhaps she was more tired than she originally thought. The man was cleaning a tiny cut, not making love to her.

He leaned closer, using a cotton swab to gently clean the cut. ''What were you thinking about out there in the pool—right before you started to go under?''

His breath was warm on her cheek. Tess shook her head. Concentrate on his words, not on what he was doing to your body. ''I don't know. I don't remember much. It's pretty much a blur.''

As she spoke, Tess was conscious of how close he was, his mouth inches from hers. It would be so simple to lift her head and quickly brush her lips across his, and then run her tongue along the swell of his bottom lip.

She tightened her fingers on the edge of the sheet. What was wrong with her? Was *this* the kind of person she was?

''Do you trust me enough to try something, Tess?'' he

asked, breaking into her thoughts. The deep smoothness of his voice, combined with its sweet underlying raspiness, seemed to weave a seductive web around her, lulling her and surrounding her with its hypnotic tone.

Tess nodded numbly, trying desperately not to think about what she'd like to suggest they do. She felt like melting butter.

He continued to work on the cut, and she watched his lips move. "Don't force anything. Just let whatever is inside your head come out. Allow it to come out on its own."

She nodded again. Waiting.

"Close your eyes and concentrate on my voice."

Tess did as he asked. It was easier to comply than continue to stare up at his face and contemplate what she couldn't have. She settled back, feeling the cool sheet against the back of her neck.

"Good, now I want you to think back when you were in the pool. You're swimming, and the water feels good against your hot skin. It washes over you, cooling and cradling you." He paused a moment before continuing. "Everything—your arms, your legs, your breathing—everything is working together for the same purpose. You feel warm. You're secure. You feel totally safe."

Tess was surprised she truly could visualize exactly what he was saying. "You're swimming. No other thought except moving your arms and legs. You're enjoying yourself. You can feel the afternoon sun against your upper back, and the water runs over you and around you, cooling you. Comforting you."

Tess smiled, allowing the sensations to take over. And then, out of nowhere, an image popped into her brain. An image of herself strapped to a table, tubes and needles stuck in her arms—in her legs—in her neck. Her legs jumped, and in a haze, she looked up, watching as the figure of the ghost, cartoonish in its shape, hovered and floated overhead. She grimaced. What did it mean? The ghost reached out to her, but he was too far away.

A small whimper slipped between her lips, and Tess tensed. The tempo of her breathing quickened, the sound harsh and rasping in her ears.

Next to the bed, Ryan noticed the change immediately. He shifted closer, reaching out to stroke her forearm, trying to impart a sense that she wasn't alone. That he was there with her.

He continued to talk, "You're perfectly safe, Tess. No one can hurt you." He watched her eyes move rapidly back and forth beneath her eyelids. "Nothing is going to happen. Nothing will hurt you. You are in total control. You can wake up anytime you need to."

Beneath his fingertips, her muscles relaxed, and he could see the tension seep out of her shoulders. Her breathing slowed to normal. She was responding to him. Trusting what he said.

"Tell me what you see now, Tess?"

"Firecrackers. Thousands and thousands of firecrackers, all going off at once." Her voice shook with a touch of wonder. "It's beautiful. They're filling up the sky. It's like one big giant celebration." She paused as if listening to something. "I can hear people shouting and clapping," she said dreamily.

"I want you to concentrate on the voices, Tess. What are the people saying?"

Concentration knitted itself between her delicately arched brows. Ryan could feel some tenseness return to her body. "I can't make it out. They're shouting, but the words aren't clear." Suddenly her entire body jumped as if jolted by an electric wire.

Ryan touched her cheek, stroking her skin's velvety smoothness. "You're okay, Tess. Just tell me what's happening. You're safe."

"Oh, God! Oh, my God!" she gasped. "Someone's dead!" Her voice was harsh, strangled, but her eyes remained shut. She remained in a deep trance.

"Tell me who is dead."

"I—I don't know." Her head lifted as if she was trying to see something. "I can't see his face. But he's dead. I can tell he's dead. Everyone is standing around him. People are crying." Confusion flooded her delicate features. "No, wait, it isn't terrible. It—it's a good thing. I'm glad he's dead."

Ryan watched as anger and sadness fought for dominance on her face. Some kind of battle raged inside her. She was torn, unable to decide how to feel. How to react.

Ryan fought an overwhelming urge to gather her into his arms, to hold her and comfort her. To tell her that everything would be okay. That he'd help her figure things out.

But at the same time, he knew it was wrong to even consider offering her comfort like that. It was impossible for him to step across the invisible barrier erected between them.

She was his patient, and no matter how personal her pain and anguish seemed, Ryan knew that he could not allow himself to become personally involved. He had to maintain his distance.

Her teeth chattered and her limbs trembled violently beneath the sheet. "Oh, God, he's been shot. And there's blood everywhere." Her hands came up in front of her face and air hissed between her teeth. "Oh no, it's on me! I've got blood all over me. Get it off! Get it off." She frantically tried to wipe the imagined blood off on the sheets, her hands twisting and rubbing frantically on the sheets.

Ryan tried to gently restrain her frenzied movements, but she pulled away, sat bold upright and opened her eyes.

She stared at him, her pupils wide, her expression crumpling.

Ryan knew that he needed to calm her, to give her a

feeling of being safe. He continued to speak quietly, his words reassuring. Soothing.

But the look in Tess's eyes remained wild, and tears streamed down her face. She leaned forward, wrapping her arms around him and burying her face against the side of his neck. He could feel her tears on his skin.

"I don't understand," she sobbed against his neck. "Please help me understand."

Ignoring the voice that warned him not to, Ryan wrapped his arms around her, pulling her slender frame close. He gently stroked her back, trying to make her feel safe and protected.

His fingers tangled in the luxurious strands of white-gold hair streaming down her back. He could smell the sweet fragrance of soap in her hair, and he felt a tightening in his groin. A sign of danger.

As he fought against the reaction, Tess dropped her head back and stared up at him through tear-filled eyes. Eyes that turned an astonishing crystal green.

Her lips trembled and softened, parting slightly. They were inches from his own and a slow heat built inside Ryan, a heat so hot that it seemed to singe his lungs with each inhalation, making him feel as though he would never again catch his breath.

And even as the voice inside his head cautioned him to remember who and what he was, Ryan found himself slowly losing the battle, forgetting everything he'd promised himself he wouldn't do.

He dipped his head and brushed his lips across hers, savoring the taste. A taste like new honey on a hot summer's day, smooth and sugary, with a warmth that reached so deep inside him that he thought he might surely die.

But when Tess responded, her lips moving beneath his, her hands tunneling deep into his hair and her mouth making soft, urgent little sounds of need, Ryan froze and then pulled away.

My God, what was he thinking? Had he gone completely and totally insane? Lost his objectivity? His sense of professionalism? His heart pounded in his chest, and he shook his head as if clear the heavy, mind-numbing fog that threatened to engulf him. "Damn! I'm sorry, Tess. I had no right to do that."

"You don't need to apologize for anything."

He turned away and then turned back again, unsure what he wanted to do or say. But he knew he needed to do something.

"That was wrong. *Totally* wrong. I don't know what I was thinking." He raked a hand through his hair.

Tess watched him, her hair in wild disarray from the stroke of his hand. Her eyes were troubled. "Why did you stop?" she asked, and then laughed something soft and shaky. She lifted a hand and wiped a tear off her cheek. "You weren't doing anything wrong. I wanted you to kiss me. Actually, I *needed* you to kiss me."

"You might have wanted me to, but I stepped over the line."

She smiled, the tears drying on her face. "What's the matter? Didn't you like it?"

"It's not a matter of me liking it or not. I'm your doctor. I need to maintain a professional distance and I forgot that for a minute. I can't treat you one minute and then kiss you the next. It's totally unethical."

She shook her head. "We already discussed this. I'm not looking for a doctor. There was nothing wrong with us kissing. Other than the fact that it was too short."

Ryan didn't want to argue. He knew in her confused state, Tess wouldn't understand. Besides, it wasn't her responsibility to keep the line between them clearly defined. That was his job, and he'd failed.

He quickly cleaned up the supplies he'd used, leaving the antiseptic on the small table near the bathroom in case she needed it in the morning. He tried desperately to regain control of the emotions raging inside him.

He would not forget his role again. No matter how vulnerable or beautiful Tess was, she could not be subjected to him trying to fulfill his own needs at her expense. This was about her getting better, not him satisfying his desires.

Tomorrow he needed to find someone else willing to treat her. Someone who could help her overcome her memory loss and help her heal. But he knew that person wasn't going to be him. It was too dangerous for the both of them.

Somehow, Tess had touched a chord within him, unleashing feelings he hadn't realized existed. She'd brought out something in his own psyche that had pushed him over the edge, allowing him to break a sacred trust between doctor and patient. It would never happen again.

TESS WOKE. One minute she was sound asleep and the next her eyes were open and she was wide-awake. She was disorientated for a minute, unsure where she was other than in a bed and it was dark. But a few seconds later, the light filtering in from the bathroom told her she was in Ryan Donovan's house.

Rolling over onto her back, she listened, wondering what had woken her up. The tiniest of warning bells was going off inside her head. Something wasn't right.

A light breeze, warm with a summer's taste to it, ruffled the curtains and drifted across the room to brush her face. Outside, she could hear the crickets chirping, their sound comforting.

She refocused her attention on the inside of the house. No sounds from the direction of Ryan's room. But that didn't surprise her. He'd retreated pretty quickly after kissing her last night, telling her he'd close his bedroom door to keep Jung from jumping onto her bed and snuggling up with her during the night. She grinned in the darkness. Something told her it wasn't Jung he was afraid would come visiting during the night.

She tightened her shoulders. Damn, she needed to stop thinking like that. Her survival relied on her senses being sharp, tuned in. She didn't need to be thinking about what it would feel like to make love to Ryan Donovan. He'd been pretty clear that he wasn't going to let that happen.

She shifted her attention to the downstairs. The steady tick of the clock in the living room and the hum of the refrigerator in the kitchen. Nothing else. She rolled up on her side and snuggled deeper into the pillow. She needed to get some sleep.

Her eyes closed and she started to drift. And then, right when she was on the thinnest edge of sleep, she heard it. The soft scrape of metal on metal. Barely audible, but out of place in the natural rhythm of the night.

The crickets abruptly stopped chirping. They had heard it, too. Tess lifted her head, straining to hear. Her breath stalled in the back of her throat.

The sound had come from downstairs. It was the sound of the back patio door sliding open on its metal track.

She waited. Nothing—as if someone else was waiting, too.

Tess sat up and swung her legs over the side of the bed.

Every nerve in her body tingled with anticipation. Someone was trying to get into the house. No, they were already inside. Tess knew they were here for her.

There was a scurry of movement in the downstairs hall, muffled footsteps and whispered voices. More than one person. She needed to get out. Too much of a risk to stay and fight.

She considered running down the hall to Ryan's room, of

making a stand with him at her side. But she could already hear them on the stairs.

No time. She shoved her feet into the shoes sitting at the side of the bed and headed for the window.

Down the hall, she heard Jung give a warning bark. Good boy, he was on patrol even though Ryan had barricaded him in his room. She slid the window open and started to throw a leg over the sill.

That's when it hit her. A mind-jolting blast of pain right between her shoulder blades.

Tess dropped, falling over backward. Her limbs, arms and legs, twitched and jittered uselessly.

She landed on her back. Her vision clouded. Damn, someone had hit her with a Taser. Her brain yawned and then seemed to scramble, every thought going in a million different directions at once.

She tried to focus. Tried to make her muscles do what she wanted them to do. But they couldn't cooperate. She was a defenseless infant, sprawled on the floor.

From the corner of her vision, she could see them moving toward her. Two dark shapes. But she was too scrambled, too confused to see any specifics.

She couldn't move, couldn't defend herself.

She was completely at their mercy.

SOMETHING COLD AND WET poked Ryan in the face.

''Jeez, Jung, get down,'' he grumbled, pushing the dog's wet nose out of the way. He lifted his head and listened, but the heavy hum of the air conditioner was the only sound. ''Go back to sleep,'' he ordered as his head dropped back down onto his pillow.

Jung whimpered and stuck his nose right back in his face.

Ryan sat up.

Frantic, Jung ran to the door, scratching and barking wildly.

"Okay, okay, I get the message. You need to go out." He got up. "You better not be using this as a ploy to get into Tess's room." He leaned down to scratch Jung's ear. "You're as enamored with her as I am, aren't you boy."

The dog ignored him and barked again.

Ryan opened the door and was practically knocked aside as the dog charged down the hall, headed directly for Tess's room.

Concerned, Ryan ran after him.

Two strange men, dressed entirely in black and wearing hoods, stood in her room. One of them had Tess in his arms. Her eyes were open, but she wasn't moving. Her body was limp.

"What the hell—" Ryan yelled.

Jung was already tearing at the arm of one of the men, growling and snarling, his powerful jaws clamped onto the man's wrist. The man appeared to have a gun clasped in his hand, but Ryan couldn't be sure.

The other man turned toward Ryan. "We're just here for the woman," he said. "Call your damn dog off and we'll leave."

"You're not going anywhere," Ryan said, circling to the left. "Put her down."

"Can't do that, buddy." The man moved closer to the window. "Just let us take the woman and you can walk away. It doesn't have to concern you."

"Not going to happen," Ryan said, moving closer.

The guy backed up more, his eyes focused on Ryan's face. As Ryan passed the vanity table, he palmed the bottle of antiseptic.

"Guess we do this the hard way, huh, Doc," the man said as he unceremoniously dumped Tess's limp body onto the cushioned chair next to the window. Her head lolled back, and her arms flopped to her side. Her eyes were fuzzy, as if she couldn't focus.

The man charged, head down. He hit Ryan in the stomach, sending him backward. They hit the wall together with a crash. Ryan lifted a knee, jamming it up into the man's chin. The man grunted, his head snapping back.

As he staggered upright, Ryan swung, hitting him full in the cheek. A burst of pain shot up the length of Ryan's arm, but he ignored it, going after the man with a fast right, followed by a left. The man fell over, hitting his forehead on the windowsill. He lay still. Stunned.

Ryan turned his attention on the other man. Jung had him cornered, his back against the bedroom closet. The gun lay on the floor. Good dog, he'd earned an extra treat. He'd gotten the man to release the gun.

Ryan rounded the bed.

The second intruder dived for the gun, but Ryan beat him to it, lashing out with a kick that caught the man in the shoulder and spun him around. He yelped in pain as Jung jumped on his back, sinking his teeth into the meaty part of his upper shoulder.

"Ry-an," Tess's warning was weak, barely a whisper.

He whirled around but not in time to dodge a fist from the first man, who had recovered. The blow smashed into his left temple. Bursts of light exploded in front of Ryan's eyes, and he staggered two steps back.

He shook his head, trying to clear it.

The man charged him again, knocking him into the closet doors. The doors crashed inward, sending Ryan sprawling against a collapsed rack of clothes.

"Come on, let's get out of here!" one of the men yelled.

Jung yelped as the first man landed a good kick, sending him rolling into Ryan.

The two men rushed out of the room. Seconds later, their footsteps thundered on the stairs as they ran for the front door. The door opened and then slammed shut.

Untangling himself from Jung, Ryan pulled himself up.

He ignored the sensation of red-hot needles prickling the entire left side of his face. He rounded the end of the bed, kneeling beside Tess.

"Are you all right?"

She lifted her head, her smile lopsided and halfhearted. "Sorry I wasn't much help. They stunned me with a Taser gun as soon as they entered the room."

He helped her sit up. "Who the hell were they?"

She shook her head. "I don't know. I woke up and they were in the house."

"I'm calling the police."

"No!" Tess reached out and grabbed his arm, preventing him from reaching for the phone sitting next to the bed.

"What do you mean, no? Someone broke into my house and tried to kidnap you. That's not something to fool around with, Tess. The police need to investigate."

She shook her head and weakly tried to pull herself to a standing position. She flopped back against the cushion and he didn't miss the frustration in her eyes. "No cops. If you call the cops I'm out of here."

"From the looks of things, you couldn't leave if you wanted to. You can barely sit up."

Ryan picked up the phone and dialed 911.

Chapter Five

The next morning, General Thomas Flynn watched the endless rush of cornfields whip past the car window. He
clamped his back teeth together and glanced down at his
hands resting on his thighs. They were clenched so tight his
knuckles shown white.

He forced himself to relax, sliding his finger along the
crisp crease in his trousers. How did people actually live
here? It was so far from civilization that their nearest neighbor could only be reached by getting into some kind of
junky, beat-up truck and driving miles over teeth-rattling
roads.

He shifted on the smooth leather seat, shooting his wrist
out the end of his jacket to check his watch. Six-forty. The
trip from the airport seemed to be longer than he remembered. Perhaps he should have allowed Bloom to send the
helicopter, but Flynn knew keeping a low profile was critical
right now.

He'd only visited once before, right after the center
opened four years ago, and the less contact he had with the
place the less chance there was that he'd be tied to the center
if something went wrong.

If something went wrong. He snorted in disgust. Something like their prime test subject rabbiting on them and
Bloom's bumbled rescue attempt. He leaned forward and hit

the button lowering the window separating him from the driver. The young man behind the wheel glanced into the rearview mirror and cocked a respectful eyebrow. "Sir?"

"How much farther to the Half Moon?"

"About ten minutes, sir."

"Take me directly to the police station."

The driver nodded. "Yes, sir. Dr. Bloom made it very clear that you wanted to be taken there first. He said that he'd meet you there. Perhaps you'd—"

Flynn cut off the young man's comment by raising the privacy window again. He focused his attention back on the view outside his window. He wasn't in the least interested in what the young man thought he might like to do while he waited.

At the moment, he was more concerned about how the local chief of police was going to take the story he and Bloom had cooked up regarding Tess.

It was imperative that they get Tess back within the walls of the center's lab. The sooner she was under their control again, the sooner they could proceed with their plans.

TESS ROLLED UP on her side and groggily tried to see the clock sitting on the oak bedside table.

She watched as the green digital numbers flipped over to read 7:45 a.m. She rubbed her eyes and flopped over onto her back again. Her gaze fell on Ryan, sound asleep in the chair by the window.

She smiled. How sweet. He'd agreed to sit with her last night until she fell asleep. But he must have been so tired, he'd fallen asleep sitting upright in the chair. His head was stretched back at an uncomfortable angle, and dark, unruly strands of his thick hair fell onto his forehead, giving him a slightly rumpled look.

Once the cops and paramedics were done asking their questions and checking them both over, the police had done a complete walk-through of the house and yard. They had left, promising to return in the morning with material to check for fingerprints. Not that anyone thought they'd find anything, especially when Ryan told them both men had been wearing gloves. But she knew they would be back and this time their boss, Chief Cole, would be with him. She'd been relieved last night when they showed up without the police chief.

She sat up and swung her feet over the side of the bed. A shooting pain between her shoulder blades and in her lower back reminded her of last night's tussle. She eased herself to her feet, stretching a bit to loosen her tight muscles.

Jung stood in the doorway, watching her with alert brown eyes, his bony tail thumping eagerly against the door panel.

He wanted out and his master was dead to the world. Tess figured she could do the honors and then spend a few minutes whipping up a hearty breakfast for Ryan. It was the least she could do considering how good he'd been to her.

She tiptoed downstairs and walked out through to the kitchen. Jung followed close on her heels, nearly tripping her more than once. As she unlatched the patio door and slid the screen door open, he made urgent little noises in the back of his throat. When the door was open, he bounded out, taking off for the far end of the yard.

Tess opened the refrigerator door and studied the eggs-and-bacon situation. She yawned. Maybe a quick shower would wake her up enough to do the job right. Shuffling back down the hall, she headed for the upstairs bathroom.

But as she neared the front of the house, someone knocked on the door.

She froze. Another knock, more insistent this time, hit the door. Tess took a steadying breath and stepped closer to the door. Her hand hovered over the knob. Should she open it?

She rested her hand on the knob and it twisted beneath

her fingers. She snatched her hand back as if burned. Someone was trying to get in.

Through the frosted glass bracketing the front door, she could see shadowy figures shift and move. There was more than one person standing on the front stoop.

She chewed her bottom lip. What now?

Another knock.

A hand and then a face pressed against the window. Someone was trying to peer inside. Tess flattened herself against the wall, holding her breath.

The shadow disappeared.

"They've got to be here," a deep voice said, filtering through the front door. "The doctor's car is in the driveway."

"Maybe they're out back and can't hear the bell," someone else said, this voice sounding vaguely familiar. Tess was sure that it was Chief Cole's voice.

Crouching down, she crept to the front window. She opened the drapes a slit. Two men stepped off the front stoop. A third man stood on the walkway.

As she'd thought, one was Chief Cole. The second man, totally bald and wearing an expensive suit, was the one closest to the door. But it was the third man who attracted Tess's closest scrutiny. He wore a military uniform and stood back from the other two. Every button and star gleamed in the sunlight, and he held his body at rigid attention, his cool gaze narrow and intense.

A whisper of fear brushed the back of Tess's neck and goose bumps pebbled both her arms. She had no idea who he was, but something told her he was a threat. Her fingers tightened on the edge of the drape, and she fought back a black wave of dizziness.

As she watched, the three men started across the lawn, headed for the back of the house. Two other men stepped into view, following close behind. They were younger and bigger than the other three. They wore white T-shirts with a logo over the front pocket and white pants belted at their thick waistlines. Tess knew they were the trained gorillas— the ones along to make sure she cooperated.

Before rounding the corner of the house, the military man paused and said something to the two trained gorillas. They nodded and headed back for the car.

Good. That meant they weren't coming around to the back with the other three. Fewer people for her to deal with. Tess turned and raced for the back door. She'd left it open. She needed to lock it.

Her stocking feet skidded on the linoleum floor, and as she scrambled for balance, saw the side gate start to open. Too late! She ducked behind the counter. Reaching up, she cracked open the pantry door and slipped inside, closing the door after her. It was dark inside. Dark and crowded. She pushed her way to the back, holding her breath.

Two seconds later, someone pounded on the patio door.

"Hello in there!" Chief Cole shouted.

Tess sank into the farthest corner of the closet, clutching her arms around her legs and struggling to quiet her breathing. How long before they gave up and left? How long before she was safe?

RYAN SAT UP with a start. He glanced around, slightly disorientated. What the hell was he doing sitting in the spare bedroom?

The taste in his mouth and the stiffness in his joints told him that he'd fallen asleep in the chair. A quick glance at the bed confirmed his worst fears. It was empty, meaning he'd either slept through a second abduction attempt or Tess had taken off.

He doubted it was the first scenario. From what he'd witnessed last night, Tess wasn't about to go anywhere with anyone peacefully. More likely she got it in her head to take off on her own.

She'd been amazingly calm and coolheaded during the abduction attempt. But when the cops and the paramedics came, she'd been spooked and angry, almost sullen when answering their questions.

Bam! Bam! Bam! Someone was pounding on the back door.

Jumping up, Ryan ran down the stairs. He could hear Jung adding to the racket by barking and howling interchangeably. Maybe Tess had locked herself out.

Entering the kitchen, he saw three men standing under the shade of the awning at his back door. Two he recognized—Sidney Bloom and Chief Cole. The other man was dressed in an immaculately creased army uniform with three silver stars gleaming on the perfectly braced epaulets on his shoulders.

Ryan slid open the door, not missing the fact that it was already unlocked. Had Tess really walked out?

"Sorry to bother you, Ryan," Bloom said. "But I needed to talk to you and I saw the car parked out front. I knew you were here."

Ryan got the impression that Bloom was nervous, on edge.

"We had a little excitement here last night, and I ended up falling asleep in the chair." Ryan glanced around the kitchen. No sign of Tess. It didn't even look as though she'd eaten. No coffee in the pot or dishes in the sink. A knot of concern settled into the pit of his stomach.

"We were wondering if we could speak to your guest," Bloom said. "The young woman, Tess. She's still here, isn't she?"

"Guess you've kept abreast of who comes and goes at the house, huh, Sidney?" Ryan opened the door wider and stepped aside. "Why not come inside, it's cooler."

Jung scooted around all three men and ran right for the pantry door. His butt hit the floor and he lifted a paw to scratch the wood panel. He whined pitifully.

Ryan ignored him and waved the three men into his kitchen. They entered, looking tense. Ill at ease.

"I don't have all day," the general said, his impatience obvious.

"Of course not." Bloom's gaze darted to Ryan. "Ryan, this is General Flynn." He waved a hand in Ryan's direction. "Dr. Donovan joined our staff a few weeks ago."

They exchanged brief handshakes, the general's flint-colored eyes seeming to sear into Ryan, a blatant attempt to intimidate. Ryan didn't bite, and he put a little extra squeeze into his handshake.

"It's a pleasure, Doctor."

"Likewise." But Ryan knew that whatever pleasure the general was referring to had nothing to do with meeting him. The man seethed with impatience. "What exactly did you want to talk with Tess about?"

"Private business," Flynn snapped. "But if you must know, I'm here to take her home."

"Take her home?"

"General Flynn is Tess's father. He's been worried about her since she disappeared several days ago." There was no missing the slight tinge of nervousness in Bloom's voice.

"Tess mentioned that her father was dead," Ryan said slowly. "She still has huge gaps in her memory, but she was pretty clear that her father was dead."

Bloom and Flynn exchanged glances.

"That's part of her delusions," Flynn said. "Where is she, Doctor? I need to know she's safe."

"I'm sorry, she's not here. When I got up this morning, she was gone."

From the other side of the kitchen, Jung's whine got louder.

"What's wrong with the damn dog?" Chief Cole asked.

Ryan moved over to the pantry. "His treats are in there. He's just reminding me that I haven't given him one of his treats."

Chief Cole grunted, making it obvious what he thought of dog owners who spoiled their pets with doggie biscuits.

Ryan opened the pantry door and grabbed the box of treats sitting on the middle shelf. As he stepped back, something red caught his eye. He frowned and peered deeper into the closet. What the hell?

Crouched down in the farthest corner of the closet, between a twenty-pound bag of potatoes and a canister of dog chow, sat Tess. He opened his mouth, but she quickly put a finger to her lips and shook her head. Her message was clear.

Perplexed, Ryan slipped the box under one arm and closed the door. Jung didn't move from his position in front of the pantry door. Doggie treats had definitely lost their appeal. He whined again, drawing the final note out like a true hound in distress.

"Come, Jung," Ryan ordered, shaking the box.

Jung glanced over at him, his brown eyes seeming to say *Back off, buddy. I've got a wicked game of hide-and-seek going here and you're ruining it.*

Ryan reached over and grabbed the Lab's collar. He had to practically drag Jung across the kitchen floor to the back door. The Lab's toenails skidded across the floor as Ryan pushed him out the door. He threw two biscuits out onto the patio and then slid the door closed.

"Have a seat, gentlemen."

Normally he would have invited them all into the living room, but something told him that Tess wanted to hear what they had to say. Hell, he was curious, as well. He had no idea why Tess was cowering in the back of his pantry, frightened of the men who had entered his house. But he was smart enough to know that there had to be a good reason for her fear.

He opened the refrigerator and grabbed a pitcher of iced tea, setting on the table. "What's this all about?"

"The general's daughter disappeared. He's been concerned about her whereabouts and when he heard she was here in Half Moon, he came to pick her up."

"How did he know she was here?" Ryan leveled a glance in the general's direction. The man stared coolly back, a thin line of anger bracketing his lips. An uncomfortable chill slid up the middle of Ryan's back. This was a man who was used to getting his way, and he was positioning himself to get that now.

"I saw the news clip on the accident and heard about the appearance of a young women who didn't know her name."

Ryan frowned. "But there was no picture of Tess on the TV."

"The description they provided fit the description of my daughter."

"So, you're not positive she *is* your daughter?"

Ryan forced himself not to glance in the direction of the pantry. Something in the general's face told him that the man was waiting for exactly that kind of reaction.

"I'm not positive," Flynn said begrudgingly, "but my daughter's name is Tess."

"It's critical the general locate his daughter," Bloom said. "She has a lot of serious problems."

"What kind of problems?"

Bloom pulled a thick file out of his briefcase and dropped it onto the table. "General Flynn was kind enough to bring a copy of his daughter's psychiatric file. I've looked it over. This is a young woman with a long history of very severe psychiatric problems."

"Which might explain the dead man in the cornfield," Cole added, setting his glass down.

Ryan shook his head. "I'm sorry, but there's no way Tess is responsible for the death of that man." He tapped the file in front of him. "I don't care what kind of crap is in this file."

"The Ryan Donovan I know doesn't jump to conclusions without reading all the evidence," Bloom said. "Read the file. She's a paranoid schizophrenic, suffering from auditory and visual hallucinations. She's attempted suicide five times, and she has physically assaulted her father, two boyfriends and a whole line of different hospital staff over the past five years. She even tried to stab an orderly while escaping from the last facility she was in. She was there on a seventy-two-hour court-ordered evaluation. You know what that means."

Ryan stood up. This was just getting worse. He knew only too well what a court-ordered evaluation meant. A person didn't get committed unless he or she was totally out of control. Unless he or she was suicidal or homicidal.

He raked a hand through his hair. "We can't be talking about the same person." He paused, his eyes connecting with the general's. "I'm a good clinician. I've spent time with this woman—not just a session or two in my office. It's ridiculous for me to even consider the possibility that she's psychotic or capable of the level of violence you're talking about."

Flynn smiled coldly. "Believe me when I say that I know my daughter, too, Doctor. Perhaps better than you." He reached over and tapped the psychiatric file. "Do as Dr. Bloom suggests—read the file. My daughter is capable of the things Dr. Bloom describes."

Ryan shook his head again, refusing to buy any of what they were saying. "I'm sorry, but again we have to be talking about two different women."

Flashing a look of disdain, Flynn flipped open the file and pointed to a photo stapled to the inside front cover. "Is this the woman currently staying at your house?"

Dread tightened around Ryan's throat. There was no mistaking the stunning cloud of white-blond hair. He leaned closer, studying the photo. Tess's face stared out at him from the photo. She had a more sophisticated, polished look. Her trademark hair was twisted up off her smooth porcelain shoulders, and soft, wispy tendrils escaped to frame a classically oval face and wide expressive green eyes.

"Is this the woman?" the general demanded.

Ryan dragged his eyes away from the picture. "Yes, that's her."

"I thought so." Flynn sat back. "You need to understand something, Doctor. Tess was a difficult child. A violent teenager prone to both verbally and physically aggressive behavior."

"Most teenagers go through a rebellious stage, General," Ryan protested. "In our society it's almost a rite of passage."

Flynn smiled indulgently. "Tess rebelled at age eight. She was plagued with horrible nightmares from birth on. But she was always bright and articulate. Perhaps tragically bright. She was admitted to Rochester Institute of Technology when she was only seventeen. It was there that she experienced her first psychotic break."

"How?" Ryan asked.

"Her first semester, campus security found Tess on the roof of the high-rise dorm, stark naked and covered in paint. She insisted that she was involved in an ancient tribal ritual that made it imperative that she jump off the high-rise and soar out over the campus. She had to be restrained by three security men."

Ryan swallowed hard. Surprisingly, the scenario didn't seem that far-fetched. He'd heard and seen enough similar incidents in his own practice. Had her earlier appearance at the Carson's farm, naked and confused, been the first indication of a new break? The thought threw him. How could he have been so wrong about her? How could he have missed the clinical signs?

"Tess is quite good at manipulating people," Flynn said, as if picking up on Ryan's train of thought. "I'm not at all surprised you weren't able to pick up on her psychosis. She has moments of very rational behavior."

"But she wasn't so rational when she killed the driver of that car, was she?" Cole asked, sounding like a one-note recording.

Ryan turned on the police chief. "You've wanted to pin this on her from the moment you met her. What's your problem?"

A part of Ryan knew he was being unreasonable. Unwilling to look at the evidence with an open mind. But he was angry. Angry that he'd missed the evidence. Angry that any of this had to be true.

"In case you've forgotten, Doc, the man is dead," Cole said.

"How do you even know she was with him?"

"Because I hired him to bring Tess here to Half Moon," Flynn said.

"You what?" Ryan whipped around to face Flynn. "Hired him? Why?"

"His name was Trevor Vaughn. He was a registered nurse I hired to transport Tess here to the center. I heard about some of the experimental work being done here, and I thought it was worth the effort to see if Dr. Bloom could help Tess."

A wave of suspicion brushed the back of Ryan's neck, and his clinical radar went off with a silent wail. Something was not right. Flynn's story didn't fit what Ryan had witnessed at the crash site.

He kept his face impassive as he studied the General. The weariness and concern on the man's face seemed forced, as if he was playing a role.

"Vaughn was supposed to hire two other professionals to assist him with Tess's transfer. But it seems that he decided to pocket the money rather than hire additional help. It's a mistake that seems to have cost the man his life."

Ryan knew there were huge inconsistencies in what the man was saying. The story didn't ring true. "It isn't often that a person crashes through a fence in an attempt to get *into* a facility."

Steel-colored flecks of anger flashed in Flynn's eyes, but he hid them as quickly as they appeared. "Perhaps Tess forced Vaughn to crash through the fence when she realized she was about to be incarcerated in another facility." He shrugged. "If she overpowered him with a gun, he wouldn't have had a chance."

"Where would she have gotten a gun?"

The angry flecks were back in Flynn's eyes. "How should I know, Doctor? Like you, I wasn't there. We can only make educated guesses at this point—until we're able to talk to Tess, that is."

"I find it interesting that you are all ready to pin this on Tess. Nothing you've said proves that she's capable of killing a man in cold blood," Ryan said.

Flynn threw up his hands. "Obviously nothing will convince you, Doctor, and I don't have time for this nonsense. Where is my daughter? We're leaving now." He pushed back his chair and stood.

Ryan got to his feet, too, not backing down from the man's hostile stare. "Last time I looked, General, this was still the United States. That gives Tess some rights. And one of those rights is to say where she goes and who she goes with."

Bloom cleared his throat nervously and pulled a thick document out of the front of Tess's file. "Uh, actually that isn't quite true, Ryan. General Flynn has full guardianship over his daughter." He opened the document and handed it to Ryan, adding, "It's for her own protection. The courts have determined that she's a danger to herself and others."

Ryan glanced over the paperwork, acutely aware that they'd played their ace in the hole. The cold satisfaction on Flynn's face told him that the man had been waiting for just this opportunity. He knew that Ryan understood only too well what such a court order meant—essentially, that Tess had no rights. She was a person without any decision-making ability in the eyes of the law.

"She's not going anywhere until I've had the opportunity to talk to her," he said firmly. "Let me talk to her alone and then she'll come with you. At least until we get this straightened out."

The general's eyes darkened and the muscle in the center of his lean cheek jumped. "I want my daughter now, Donovan."

"Well, we're going to have to do things my way," Ryan said, his voice soft and deadly. "Tess deserves some degree of dignity. And that means you wait outside while I talk to her."

"I thought you said she wasn't here."

"I lied."

A cold smile crossed the general's face. For a moment Ryan thought he'd refuse, but finally he nodded and moved to the patio door. He paused before stepping outside. "You have exactly two minutes to convince her. But don't ever try to cross me again, Doctor."

Ryan closed the door, already trying to figure out how to get Tess to cooperate, at least until he was able to pull some strings and find out what was going on. He didn't want her hurt and there was no question that Flynn was going to force the issue no matter how cooperative or uncooperative she was.

Ryan knew he needed more time. Time to investigate how

legal and binding the court papers were. Time to see if Tess had any other options.

But he only had two minutes and something told him that Tess was just as stubborn and impatient as the man who was here to whisk her away.

Chapter Six

Tess seethed with outrage. Who the hell did Ryan Donovan think he was, making promises he couldn't keep? He had no right to speak for her.

She hit the flat panel of the pantry door and it swung open in his face. She could barely contain her fury, and from the calm expression his face, she could tell he had anticipated just such a reaction from her. That in itself irritated the hell out of her.

He stepped aside as she blew past, his gaze coolly assessing, but Tess wasn't in any mood to be reasoned with. Or worse yet, placated.

"Before you rip me a new one, hear me out," he said softly.

Tess whirled around, anger tensing every muscle in her body. "How dare you promise them that I'd go with them. Are you totally nuts?"

"I gather you heard everything we discussed," he said calmly.

Tess pulled a face. "I was less than three feet away. Of course I heard everything. And from the looks of things, you bought every outlandish lie he fed you."

"Not entirely."

"You could have fooled me."

He leaned one broad shoulder against the doorframe and

folded his arms. "I'm not left with a lot of choices, Tess. They have evidence to show that Flynn is your father. He has a pretty detailed psychiatric file on you and a court document giving him guardianship. If you can disprove any or all of this, I'll stand by you to the end. But you need to give me something to work with."

"So a lousy piece of paper is more important than what you feel in your gut?"

"Be reasonable, Tess. They—"

"Be reasonable?" She leaned in, poking her finger into the center of his chest, her sense of betrayal so intense, so hurtful that it seemed to shred her insides. "You mean you want me to accept what that man is saying about me? Believe that I'm some kind of psychotic nutcase? A person so dangerous and so deranged that I can't even be trusted to make my own decisions?"

Her hand tightened into fist against his chest. She closed her eyes, trying desperately to regain control. If she lost it now and started screaming, she'd never prove anything. He'd believe Flynn.

"Easy, Tess."

She sucked in a calming breath. "If you think, for even one minute, that I'm going anywhere with that man, you're crazier than he says I am."

"Look, you're getting too worked up over this. We need to sit down and talk about this rationally."

She dropped her hand, her shoulders slumping. "I'm as rational as I can be in the circumstances."

"All I'm asking is that you go along with them until I have a chance to figure out what's going on. Flynn is not going to hurt you. He thinks he's rescuing you. Humor him." He ran a hand through his hair, as if stalling while he tried to figure out how to convince her to do things his way. "Hell, if you can't humor him, humor me. Give me a little time to track things down. Let me do a little investigating. I promise you, I'm not turning my back on you."

"I'm not in a mood to humor *you* or anyone else." Tess moved to stand in front of the patio doors, not caring if the general saw her through the glass or not. She stared defiantly out at him.

Although the morning sun reflected on the glass and probably blinded Flynn from seeing what was going on inside the house, he stood facing the door, his shoulders braced, his hands clasped behind him at parade rest. His gray eyes seemed to bore holes of white heat through the glass, and Tess stared back at him.

She could feel his impatience soaking into her body, tightening her stomach. She wasn't sure how, but she knew that they'd been engaged in a similar mental standoff in the past. This had an all-too-familiar feel to it.

She swallowed against the fear rising in her chest. A fear so raw and intense that she knew that, in spite of not remembering Flynn, of not recognizing him, she couldn't trust him under any circumstance. No matter what Ryan thought, cooperation was impossible. Dangerous even.

She turned and faced Ryan again.

"I promise you, I won't walk away. I'll stay with you," he said. "I'll dig until I find out what's going on. I have contacts—people I can call to get information on Flynn. I can call the hospitals he says you were treated in. I can talk to the doctors who have worked with you over the years. But you need to give me more time, Tess. I can't make it happen just like that."

He snapped his fingers, and his eyes, those brilliant blue eyes pleaded with her to see things his way.

Tess sighed and shook her head. "For a shrink, you really don't listen too well, do you? I don't have time to waste waiting for you to figure out what's going on. I *cannot* go with that man. I can't explain it and I can't make it any clearer than what I've already tried to say. I just know that if I go with him, I'm lost. There will be nothing left of me when he's done.''

She could see the disbelief in Ryan's eyes. She knew that at that moment he believed she was lost to him, that she'd drifted away and lost touch with reality.

Tess felt as though her heart might shatter into a million pieces of fragile glass. There was no way she was going to be able to reach him. ''It's all right, Ryan. I appreciate all you've done for me up to this point. I'll take it from here.''

She brushed past him, headed for the front of the house and freedom. Ryan fell in step behind her.

''Running isn't going to solve anything, Tess. They'll only come after you. Can't you see that they're concerned about your welfare.'' He grabbed her shoulder, halting her retreat.

Tess whirled around, anger replacing the pain she'd felt a minute ago. ''My welfare? You think that man out there, the one claiming to be my father, cares one whit for my welfare?''

She could see a flicker of something, perhaps confusion, maybe even uncertainty, cross Ryan's face. She knew, without him saying anything, that he was bothered by Flynn's attitude, too.

''You have to help me understand, Tess. Help me support you. I can't do that unless you spell things out.'' Frustration clouded his face. ''All you've given me are a bunch of vague, unsubstantiated reasons for believing that Flynn wants to harm you. You have to know on some level how crazy all of this sounds. Give me some hard facts to hang those feelings on.''

But Tess didn't have anything to give him other than her raw emotions, her deep-seated fear that if Flynn managed to get her to go with him, he'd destroy her. She would cease to exist.

She turned and put her hand on the doorknob, pausing for a moment. "Can you honestly tell me that you trust those men implicitly?" Her voice trembled slightly. "Can't you put aside your skepticism, your suspicions, for one minute and *just believe* me?"

Ryan reached out and covered her hand with his. She felt his sincerity, his need to make things right pulse with the heat of his hand. "I want to, Tess, I really do. But you haven't given me anything. I know you're hurting right now, but you've said yourself that your memory is gone. Wiped clean. How can you trust the feelings you're having, knowing those feelings could be flawed?"

Tess shook her head, a deep sadness threatening to swallow her whole. He couldn't trust her any more than she could trust him.

She reached up and touched the side of his face, the briefest brush of her fingertips along the roughness of his jaw. "You should shave," she whispered.

He reached up and covered her hand with his, holding it to his cheek. The roughness of his skin scraped as he turned his head, his lips pressing intimately against the center of her palm. She felt the scorching heat of his mouth touch the center of her hand, his tongue lightly tracing her lifeline as if memorizing it.

She closed her eyes, savoring the feel of him, knowing that it might be the last time she ever felt his lips on her skin.

She leaned her head forward and touched her forehead to his chest. "Is your job so important to you that you can't believe what your own heart is telling you?" she asked. "Is it really that easy to sell me out?"

He had no answer.

Tess slipped her hand from his, opened the front door and walked out onto the front steps.

RYAN BRACED HIMSELF against the surge of pain that raced through him at Tess's comment. His hand dropped to his side. How could he make her understand that he wasn't selling her out? That he wanted with all his heart to believe what she was saying to him.

He heard the patio door slide open.

"Stop right there, Tessa. Don't even think of running."

Ryan saw Tess's spine stiffen in response to her father's demand. Obviously Flynn had gotten impatient.

"Stop her, Donovan!"

She shot Ryan a quick glance. "Decision time, Doc. Whose side are you on?"

Ryan held her gaze but addressed Flynn, "I thought I made it clear that you were to wait outside, General. Tess needs to make this decision on her own without any pressure from you. Now back off."

He could see surprise register on Tess's face, the slight widening of her eyes and the small arch to one eyebrow. She hadn't expected him to stand up for her. She had expected him to simply step aside. It hurt to know that she expected him to feed her to the wolves.

He moved to block Flynn.

"There are no decisions to be made, Doctor. Tess is leaving *now* and with me." He crooked his finger and motioned for her to come.

The arrogance of the gesture grated on Ryan's last nerve. If the man *was* indeed her father, Ryan could well understand Tess's distrust of the man.

When she didn't immediately obey, a silvery flash of anger darted into Flynn's eyes. "There's no need to make this more difficult than it already is, Tessa."

"This isn't going to be difficult at all, General," Ryan assured him. "Mainly because Tess will be leaving with me. If you're set on her going to see a doctor of your choosing, so be it. But I'll accompany her to that appointment."

"Get out of our way, Donovan," Flynn said curtly. He snapped his fingers at Bloom, and Ryan watched his boss move up to stand next to Flynn. There was a syringe in his hand.

Rage heated Ryan's insides and he stepped out onto the steps, sheltering Tess with his body. "All right, this has gone far enough. You are not going to take her by force." He pointed at Bloom. "Put the syringe away. This is not the way to handle things."

Beside him, Tess's hands tightened into fists, and he felt her body shift, her weight coming forward onto her toes. She was going into fight mode. The situation was escalating out of control. He needed to get everyone to calm down. To think things through.

"You had your chance to convince her to come quietly. Now we'll take over." Flynn's cold eyes settled on Tess. "Don't fight me, Tessa. Just let Dr. Bloom give you some medication to help you relax."

"If you come any closer, I'll shove that medication where it'll do the most good," Tess snapped, moving backward, one step at a time.

The two men lounging against the side of the limo straightened up. They were big, muscular and decidedly mean looking. Ryan didn't need anyone to tell him that they were the two goons hired to handle Tess if the situation turned physical. Although they were both probably trained in nonviolent-restraint techniques, they looked a little too eager to mix it up.

Tess moved out onto the lawn, and the two men split up, started circling her from opposite directions. She was effectively surrounded, hemmed in. But she didn't appear overly apprehensive. Perhaps she had no idea what was about to happen.

"Tess, stay near me," Ryan warned. He glanced at Bloom. "This does not have to happen like this."

Bloom ignored him, his attention focused on Tess. "Your part in this is over, Ryan. Get out of the way."

Both men moved toward Tess, but Ryan stepped between them. "Look, I think everyone needs to just chill out." He motioned again for Tess to step behind him. "You're scaring her, making things worse. Back off and let me deal with this."

"I've already told you we're done doing things your way, Donovan," Flynn snapped. "If you continue to interfere, I'll have the Chief arrest you. Now move!"

Ryan shot a glance in Chief Cole's direction. Was the lawman really going to allow this insanity to continue?

Cole stood off to one side, his expression mildly amused. Apparently he wasn't about to jump into the fray, but he also wasn't about to put a stop to it. He shrugged. "Sorry, Doc, but the general's got a point. His papers are in order. Totally legal. He's got the right to insist that his daughter accompany him. So I suggest you move aside and let him get about his business."

Flynn darted out a hand, reaching around Ryan and grabbing Tess's forearm. He yanked her toward him. She screamed and kicked out, her foot connecting with his shin. Flynn grunted but hung on.

Ryan tried prying the general's fingers off Tess's arm, but he found himself grabbed from behind, a beefy arm closing around his throat. The arm tightened, cutting off his oxygen. One of the goons had him in a bear hug.

He struggled, using his larger frame to yank the man off balance. They shuffled back and forth a few clumsy steps until Ryan managed to slip an arm up and around the man's head. He jerked backward and then leveraged the goon forward, flipping him over his shoulder. The man hit the ground with a satisfying grunt.

But before he could straighten up, Ryan was hit by the second man, a quick blow to the back of the head. He stumbled forward a few steps as a wild array of white and yellow lights exploded in his head and he fell to his knees.

"Ryan!" Tess screamed again, her desperation palpable. It tore at him, spurring him on. He shook his head, trying to clear it. Through a haze of pain, he could see Flynn wrestling with her, her long legs flying in a desperate attempt to keep Bloom from approaching her with the syringe.

Across the short distance between them, her gaze locked on him. They pleaded with him to help her. To do something. Anything. He tried to throw the two goons off him, but they bore down harder.

Flynn wrapped his arms around her, holding her secure against him, his face a mask of determination. He nodded at Bloom and the man stepped gingerly closer.

"Ryan! Don't let them take me!" Tess begged. She tried to twist out of Flynn's arm, but he jammed his knees into the back of hers, buckling her legs from beneath her.

Rage ripped through Ryan, sending a jolt of adrenaline through his system. He threw the two goons off him and pulled himself to his feet, struggling the short distance to reach her.

The needle was inches from Tess's thigh. Ryan clamped a hand on Bloom's shoulder and jerked him backward. But then it was if he was hit by a tree from behind.

His legs went numb and he dropped to his knees again. As he pitched forward onto his face, he saw one of the goons slap a blackjack against his meaty palm and grin. Ryan's left cheek hit the grass and his head bounced.

Ryan reached out and touched Tess's shoe. But he couldn't move. Someone had dropped down to sit on his back and someone else had jammed his foot on the back of his neck, effectively pinning him to the ground.

"Let her go," he said, his voice sounding faraway even to his own ears. He spit dirt and blood.

He watched helplessly as Flynn subdued Tess. She struggled, but he was too strong for her. She threw her head back, attempting to head-butt him. But he seemed to anticipate her every move and he tightened his grip.

Bloom moved toward her.

"Don't do this, Sidney," Ryan said.

Tess whipped her head in Bloom's direction. Her lips were drawn back over her teeth like a cornered animal. "Don't come any closer!"

Not waiting a moment, Bloom stuck the needle in Tess's right hip, injecting her right through the fabric of her pants. Air hissed between her teeth.

"You bastard." Her voice was fractured, broken, but Ryan could still hear the edge to it, the touch of defiance.

His heart hammered in his chest, and he tried again to throw the man off him. But whoever was on him held firm.

Tess tried to jackknife her body, but Flynn held her easily.

"You can't do this to me," she protested.

"We just did," Flynn said, his expression bland. Emotionless. He snapped his fingers at one of the goons. "Get her in the car. And sit next to her. I don't trust the medication to keep her quiet for long."

"It won't," Tess said, her voice still edgy, but Ryan could see that the drug was already having an effect. She shook her head as if dazed and blinked rapidly several times as if her vision was clouding.

Whatever they had given her was powerful.

She looked around, as if confused, unable to focus. Finally her gaze settled on him. "I—I'm not crazy."

The words were slurred and jumbled. She squeezed her eyes shut for a minute, as if trying to concentrate. Finally she opened her eyes and tried again, each word distinct. Every syllable was heartrendingly clear. "Don't believe what they're saying about me."

"I don't, Tess. I believe you." He reached out and

touched her foot, and Tess could feel the pressure of his fingers through the fabric of her socks, the warmth of his fingers soaking through to her toes. Even though she knew she had lost the battle, she was comforted. He was close. He believed her.

"How touching," Flynn sneered. He picked her up and the comforting touch of Ryan's hand disappeared. An emptiness cloaked her, leaving her cold.

Tess slipped into a deep hole, her world starting to fade around the edges. Her head lolled back against her father's shoulder and her eyelids fluttered. Her mouth moved, but no words came out.

She could hear Ryan talking, that deep, beautiful voice of his reaching down into the pit she was getting sucked into and trying to pull her back to the surface. "It's all right, Tess. Don't fight it. Just let go. You're all right. I won't let them hurt you."

She tried to lift her head, to tell him that she'd hang on. That she wouldn't give up fighting no matter what. But when she tried to reach out to touch him, he seemed miles away, and it was as if someone had slipped a hundred-pound-weight around her wrist, keeping her from lifting her hand.

She shook her head violently, rolling it back and forth. "N-no! Not okay. Not—not all right. Don't le—let them take me away. You promised, dammit."

Tess saw the distress on Ryan's face, the tortured concern. He opened his mouth as if to say something more to her, but the darkness, a yawning emptiness snatched her, pressing her down.

She heard Ryan's voice from somewhere far-off, a voice that promised her she wouldn't get hurt, that she'd be safe.

She wanted to stand up and rage back at him. To make him understand that she wouldn't be *okay*. That she'd never be safe as long as Flynn had her, but she didn't have the strength.

All feeling leaked out the tips of her fingers, and her tongue, ten sizes too large for her mouth, seemed to choke her. Every muscle in her body froze and she was unable to move.

And as her vision completely shut down, Tess wondered if she'd ever see Ryan Donovan again.

Chapter Seven

The goon sitting on Ryan got up, allowing him to pull himself to a sitting position. Ryan used one hand to keep himself from falling over and, as he leveraged himself to his feet, stumbled several steps before regaining his balance.

The two goons ignored him, working together to load Tess into the back seat of the limo.

Ryan turned to Flynn. "Are you taking her to the center?"

"Hardly," Flynn scoffed. "After this fiasco I have no desire to have Tess involved with anyone at the Bloom Research Facility. We'll be leaving on my private jet shortly. She'll return to the facility she was in before I had the misfortune to think anyone in Half Moon, Iowa, would know anything that would be of any help to Tess."

"What facility are you taking her to?"

Flynn laughed. "Nice try, Doctor." He bent down to climb into the limo, but then he stopped and straightened up. His gray eyes were cold mirrors of ill-concealed rage. "Don't make the mistake, Doctor, of thinking that your concern and your misguided loyalty to Tess will be tolerated. If you try to find her, I will press harassment charges." He turned away, adding, "If I'm not mistaken, legal difficulties of that nature could result in one having their license revoked."

Ryan stepped closer. "Don't threaten me, Flynn. It will be a cold day in hell before I forget what happened here today. Plan on looking over your shoulder and finding me standing there."

"A shame," Flynn said. "A man should know when his career is about to tank." He climbed into the limo and slammed the door.

Ryan moved around to the other side. Bloom had the door open, giving final instructions to Chief Cole. Most likely something about making sure that Ryan didn't try to follow the limo. He bent down and checked on Tess.

She lay between the two orderlies, her hair in disarray, several strands caught between her lips. Her eyelashes were dark spikes across the paleness of her cheek, and she lay with her legs drawn up and her fists clenched in front of her, as if she'd simply quit in the middle of a fierce battle.

Even after the ordeal she'd been through, she looked beautiful and defenseless. Vulnerable. Ryan's heart tightened.

Bloom stepped in front, blocking his view. "Leave it alone, Ryan."

"I can't leave it alone," Ryan said, incredulous that his former mentor would even consider asking him to do such a thing. "Any way you look at this, it's wrong."

"Not according to the authorities," Bloom said. "You tried to help her, and now her father is taking over."

Ryan stepped closer. "Something's wrong with that guy, Sid. Don't let him take her. Let me at least call a few friends, check things out. I'm getting really bad vibes here."

Bloom waved a hand dismissively. "You're too emotionally involved with this woman to see things clearly." He climbed into the back of the limo. "Perhaps your behavior today explains what happened in Boston. I advise you to get your act together before you find yourself looking for another job."

The door slammed and the limo shot down the driveway. A few seconds later, it roared off.

"So not only have you gotten yourself beat up, you've alienated your boss. Not bad for a single day's work," Cole remarked.

Ryan stared after the limo. "You're not much of a lawman, Cole, if you'd stand by and let a bunch of thugs manhandle a woman like that."

Cole climbed into his car. "Still trying to push buttons, huh, Doc?"

"I thought you wanted Tess down at the station for questioning."

"Oh, I know where to find her if I need to talk to her." He tipped his hat back on his head. "Now don't you be thinking about following that limo, Doc. I'll be trailing behind it to the airport and if I see that fancy little sports car of yours anywhere near it I'll be running your ass in." He started his car's engine and leaned an arm out the window. "We understand each other?"

"I understand the sad fact that they've bought you off."

"Man's gotta make a living, Doc. But you didn't hear that from me." He put his car in Reverse and backed slowly down the driveway. He waved as he took off in the same direction as the limo.

Ryan glanced down at himself. He was covered with grass and dirt. He swiped a hand across his mouth, coming away with blood.

He needed to clean up and get out to the center. If he couldn't follow Tess, he could at least start making calls, finding out where her father was taking her. He still had a few contacts that would help him out.

Tracking Tess down wasn't going to be easy, but Ryan had no intention of leaving her in the hands of the man who treated her so brutally.

AFTER SHOWERING and dressing, Ryan ran to his car and slid into the front seat. He slipped his cell phone into its carrier and backed out of the driveway. As he jammed the shift into Drive, he dialed the center.

He paused at the end of the driveway, punched in the extension for the hematology lab and waited.

He heard the click of the transfer and a few seconds later an impatient voice snapped, "If you people don't quit bothering me, I won't get anything done down here."

Relief washed over Ryan. His friend, Craig Freedman, the head of the hematology lab was exactly who he wanted to talk to. "You sound a little stressed, Craig." He forced a touch of humor into his voice.

"Donovan," Freedman growled, his tone warming a millimeter. "Damn clerk called in sick again, and they didn't send me a sub. I'll be stuck answering the phone all day, and to add to the indignity, people keep sending me stupid lab requests on inadequate drops of blood. What the hell do you want?"

"The results on a stupid lab request, of course."

Freedman grunted. "What's the name?"

"Doe. Tess Doe."

"Hang on and I'll see if it's done." Ryan could hear the man's fingers fly over the keys of his computer as he searched the file. "Got it. A BCC, Tox screen and drug panel, right?"

"That's the one. Anything of interest show up?"

"Actually, yes. Your little lost lamb had a snootful of what you shrinks used to call a *sleep cocktail.*"

"Thorazine?"

"Yep. In addition to Nembutal, Seconal, Phenergan and Veronal."

Ryan whistled through his teeth. "I didn't think anyone was using that particular combination anymore. Not since the sixties anyway."

"Well, either you've got a Rip Van Winkle doc treating this patient or someone who didn't attend the lecture in med school that talked about the unethical use of certain drug concoctions."

"Did you find anything else?"

"That's not enough for you?"

"Come on, Craig. What else did you find?"

Craig sniffed. "Good thing your patient holds a certain fascination for me. I ran a couple of other tests to see what I'd find and, lo and behold, I actually found something."

"What?"

"You've got me."

"What the hell is that supposed to mean?"

"Exactly what I said. I have no idea what I found. She's got some kind of new chemical compound swimming around in her bloodstream. An unknown. It's got some similarities to Thorazine, but it's a total hybrid. In other words, a new drug."

Ryan gripped the wheel tighter. "You're sure?"

"Of course I'm sure," Craig snapped.

"Send me up a copy of the findings, all right?"

"They're on their way to your office as we speak. You'll find them on your desk as soon as you get your hide in here."

He wrapped the conversation up a few minutes later and replaced the phone in its cradle. He sat back, a sense of unease niggling at the back of his neck.

An unknown compound. A new drug.

Something was definitely going on and he wanted to know what.

THE ROOM WAS STERILE WHITE. A combination of glaring white walls and steel, a dazzling white-tiled floor and stark, whitewashed furniture with shiny steel knobs and hinges.

General Flynn clasped his hands behind his back and settled into a comfortable parade rest. Staring through the stretch of glass that separated the control room from the examination room, he considered the form stretched out on the stainless-steel table in the middle of the room.

Tess lay on her back, her arms and legs secured to the table with leather fleece-lined cuffs. She was dressed in a pair of thin green hospital pants and a white tank top.

A strap across her forehead kept her head from moving from side to side. Not that it was necessary at the moment as she was unconscious and totally limp. A pair of high-tech headphones were clamped over her ears, sealing out all noise from the room.

Flynn knew that a preprogrammed tape was being filtered through the headphones—a tape with his voice on it. He knew the prerecorded message was telling Tess what he expected of her. A job to be carried out in less than a week.

So little time. So much to accomplish.

A technician, dressed in a white lab coat, stood near the head of the table and Flynn watched as the woman efficiently injected the end of a needle into a small glass vial and drew up a liquid. When she withdrew the needle, she used one bright-red-tipped finger to flick the barrel of the syringe, eliminating any air bubbles.

Turning, she swabbed an alcohol pad over the rubber stopper on the IV tubing connected to Tess's arm. She removed the cap on the syringe and then stuck the needle into the rubber diaphragm of the IV tubing, pushing in the plunger.

The medication slid effortlessly into Tess's body.

"You're sure she's totally unaware of anything going on around her?" Flynn asked, not bothering to turn around.

"Yes," Bloom said from somewhere behind him. "I find that she responds best to your voice when she's in a deep trance. If she's in a light sleep, she fights too much."

Flynn glanced at the TV monitor mounted over the glass.

It framed a close-up of Tess's face. Her skin was startlingly pale. She hadn't gotten much sun these past six months, not when she'd been locked up deep within the top-secret basement of the center.

She was indeed beautiful. Untouched almost. Flynn understood well Ryan Donovan's desire to be her champion. But the young doctor had no idea what he'd stumbled into, and if the good doctor didn't watch out, he wouldn't be stumbling into anything ever again. He'd be dead.

It was a good thing that Bloom seemed to be somewhat in control of the young man's curiosity. Flynn had a strong feeling that in any other situation, Donovan would be someone to be reckoned with. Thankfully, the low-level researcher had no knowledge or access to this part of the research facility.

Flynn turned back toward Bloom. The doctor stood over the shoulder of a technician who was monitoring one of the computers giving him a readout on Tess's physiological reactions to the medication.

"What happens if she's not ready in time?" Flynn asked.

"She'll *be* ready," Bloom said, not bothering to look up. "I've already planted the trigger word in her memory. A few more sessions and I'll be able to reintroduce the memories we had to wipe clean earlier."

"And if she's not ready? What then?"

There was no missing the flicker of impatience that slid across Bloom's face. But Flynn had to give the man credit. Before lifting his head, he carefully composed his face. "We'll do what we always said we'd do. We'll use McCaffrey. He's her backup."

"That has the potential to cause more problems at this late date. He doesn't have the connections with Starling that Tess has."

"No, but we planned for that possibility. McCaffrey is on the guest list as Tess's date for the reception. He'll have the access he needs should Tess not be able to fulfill her duty for whatever reason. We agreed from the start that Tess could get the closest, but that McCaffrey was our ace in the hole.''

The technician interrupted by pointing to the monitor. Bloom nodded and reached down and flicked a switch. ''Marsha, give her another five cc's please.''

The nurse inside the examination room nodded and drew up the medication, injecting it into the IV tubing.

Flynn turned halfway around and studied his stepdaughter's body strapped to the examination table. ''Is it safe to increase her dosage like that? I mean, she's been without the drug for an entire day and then some.''

Bloom ignored him and reached over the technician's shoulder to tap the tip of his pen against the monitor screen. ''Run a comparison on that reading with her initial EEG.'' He straightened up and glanced at Flynn. This time he made no effort to hide his irritation at another interruption. ''Perhaps, General, you'd prefer to wait in your suite. I'm a tad busy at the moment. I'll meet you later to give you a rundown on the results from this reprogramming session.''

Flynn nodded. He wasn't stupid, he knew when he was being dismissed. Medicine was definitely *not* his area of expertise, and he didn't want to slow things down even more by asking mundane questions. ''I'll be awaiting your report.''

As he left the room, Flynn overheard Bloom ordering another increase in Tess's loading dose. He could only hope that Bloom was as good as everyone said he was. Starling and his crew of renegades needed a wake-up call they'd never forget and if things went the way Flynn wanted them to, Tess Ross would deliver that message in a way that no one would ever forget.

UNDER THE CLOSE SCRUTINY of the stone-faced armed security guard positioned at the inner gate leading to the Half

Moon Research Center, Ryan swiped his ID badge through the security box next to the guard hut.

The light on the box changed from red to green.

The gate swung open. "Have a nice day, Dr. Donovan," the guard in the booth said.

Ryan nodded and released the brake, giving the car a little gas. As he drove through and headed for lot A, the guard's attention had shifted to the computer in front of him. His fingers flew across the keypad. Ryan knew the man was recording his car license plate and arrival time. He also knew that his entry was already being flashed ahead to the security team within the facility.

When he had first arrived at the center, Ryan had been somewhat amused at the high level of security. Although Bloom had mentioned they did handle some military projects on occasion, Ryan had gotten the impression that they were usually low-level projects, nothing that required this degree of precaution.

Ahead, the glass and steel structure of the Bloom Research Center loomed among a grove of lush trees, winding walkways and carefully tended gardens. As he passed the small driveway leading to Dr. Bloom's private entrance, he noticed the back end of a black car jutting out from behind the thick hedge hiding Dr. Bloom's parking lot and private entrance. Could it be? Was it possible that it was the same car they'd loaded an unconscious Tess into less than an hour ago?

He slowed, craning his neck to get a better view.

If it was the same limo, what was it doing here? It meant that Bloom and Flynn had lied. No big surprise there, but it was hardly what Ryan had expected. It meant that Tess had been brought to the center in spite of Flynn's assertion that he was taking her back East to another hospital.

He clicked on his signal and turned into lot A. Not many

of the slots were filled yet. Bloom had told him that July was vacation month. A lot of people were out of town.

Exiting the coolness of the air-conditioned car, he locked up and walked the short distance to the canopied entrance of the center. By the time he reached the door, the humid morning air had caused his shirt to stick to the middle of his back.

Ryan inserted his badge into the slot in the door handle. A few seconds later, the door clicked and he stepped into the main lobby.

He walked across the slate floor to the receptionist's desk. To the right stood a luxurious cluster of butter-soft couches and chairs. Ryan knew they were butter-soft because he'd sunk into one when he'd visited the center a little more than two months ago.

He'd sat there for forty minutes until Bloom showed up to escort him inside the center for his tour. He hadn't realized then, but he wasn't allowed to just wander around the research facility. Someone was always at his side during that initial phase. Now they tracked him like all the employees— through his identity badge.

"Good morning, Pam," he greeted to the young woman seated behind the receptionist's desk. Ryan had a sneaking suspicion that even Pam was a highly paid, thoroughly trained security guard.

"Good morning, Dr. Donovan. Warm enough for you?" She flashed him a pleasant, totally professional smile and pushed a small black box across the countertop toward him.

"Too warm to be in a suit and tie, if that answers your question." Ryan hefted his briefcase up onto the gray-and-white-flecked granite countertop and pressed his thumb to the electronic print pad.

He drummed his fingers on the aluminum of his briefcase while he waited for the computer to run a check on his thumbprint.

Pam tilted her head and then nodded. "You're clear to go in, Doctor."

Ryan grinned. "You're positive I'm not an impostor?"

Pam smiled politely back, but it had an almost remote, chilliness to it. Apparently joking about security issues wasn't on the research staff's list of approved conversations.

"Have a nice day, sir." She returned her attention to the computer screen in front of her. Ryan knew he'd been dismissed.

He turned to leave and then paused, remembering the limo parked in Dr. Bloom's private lot. "Is General Flynn still here or has he left for the airport? He seemed interested in some research data I mentioned to him yesterday."

For a nanosecond, Pam's fingers froze over her keyboard. But then she glanced up, her eyes innocently questioning. "General Flynn? I'm sorry, I'm not aware of anyone with that name registered as a guest here at the center." Her fingers flew over the keys again. "But let me check for you." She paused a moment and then shook her head. "No—no one by that name here at the center."

Ryan shrugged. "Guess I was wrong."

She nodded. "Yes, it would appear so." She waited. "Was there anything else I could do for you, Doctor?"

"No, that's all. Thank you."

He turned and walked through the steel door leading to the offices. His nerve endings tingled. Flynn was in the building. And if Flynn was in the center, then so was Tess.

Chapter Eight

Groggy, Tess tried to roll up on her side, but she found herself pinned and unable to move more than a fraction of an inch in either direction. Something tight and incredibly uncomfortable held her flat on her back.

She opened her eyes and the light hit her eyes like a laser. A sharp zing of pain ripped directly to the center of her skull. It was like having someone tear her brain in two.

She squeezed her eyes shut and moaned softly. Even the sound of her own voice was painful. She tugged at her wrists, but there was no budging them. She tried moving her feet. No luck. They were secured, too.

She lay still, panting slightly as she attempted to push away the confusion and pain pressing down on her. It was like trying to slog through a sea of warm, sticky molasses.

Lifting her head, she opened her eyes a crack and stared down at her body. Damn, they'd secured her to the bed again.

Leather straps, padded with white fleece, were buckled around all four of her extremities, drawn so tight that her skin was raw and reddened. But it was the strap across the middle of her chest that kept her from moving in either direction very far. It would also keep her from bending down to use her teeth to unbuckle the restraints.

She rolled her head on the lumpy mattress. No pillow and

no hair clip. They weren't taking any chances. She lifted her head and glanced in the direction of the camera overhead. The red light below the lens winked at her.

She dropped her head back down and closed her eyes against the relentless glare of the overhead lights. They never turned the lights off and they were usually accompanied by a droning voice. A voice loud enough to keep her awake but incoherent enough so that she wasn't sure what was being said. It was all done to keep her off balance, teetering on the edge.

But today the loudspeaker was unusually silent. Nothing, not even the smallest, most inconsequential sound penetrated the heavy steel walls of her padded cell.

Tess shifted her position on the cot and wiggled her toes, trying to get the circulation going. Her captors also kept her off balance by varying the room temperature. They were currently on a cold kick. Not cold enough to make her shiver, but cool enough so that she was uncomfortable.

As she contemplated her predicament, the steel door buzzed and someone stepped inside. The doctor, the one Ryan had called Bloom, walked over to stand next to her. Following close on his heels was the woman who administered most of the medication they'd been shooting into her system.

Tess's stomach clenched at their appearance, but she kept it from showing on her face. She refused to give either of them the satisfaction of knowing the dread that washed over her at the sight of them.

"And how are we feeling today, Tess?" Bloom asked, his smooth, melodious voice immediately tying her stomach in a knot.

"I don't know how *you're* feeling, Doc, but I feel pretty lousy. But then you knew that, didn't you?" Tess's voice cracked and her throat felt drier than dust.

Bloom smiled benignly. "You'll feel right as rain soon."

"Of course I will. You'll just shoot me full of more of your bug juice and I won't care how I feel, right?"

"Medication, my dear, medication," Bloom corrected. "You're sick. We're simply helping you recover."

"I'm not sick." Tess frowned. "I just have trouble remembering things."

Bloom smiled indulgently. "Exactly, and that's why I'm here. To help you regain your memory."

"I'm not an idiot, Bloom," Tess said. "You and your drones are more interested in pulling the wings off butterflies than you are in helping me."

Bloom's smile turned amused. His assistant's face, a Nurse Ratchet wannabe, remained impassive.

"Are you feeling like a butterfly today, Tess?"

"I'll tell you how I feel. I feel like getting up off this table and squeezing your scrawny pencil neck." Tess knew what she was saying was nothing more than reckless bravado, but it was all she had left in her arsenal right now. And somehow she knew that she needed to keep herself pumped up. Angry. She couldn't lie back and surrender. Anger gave her an edge and seemed to keep her mind sharper.

Bloom seemed amused. "My little soldier. You make me proud." He reached down and tugged on the strap on her right wrist. Pain shot up her arm.

Tess struggled to wrap her mind around what he said. Soldier? He'd called her a soldier. Why?

"Just let me up and I'll show you proud," Tess said, forcing the words out from between stiff lips.

Bloom reached out and patted her cheek, his fingers cold and impersonal. "Such harsh threats. You really should work on that temper of yours." He laughed. "But first you have a job to do."

He glanced over his shoulder at the nurse behind him and held out a hand. "The syringe please."

Tess tried another tack. "Is Dr. Donovan okay?"

"You took a liking to my young assistant, didn't you?" Bloom paused and regarded her for a moment. "I'm not surprised. Women have always been drawn to Ryan. His looks, his quick intellect. You wouldn't be immune to it, either. I knew that."

Her muscles tensed. He knew that? What did that mean?

"I liked his honesty. The fact that he stood up to you and Flynn. I like that he saw through your lies."

Bloom's amusement was obvious. "Honesty? Now that's rich. Ryan does exactly what I tell him to do. No more. No less."

Dread squeezed Tess's heart. What was Bloom saying? Had Ryan been sent to string her along? Had it all been an act? She squeezed her eyes shut, battling the thick wave of despair that threatened to engulf her. She should have known.

She opened her eyes and dully watched Bloom swipe an alcohol swab across the rubber stopper on her IV and then slide the needle through. The ice-blue liquid slid through the barrel into the plastic tubing, and a familiar light-headedness flooded Tess's brain.

She fought the sensation, concentrating hard to keep her head above the dark waters lurking below consciousness. But she lost the battle even faster than last time. The drug was grabbing hold of her with the strength and viciousness of a wild beast. Either they had upped her dose or her body was metabolizing it at a faster pace, lapping it up like a favored treat. Her grip slipped and she was again sucked beneath the cold surface of unconsciousness.

Her last thought as she slid under the dark, oily barrier was of Ryan Donovan. The chiseled angles of his face and the sharp intelligence of his eyes. His damned expression of compassion. But now she knew it was a lie. A total put-on.

The vision pulled at her, and for a moment, Tess felt as

though he were trying to speak to her. Trying to placate her with a whispered promise of watching out for her and seeing that she came to no harm.

She fought the pull as her emotions betrayed her and tears prickled at the back of her lids. Several tears slipped from the corner of her eyes and the feel of betrayal was hot on her cheeks. Damn him! He'd lied to her. He'd been with them all along.

SEVERAL FLOORS UP, Ryan paced his office. He had no idea where they had stashed Tess, but he knew, without really knowing how, that she was somewhere inside the center. It wasn't just the fact that the limo was parked outside Bloom's private entrance. It was as if his body knew she was here and it was screaming the information to him, every nerve ending jumping and surging with energy.

Studying the results of Tess's lab results hadn't gotten him very far. The new drug eluded him. Its properties were so similar to Thorazine that it could be its twin. But there were still some structural differences that told him the effects on Tess would be different. Along with the concoction of other drugs, the effects would be devastating.

He reached up and rubbed his eyes, a flash of annoyance ripping through him. What made him think any of this would be of any help to Tess now? He dropped into his desk chair. How could he get into the bottom portion of the lab without being seen?

He had stood up to pace again when the door to his office opened and his secretary, Alice, stuck her head in.

"Morning, boss," she greeted him. "Sorry, I wasn't here when you arrived, but I had some errands to run."

"Not a problem." He wanted to pump her for information, but he wasn't sure how much he could trust her.

She tilted her head and gave him an inquiring look. "You look perplexed. Something I can get you?"

He shook his head. "No, I'm fine."

She raised an eyebrow and then started to close the door again. "Okay, I'll be out here if—"

"Alice?"

She opened the door again, her expression expectant.

"Do you know what kind of research they're conducting in the lower labs—the ones that are off-limits to everyone else on the first two floors?"

"No, and I don't want to, either." Alice glanced over her shoulder as if worried that someone might overhear. "Tammi—she works over in data processing—told me she thought they were fooling around with anthrax and the Ebola virus." She frowned and her voice dropped to a hush. "You don't think that's true, do you? I mean, if anything happened, we'd all be killed."

Ryan leaned against his desk. "It seems unlikely. But then again, everything is pretty hush-hush around here. Have you ever talked to any of the staff that works in those labs?"

Alice shook her head. "They seem to be on a different shift from us. I'm not sure if they even enter the research center the same way we do. From what I've heard, they have their own elevator—they enter through the doors at the back of the center. By the loading dock."

Ryan figured that her information made a lot of sense. From what he'd been able to tell, the elevator in the main portion of the center didn't even go to the sublevels. And the stairs he used to get to the second floor didn't go down below the first floor.

"Guess there isn't much I can do about it even if that's what they're doing. Jobs aren't easy to come by here in Half Moon," Alice grumbled. "And none of them pay as well as this one."

Ryan nodded. He knew Alice had a son, a three-year-old, who she was raising alone. From what he'd been able to gather, she'd had him when she was seventeen, which he instinctively knew made life harder for her.

"If you want, I could ask Brian if he knows what's going on down there."

Ryan knew she was referring to her boyfriend, a computer geek who worked in the computer-data complex. "You think he knows anything?"

"Brian's not the type to take things at face value." She laughed nervously. "He has an insatiable curiosity. He's been snooping—trying to figure out a way to find out what's going on down there. I don't know how he did it, but a few days ago he figured out a way to code his security badge so he can go down there—to the sublevels. He wants to look around."

Ryan felt a stir of excitement. "Do you think he'd recode my badge if you asked?"

Alice looked surprised that he'd make such a request. "I guess he could. You want me to ask him tonight?"

"Any chance he's in his office right now?"

Alice looked slightly flustered. "Now? This minute?"

Ryan nodded.

"I—I guess so. You want me to give him a call?"

He stood up. "Let's walk down and talk to him face-to-face."

If the guy knew how to reprogram the security badges, Ryan didn't intend to waste any more time. He needed to convince Brian that he had to get down into the lower labs today. Tess was waiting for him, and he was determined not to forget his promise not to abandon her. He refused to leave her in the hands of the person she feared most in the world—her father.

He only hoped he'd reach her in time.

Chapter Nine

Less than an hour later, with one newly programmed security badge in his hand and another in the pocket of his lab coat, Ryan slid his card into the security slot next to the bank of elevators leading to the subbasement labs. The extra card in his pocket would hopefully serve as Tess's ticket to freedom—if he was able to locate her in the labyrinth of labs occupying the lower levels.

Alice's boyfriend had given Ryan a quick rundown of what he knew about the subbasement setup. They had studied a series of computer blueprints, agreeing that Tess was probably being held on Sub Level 5. The diagrams seemed to indicate that Level 5 was made up of several secure cubicles—sufficient security to house prisoners. There was no doubt in Ryan's mind that Tess was Flynn's prisoner.

He held his breath as the security system scanned his card, matching his photo and coding to the computer scan of his face. The wait seemed overly long and Ryan itched with anticipation, waiting for alarms to sound or a heavy hand to clamp down on his shoulder. But a few seconds later, a green light flashed, and the elevator doors slid silently open.

He stepped inside, relieved to find the cubicle empty. He punched the button for Sub Level 5, forcing himself not to fidget, acutely aware of the dual cameras mounted in the front and back of the elevator, watching his every move.

The elevator moved smoothly downward, the lights overhead blinking their descent. Ryan breathed a sigh of relief, figuring he was home free. But then, the elevator slowed. The panel overhead indicated they were stopping at Sub Level 3. He was going to have company. He moved to the back of the stall, lowering his head.

The doors slid open and two men, engaged in a lively debate and dressed in crisp white lab coats, stepped on board. Both nodded absently to him but kept on with their exchange, arguing about some recent data recorded on a clipboard one of the men held. Ryan kept his nod brief and distant. He didn't want to find himself pulled into their conversation.

One man stabbed the button for Sub Level 6 but then quickly pressed a finger on the Door Open button. He glanced apologetically in Ryan's direction. "Sorry. Our colleague is right behind us."

Ryan nodded politely, but clenched his back teeth hard enough to crack them. Damn, just his luck. The longer he was in their company, the better the chance that he'd be discovered as an imposter.

The man with the clipboard turned slightly toward him. "You new?" he asked.

Oh great, a conversationalist.

"Started a few weeks ago." Ryan kept his tone flat, uninterested. Hopefully the guy would take the cue and realize he wasn't interested in socializing.

No such luck. "What department are you in?"

Anxiety raced through Ryan's veins. Now what? His gaze brushed across the computer printout sheet on the man's clipboard. "I work in Research and Design."

Both men groaned. "Oh, so you're the one who tortures all of us with this crap."

"Yeah, that's me." Ryan shifted positions and jerked his head toward the corridor. "You think your friend is coming any time soon? I have a few people expecting me downstairs, and I sure hate to be late when I'm one of the new guys." He added a smile in an attempt to take the sting out of his complaint.

The quiet guy leaned forward and glanced down the hallway. He shook his head and the talkative one snorted in disgust. "The hell with him." He took his finger off the Open button and hit the Down button. "Ya snooze, you lose."

The doors slid shut and the elevator jerked slightly before starting downward.

"How do you like things so far?" the chatty guy asked. He had turned almost completely around, apparently more than a little interested in the new guy's take on the job.

"Not bad." Ryan shrugged. "No worse than any other job I've ever had."

"What do you think of the security?"

I'll let you know when and if I ever get myself and Tess out of here, Ryan thought ruefully. "Pretty standard."

The two men exchanged amused glances. "Guess you haven't been strip-searched yet."

"No, can't say I've had that pleasure." A bell dinged, announcing that they'd arrived on Sub Level 5, and the doors slid open. "My stop. Nice meeting the both of you." Ryan moved to get around the two men. He paused. "Uh, the loading dock… Where is that exactly?"

"Three levels back up the way we came."

The door slid shut on the two men.

Ryan checked the corridor. Empty. A sign on the wall announced that the Holding Facilities were to the left.

Ryan turned. He was fairly certain they'd secret Tess away in some kind of holding area.

Within minutes, Ryan found himself faced with a double

row of doors on either side of the long corridor. Twenty to twenty-five holding rooms stretched the length of the hall. To search them all would take precious minutes Ryan knew he didn't have. Anxiety squirted through his blood.

Every minute he stayed in the subbasement meant another opportunity for Bloom and his men to discover his treachery. But he had to find Tess. Something told him that she was close. He couldn't leave without finding her.

Each door had a tiny window. It was the only way to see into the rooms. A quick check of the first window revealed a narrow cell. The walls were padded and the floor was stainless steel. The room was empty.

His heart rate increasing and his breath coming in short pants, Ryan moved to the next door.

A THICK FOG SWIRLED around her and a chilling breeze brushed her cheeks. Tess lifted her head and sniffed. The smell of copper hung heavy in the damp air, and its presence sent a shiver of fear down her spine.

Steady, girl, she thought. *You're dreaming. Just one more nightmare to get through.*

She took a tentative step forward and her heart leaped into her throat, almost choking her. Something wet and sticky pulled at the soles of her bare feet.

Don't look down, her mind screamed. *Keep your eyes straight ahead!*

But she looked anyway, and a low moan slipped from between her lips. Spreading out beneath her lay a pool of red, a dark liquid carpet of something red and slick.

Her mouth went dry.

Oh God, please tell me that isn't blood. Please don't let it be blood. Hot tears stung the corners of her eyes and slid down her cold cheeks.

The smell of copper, thick and heavy, swept up her nose, and her stomach turned over with dread. Blood. Gallons and gallons of blood. It rose around her, covering her feet and sucking greedily at her ankles.

I'm going to drown in it, she thought. I'm going to drown in a sea of blood.

She sloshed through the viscous liquid, and up ahead, the mist parted. In the distance she saw a black man standing on an embankment. He motioned to her, waving at her to come closer.

Tess squinted, trying to see his face, but the mist seemed to hide him. He gestured again.

She waded deeper, pumping her legs through the heavy liquid as it swirled and sucked at her, threatening to pull her beneath its shimmering surface. She fought the tide.

As she drew closer to the man, his figure seemed to waver, the lines of his body disappearing and then reappearing.

Wait! Tess called. *Wait for me! Don't leave.*

But the man's body changed, morphing into something strange and ghostly. Tess stumbled.

Suddenly the man became something familiar. Something from her childhood. *It's Casper the Friendly Ghost,* she whispered. *Wait for me, Casper.*

But he drifted upward, just out of reach.

Crying, Tess stood on tiptoes and reached for her childhood hero. He drifted higher.

Tess struggled to reach him and then tripped. Someone or something lay beneath the surface of the sea. As she watched in horror, a hand rose up out of the ocean of blood.

Whimpering, Tess scrambled to get away, but the fingers reached out and clamped themselves around her throat. She screamed as the hand pulled her beneath the roiling blood-red surface.

RYAN HEARD THE SCREAM of total terror. He knew without question that it was Tess.

He tore down the corridor, following the frantic sound.

His hands trembled with rage as he slid the security badge into the slot outside the steel door. "Come on! Come on!" he said.

He watched impatiently as the light shone a steady red until it finally blinked green and the door slid open.

He stepped inside the tiny cell, taking in the sterile white of the room and the single stretcher clamped securely to the floor.

A woman with a cloud of shimmering blond hair lay strapped helplessly to the bed. Ryan ran to her side.

When he touched Tess's cheek, she opened her eyes, and Ryan watched as the confusion clouding the surface of those exquisite jade-colored eyes disappeared. She stared at him, every muscle in that beautiful body tensing against the restraints holding her secure. And he knew the exact moment she recognized him, a single instant when her pupils constricted and she tried to lift her head off the cot.

There was a momentary flash of unmistakable joy, followed by a cold look of caution. He hoped the caution would fade and disappear, but it stayed. The fact that it stayed told Ryan that Bloom had been busy. He'd been pumping her full of nasty drugs, trying to destroy what little trust Ryan had managed to build in Tess.

No doubt the doctor had backed her into a corner and worked on the tiny wall she'd built around her faith. Ryan had a feeling it wouldn't have taken much to topple it. Something told him that he was starting back at square one.

"Come back to gloat a little?" she asked, her voice hard, unforgiving. "To make sure you did the job right the first time?"

He put a finger to his lips and shook his head.

Her gaze immediately jumped to the camera overhead, and a tiny glimmer of confusion reentered her eyes. She wasn't sure what he meant, but at least she understood that the room was monitored.

She lay back, but Ryan didn't miss the reemergence of wariness in her gaze. She wasn't about to believe anything he said, and Ryan knew without a doubt that Bloom had filled her ear with some kind of garbage about him.

Bloom wanted her vulnerable. Totally dependent. And in order to make sure that happened, he would have worked to destroy any lingering feeling of trust she felt for the one person who had tried to save her—Ryan Donovan.

He knelt down beside the bed and whispered in her ear, "A friend is sending a loop of video to their camera—it shows you sleeping. But if they catch on, we're toast. So, we need to work fast. Nod your head if you understand?"

She nodded.

Ryan reached across and started to undo her restraints. Beneath his hands, every muscle in her body was tense and coiled to spring.

As soon as her arms and chest were free, she sat up and worked on her left leg while he concentrated on the right. Before he could help her with the IV, Tess yanked it out, throwing the needle and tubing on the bed.

"So much for following proper medical procedure," he mumbled, digging into the pocket of his pants and pulling out a handkerchief. He handed it to her and she nodded her thanks, slapping it over the small puncture wound in an attempt to stop the bleeding.

"Let's go," she said.

Ryan nodded and headed for the door. But he had barely gone two steps when something hit him from behind. Hard.

He stumbled forward two steps before he realized that Tess was on top of him, her arms wrapped around his neck from behind. She had clamped both legs around his waist, tightening them with excruciating strength. As he struggled to straighten, she jerked back on her arms, cutting off his oxygen.

"What the h—" He tried to turn around, but she clung

to him with the tenacity of a tiny flea riding the back of the bull.

She leaned forward and whispered in his ear, "I fell for it the first time. I'm not so stupid I'd fall for it again. What are you up to?"

He tried to answer, but she tightened her arm across his windpipe. He thought about dumping her over his shoulder to get her off, but he didn't want to hurt her. But he wasn't going to be able to reason with her if he blacked out from lack of oxygen.

"I'm not part of this," he managed to croak. He knew that their time was running out.

"I think we played this scenario out once already. What kind of sick game are you all playing?"

Feeling their time ticking away, Ryan bent forward and let gravity pull her body upward. She scrambled to stay pinned to his back, but Ryan didn't give her a chance. He reached behind, grabbed her under one arm and gave her a hard yank, lifting her up and over his shoulder.

She sputtered and kicked, but Ryan ignored her, setting her down directly in front of him.

"Calm down," he warned. "In case you missed it, I'm trying to rescue you."

Her chest heaved and her breath came in short, little pants. She fell back a few steps and dropped into a crouch, her body with all its sweet familiar curves signaling that she was ready to defend herself should he step any closer. Her eyes regarded him with open suspicion.

Ryan knew they were in a standoff. But how could he convince her that he wasn't part of this crazy plan to hurt her? To drug her and play with her mind? She wasn't in any frame of mind to allow her to trust anything he said. And if he didn't get her out of there soon, they'd both be sitting in one of Bloom's cells.

"Tess, I promise I'm not going to hurt you. I'm here to help." He took a step toward her, but she stiffened.

He stopped, rethinking his approach. "Look, I know it's hard for you to trust me, but we don't have a lot of choices here. They're going to figure out that's a loop playing in the system soon and when they do, they'll be piling in here pretty fast."

"And then what? Do I get strapped to the table, pumped full of drugs again and then you come in and we start the rescue game all over?"

She'd stumped him with that question. Hell, Ryan knew he'd think the same thing if he was in her shoes. But he had to convince her somehow.

Pain shadowed her eyes. "Bloom told me what it was all about. The whole sick scene at your house. It was all an experiment to you. A chance for you to see if you could convince me that you were helping me. You recorded everything. Analyzed it." The realization of what she'd said seemed to hit her hard and tears swam in her eyes. She choked and swallowed hard.

He shook his head. "Tess, listen to me—"

Her momentary weakness angered her, and she slashed at the tears with the back of her hand, wiping them along the side of her thin green pants. She bit down on her lower lip to keep it from trembling.

"Shut up," she demanded. "You like doing that to people, don't you, Dr. Donovan. You like getting them to trust you and believe in you. You like analyzing things and seeing how people tick. Well, you're not going to fool with my mind anymore."

She stepped backward another step and he could see her almost stumble. She'd been through so much, and Ryan knew she was more than just exhausted. She was wiped out, overwrought and drugged beyond anyone's limit with a dangerous concoction of psychotropic medications. But he needed her to hold it together for a little longer. At least until he was able to get her out of the center.

He kept his voice soft, trying to recreate the bond he'd established with her earlier. "I know this is hard, Tess, but I'm asking you to trust me one more time. Just reach down inside and remember how hard we worked to figure things out. Would I have done those things for you, if I wanted to hurt you?"

She rubbed a spot between her eyes as if trying desperately to concentrate. "Your damn drugs are beginning to wear off and I'm thinking clearer now." Her breath came in quick little hitches. "And I have a feeling that you'd do anything to get me to do what you wanted."

"Come on, Tess, you don't believe that. Think about what you're saying." He tried to move a little closer, but she immediately held up a hand, telling him to stay where he was.

Frustrated, he complied. Damn, the minutes were ticking by, and he wasn't sure how much longer the loop Brian had sent to the computers would last.

"I want to believe you, I really do." She put her palm against the side of her head, as if fighting against something going on inside her brain. "But I—I can't." She glanced at the table behind her and Ryan knew she was thinking about the possibility that she'd end up back there, strapped down and pumped full of drugs.

He wiped a bead of sweat off his forehead with his sleeve. Tess's face was flushed and her nostrils were flared. The air between them spit electricity.

She circled him, ready to spring if he made even the slightest move toward her. She had to know that she was no match for him physically, but she was willing to fight if she had to.

Ryan knew he could subdue her with brute strength if necessary, but he didn't want to resort to that method. She'd suffered that indignity once already. He had to convince her that she could trust him without physical intimidation.

Leaning forward, he grabbed her forearm and gently pulled her toward him. Her body tensed and air hissed between her teeth.

"Listen to me," he said. "I want you—"

The door behind them clicked open and they both froze.

A nurse, carrying a small tray with a group of syringes aligned across the top, stepped inside. Alarm immediately sprang to her severe face. Her gaze jumped back and forth between Tess and Ryan, finally settling on him. "Who are you? And what are you doing in here?"

Ryan grabbed Tess's wrists, whipped her around so that she was backed up against him. He crossed her arms on her chest and held her secure against him. "I found her trying to escape. Put down the tray and get the table ready so I can get her back into her restraints."

Tess's body was still for a brief nanosecond, and then she seemed to explode. "You lying, sneaking bas—" Her anguished wail cut at him, but Ryan ignored it, struggling to hold her.

The nurse's indecision was momentary, but then she quickly set the tray down and leaned across the table, hurrying to untangle the restraints.

Ryan winced as one of Tess's heels cracked into his shin. Damn, but she packed a wallop. She twisted her body, bowing it outward in a frantic attempt to get loose. She bent her head down and clamped her teeth into the meaty portion of his forearm. He grunted in pain, but simply dragged her along with him as he moved closer to the bedside table and the syringe tray.

As the nurse started to straighten up, Ryan pushed Tess away, grabbed one of the syringes and sank it into the nurse's hip. The woman's eyes widened with surprise, and she lunged for him, but he stepped back. She staggered a few steps and then fell. Ryan caught her before she hit the floor.

"What are you doing?" Tess demanded from the other side of the room.

He lifted the nurse onto the table and started to strip off her uniform. He glanced over one shoulder. "Get undressed."

Tess regarded him with cautious eyes. She circled around the table, keeping her distance from him. "What are you up to?"

Ryan lifted the woman's limp body and peeled off the upper portion of her uniform. "I'm getting you some escape clothes."

He pulled off the nurse's pumps and threw one of them to Tess. She caught it with one hand. She continued to stare at him.

Ryan threw her the other one and then started to shimmy the woman's dress over her hips and down her legs. She wasn't as tall as Tess, but the dress would have to do. He shot Tess an impatient glance. "If you don't hurry up and change, we're never going to get out of here. And I don't think we have enough syringes to take down every goon that walks through that door."

Tess studied him for another minute and then in a single instant, she seemed to make up her mind. She tore at the tie at the waist of her pants, stripping them off and then sliding her cotton shirt over her head. There was no embarrassment or false modesty.

Ryan struggled not to stare, but it was a losing battle. He drank in the welcome sight of her firm breasts and the gentle curve of her back, hips and belly as she bent to pull on her new set of clothes.

He felt his mouth go dry and he shook his head. How in God's name did his body manage to betray him at such an inopportune time? He pushed the thought aside. He was simply experiencing a reaction to stress.

Ryan grabbed her discarded clothes and started redressing the nurse. Tess stepped forward to help him buckle her into the restraints, and he paused long enough to slap several pieces of medical tape over the woman's slack mouth. It wouldn't hold for long and with the woman's dark hair, he didn't figure she'd fool the security camera forever. But it might buy them enough time to get out.

He looked up to find Tess watching his every move, the distrust still lurking in their green depths. "So, you think that because you've drugged her and tied her up, I'm going to believe that you're really on my side?"

Ryan reached out and gently ran his finger along the curve of her delicate jaw. She didn't pull away, but her tough, no-nonsense gaze didn't waver, either.

He sighed. "Do you remember back at my house when you asked me if my job was so all-fired important that I wouldn't listen or believe anything my heart was telling me?"

She nodded.

"Well, I needed to come and find you to tell you that my job isn't that important. I'm willing to listen. I'm willing to sacrifice everything and anything to make sure you are safe."

A small smile tugged the corners of her lush lips, and he knew he had managed to reach her.

"Do you believe me now? Even just a little?" he asked.

Her lashes, thick and dark, swept the crest of her cheeks as she paused to consider his question. Finally she lifted her head and nodded. "I'm not really sure why, but I do." She glanced toward the unconscious nurse. "Do you have some kind of plan for getting us out of here?"

He grinned ruefully. "Unfortunately, we're pretty much left with trying to walk out of here undetected."

"Oh good, I love it when my hero arrives with a well-researched, well-mapped-out escape plan."

"Hey, you got any better ideas?"

She waved a hand. "Sorry, I get a little cranky when I don't get much sleep. Let's get moving."

He eased the cell door open and checked the hall.

Empty. The cameras on both ends were off. Brian had seen to that, but there was a limit to how long they would stay off without someone correcting the glitch in the tampered program.

He nodded and slipped out, and Tess followed. She closed the door behind them and the electronic lock reengaged, clicking home with a finality that reminded Ryan there was no going back.

The hall leading from her cell to the elevator was eerily quiet. Their feet echoed hollowly on the metal decking.

Tess figured part of the eeriness was due to them being so deep underground. So deep in fact, that nothing, no noise or smells from the outside filtered down into this section of the facility.

They passed only one other person, a man in a lab coat who was more interested in the PalmPilot in his hand than the two of them. He nodded curtly to Ryan and essentially ignored her.

At the end of the corridor, Ryan punched the elevator button for up. "We need to go two floors up to get to the loading dock area. That's the only exit."

"Guess they didn't take into consideration the possibility of a fire and needing alternative escape exits," Tess said, tugging at the hem of her dress. The nurse was a good two inches shorter than her, and the dress rode a little too high on her thighs.

"I don't think they care. Everything has been designed to keep this portion of the lab as tightly confined as possible.'' Ryan's fingers drummed restlessly on the elevator panel.

She reached out and covered his hand with her own. ''We're going to get out.''

He smiled and nodded, but she could tell he wasn't convinced.

''Who's this person helping you?'' she asked. ''Are you sure you can trust him?''

Ryan checked the location of the elevator. ''He's my secretary's boyfriend. He works in the center's computer department. According to Alice, he's a little odd, a puzzle freak. He's been curious about what's been going on down here for a while, and he's been trying for months to breach the security system without being detected.'' Ryan thumbed the bottom edge of the plastic security badge clipped to his shirt. ''He reprogrammed this badge, put my picture in for some lab tech assigned down here. The man is a whiz.''

''How did he change the information in the system?''

''He simply substituted the picture from my assigned badge for this one. Essentially gave me this other guy's identity.'' He chuckled ruefully. ''This guy's file showed him as chronically late for work. So we crossed our fingers and had me come in posing as him a little early. Hopefully, the guy will stay true to form and come in late today.''

''Risky chance.'' Tess lifted her own badge and stared at the picture on it. ''It's not hard to see this isn't me.'' There was only a likeness, but she also knew that there would be no picture of her in the system. She didn't work here. She wasn't even supposed to *be here* inside the building.

''We went through the entire data bank of pictures in the personnel file trying to find someone close to your size and features. This woman was the only one even close to your general description. Lucky for you, she's on the medical staff.''

"Looks like we're running this operation on a wing and prayer," Tess said dryly.

"Guess that's what you get when you rely on a last-minute rescue."

Tess smiled up at him. "Okay with me, as long as you're the last-minute rescuer."

The elevator arrived with a ding, and the doors slid open. The car was empty.

"Keep your face away from the camera in the corner," Ryan warned. "We couldn't play with any of the other cameras. We're live from now on."

He stepped onboard and maneuvered himself so that most of his body blocked her from the prying lens.

Tess dipped her head so her cap shadowed her face and climbed on after him.

The doors closed, and they headed upward, their fate awaiting them two floors up.

FLYNN SLID OFF his uniform jacket and hung it over the heavy oak clothes butler sitting outside the bathroom door of his luxurious suite of rooms at the Bloom Research Center. Turning on the gold-plated faucet in the bathroom sink, he leaned down and splashed cold water on his face. He straightened up, leaning his broad hands on the sides of the cool porcelain and stared at his reflection in the mirror.

Bloodshot eyes and deep lines of weariness scarred his lean angular face. He stared defiantly at the old man staring back out at him. One more year till mandatory retirement. He looked older than dirt. Not surprising considering the crap he'd put up with during the duration of his military career. Bumbling idiots. Vision-impaired drones and lackluster, boring intellectuals who drained the life out of every dream he'd ever had for the advancement of his country.

It wasn't until he was invited to join the board of directors of the conservative think tank, The Patriot's Foundation of

Family Values, that Flynn felt rejuvenated. For the first time in years, he thought that his beloved country wasn't doomed to stumble down a road of mismanagement, mediocrity and ruin.

Less than two years after taking his seat on the board, Flynn found himself totally committed to the Patriot's progressive and unprecedented vision for American government. When CEO Markus Richardson, ultraright conservative and multimillionaire, tapped him on the shoulder to spearhead the Patriot's Freedom Project, Flynn hadn't hesitated a moment before accepting the job. He had agreed to take the position of project director because he knew that Richardson would see that left-wing crazies didn't find a way to take over the Oval Office with the election of turncoat Republican Jacob Tibias Starling—the man who had readily agreed to serve as vice president of the United States and then decided that the Republican Party no longer fit his vision for the future.

Flynn reached over and grabbed a thick towel off the heated towel rack. With a heavy sigh, he buried his face in the soft cloth and dried his face with a vigorous rub.

Their ace in the hole was Tess. Flynn smiled grimly. Tess was his ultimate secret weapon.

He snapped the towel back over the rack and headed for the living room. As he reentered the elegantly appointed room, there was a light knock on the door.

"Come," he ordered.

The door opened and Bloom stepped in.

Flynn moved over to the well-stocked bar in the corner of the room. "You'll join me in a drink?"

"No, thank you." Bloom walked to one of the chairs and sank into it with a contented sigh.

Flynn busied himself with preparing his own drink. Vodka was his beverage of choice. "I'm guessing from your appearance that our guest is safely stowed in her cell?"

"She recovered nicely from the session we conducted earlier. Feisty and defiant as ever. As previous, she retains no conscious memory of the session."

Flynn lowered himself into a chair across from Bloom and took a healthy swig. "Tell me, how long before she's ready to go into operational mode?"

"Well, as you saw this afternoon, I was able to conduct the final series of programming. Essentially, that was all that needed to be done. The rest is simply fine-tuning things. She's ready whenever you need her. The command has been installed in her memory. She'll obey when she hears it."

"You're sure?"

"I'm positive."

"So you can assure us of the success of the mission?"

Bloom laughed, the tiniest quiver of anxiety evident in his voice. "As I've said before, nothing is assured. We're functioning in the cutting edge of science. But I'm relatively sure Tess will perform her duties as required."

"Starling is planning to make his announcement to switch parties and run on the Progressive Independent's ticket in less than a week. I want the lesson to be taught that day."

"And it shall," Bloom said.

Flynn raised a hand as if to make another point but was interrupted when Bloom's beeper went off.

Bloom made an expression of apology and went to the phone, punching in a number. "This is Bloom."

Flynn waited, something telling him this wasn't good news.

Chapter Ten

As they stepped off the elevator, Ryan could see the security desk. Their final barrier to freedom.

Everything looked normal. Calm. No alarms. No sign that anyone knew Tess was gone. So far, so good.

Several feet beyond the security station, Ryan could see where the cement floor ended and the loading dock's huge bay doors opened to the outside. Freedom. His heart hammered. So close, yet still so far.

The doors were open and a semi was backed up to the edge of the dock. Four men and a forklift operator were unloading pallets filled with heavy boxes and stacking them against the wall.

Beyond the parked truck, he could see the brilliant orange of the late-afternoon sun touching the field bordering the parking lot. A tinge of pink licked the edge of the horizon, and a warm breeze floated down the corridor to brush his face.

Two uniformed men stood at the final checkpoint. One had his elbows propped on top of the computer console, his expression bored and his eyes half-closed.

The other guard was younger, more alert. Hypervigilant. But Ryan had a feeling the other one, the one with the bored expression, would be the one to watch out for. He was the seasoned pro. Even now he could tell that the guard was studying them from beneath hooded lids.

Suddenly Ryan stiffened and swore softly under his breath. Tess shot him an alarmed look. "What's wrong?"

"We've got a problem," he said under his breath. "See the guy walking up the outside ramp?"

Tess nodded.

"Unfortunately, he's the owner of this badge, the man whose identity I assumed." Ryan checked his watch. "The computer pegged him as chronically late for work, but he's only late by five minutes. We need to get to the gate before him."

FLYNN WATCHED as Bloom shifted the phone from one ear to the other, his annoyance disappearing to be replaced by an expression of total horror. The doctor's eyes met his across the room but then he quickly blanked his face, a blatant attempt to hide what he was feeling.

Flynn straightened up. Something was definitely wrong.

"What do you mean she's gone?" Bloom shouted into the receiver. His gaze slid away from the general's.

Flynn sat forward. What now? The back of his neck heated. Why had he ever been convinced to trust a bunch of bumbling intellectual eggheads to carry out the most important security job of their lives? He must have lost his mind.

Across the room, Bloom's knuckles turned white as he gripped the receiver, pressing it to his ear. "She must have had help. There's no way she could have gotten out of those restraints on her own."

The doctor's eyes widened and he met Flynn's. His level of panic was palpable. Flynn stood up, the steel of his spine bringing him to attention. Within seconds, he was across the room, grabbing the phone out of Bloom's hand.

"How long has she been missing?" Flynn snapped into

the receiver. Silence met him on the other end of the phone. "Answer me, dammit!"

"We—we just checked her cell two minutes ago, General. She can't have been gone long. S-someone fiddled with the video-surveillance program. One of the nurses was found drugged and in her clothes."

"There's no way she could have done that alone. She had to have outside help." He touched a button on the phone's base and put the guard on intercom and then turned toward Bloom. "It isn't hard to bet that the culprit in this mess was your prodigy—Ryan Donovan. Where is he?"

"Donovan?" Bloom frowned. "Why would you suspect him?"

"Because I saw the way he looked at Tess when we went to bring her back. The man has a savior complex. When we get to the bottom of this fiasco we'll find him. Where is he?"

Bloom shrugged. "I have no idea." He checked his watch. "In his office probably. But he knows nothing about what we're doing in the secure labs. He doesn't even have access to them."

The guard on the other end of the phone cleared his throat. "I just checked the computer—we have a log-in time for Dr. Donovan. No log-out. He must be in the building."

"Check his office," Bloom said.

Flynn dismissed Bloom with a single look. "Find Tess. Do *not* let her or Donovan out of this building. I prefer to have them both alive, but if Donovan gives you any trouble, you have my permission to terminate him."

"Yes, sir!" the guard said. "We'll have her back in her cell pronto. You can count on my team."

"I counted on your team once," Flynn snorted. "You've already failed me." He hung up on the guard.

"How do you know it's Donovan?" Bloom pressed.

"Because he isn't the type of man that is easily put off.

I knew he wasn't satisfied with our explanation of why Tess needed to come with us. I should have had him taken into custody right then and there and saved us all the trouble of dealing with him now. His meddling has put us right back to where we were when she first escaped."

"You should have allowed me to bring Donovan into the fold. If you had agreed, none of this would have happened."

"I'm a good judge of character, Doctor. And if you truly believe that Donovan would have cooperated with what we have going here, then you're crazier than I thought."

Flynn moved over to the antique hat rack standing in the corner of the room, pulled down his uniform jacket and the shoulder harness underneath.

He slipped on the harness and then released his Glock from the spring-loaded holster. He checked it as he met Bloom's gaze from across the room. "Let's make no mistakes, Bloom. I want Tess back, and if your golden boy, Donovan, interferes in any way, he won't be interfering for long."

He slipped the gun back in its holster and exited the room.

TESS WATCHED as Ryan moved toward the security desk, his long-legged stride confident. Self-assured. He was a man who knew where he was headed and didn't have a lot of time to waste.

She followed a few steps behind him, her shoulders slightly rounded, her steps slower. She was a nurse weary from a long shift.

She waited patiently as Ryan slid his card through the slot, watching the younger guard through a fringe of lashes as he studied the computer monitor carefully. The light flashed green and Ryan started through.

"Sorry, sir, but I need to check your bag," the young guard said, holding out a hand. Tess felt the older guard's eyes shift to her. She studied the floor, rubbing her lower back as if tired. He didn't seem particularly interested in her as his attention shifted back to Ryan.

Ryan set his briefcase on the counter and snapped the locks. The young guard rifled through the contents.

Tess turned to search out the location of the man Ryan was impersonating. He was on the loading dock now, exchanging a few words with one of the workers.

That's it, buddy, she thought. *Chat a little while longer. Be cooperative and stay there a few minutes more.*

The guard laughed and pulled a girlie magazine from the stack of papers inside the briefcase. "Guess I better check and make sure you didn't hide any important top-secret documents in here."

"Be my guest," Ryan said, leaning an elbow on the counter.

Tess hid a grin. Ryan had shown a real touch of ingenuity including the magazine in the briefcase. Nothing like a few nude pictures to get men's minds off the important stuff.

The guard leafed through the pages, grinning and holding up the magazine for his partner to catch a glimpse of the models. The guard winked at Ryan. "Nice research you guys are involved in down there in the lab."

Ryan shrugged. "Just some light reading to pass the time when things get slow."

Keep it brief. Keep it casual. Don't engage him too much, Tess thought, crowding in behind Ryan. She reached up and swiped her own badge.

"Get a look at page twenty-three," Ryan urged. "She's worth the price of admission alone."

Both guards leaned over to get a closer look. Neither glanced at the monitor as the nurse's face came up on the screen. The light blinked green and Tess stepped to the other side of the security gate.

Neither guard glanced at her, their attention fully focused

on the magazine and the stunning beauty on page twenty-three.

Tess walked away, her shoulders braced so tight they ached. She was sure that any minute one of them would yell for her to stop. But no yell came.

Behind her, the pages of the magazine continued to rustle.

Up ahead, the lab tech waved to the worker he was talking to, and he started across the dock for the security desk.

Okay, time to break up the little party, Ryan. Get moving! Tess tightened her hands into fists, but she resisted the urge to glance over her shoulder to see if he was aware that the technician was now making his way toward the desk. She kept moving.

"Okay, guys, I need to get going. My old lady is probably counting the minutes until I get home. But you two keep the magazine. My personal gift to security."

"Hey, buddy, thanks," the younger guard said. "It'll make the evening pass at a faster clip."

Tess heard the briefcase snap shut and then the sound of Ryan's footsteps as he hurried to catch up to her. "That was close," she said, continuing to walk toward the exit.

"It isn't over yet. The guy arrived at the desk just as I was leaving." He nodded toward the front of the semi parked at the loading dock. "Head for the cab. We're going to need a ride out of here."

She shot him a quick glance of approval. "A little oversize, but it'll serve our purpose."

"Not so terribly oversize when you remember that we're going to need to get through the front gate."

Tess quickened her step—she'd forgotten that particular fact. There were still a lot of obstacles in front of them.

Ryan swung ahead of her, headed for the driver's side of the rig.

They were halfway down the ramp when the late-arriving technician yelled, "For crying out loud! All I did was come a few minutes late and park in the handicapped slot. Is that a reason to pull a gun on a guy?''

Tess glanced behind her. The guards had their guns drawn and trained on the technician. He was facedown on the loading dock.

Ryan yanked open the door of the cab and stepped back, allowing Tess to climb in ahead of him. As she slid past the steering wheel into the passenger's seat, a sense of relief washed over her. The driver had been kind enough to leave the keys in the ignition.

"You know how to drive one of these things?" she asked as Ryan settled behind the wheel.

"I drove a dump truck for two summers in college, working construction. We can only hope they're somewhat similar." He jammed a foot on the clutch and reached down to turn the key. The big engine rumbled to life as he threw the shift into gear.

As they started rolling, Tess checked the side mirror. Two men on the loading dock were yelling and the doors to the tractor trailer swung back to hit the sides of the truck with a loud bang.

"Keep moving," she said. "They're not looking happy."

Sure enough, a siren sounded as they pulled away from the dock and headed for the parking lot exit.

"Buckle your seat belt," Ryan yelled over the roar of the engine. "By the time we reach the main gate, they're going to be ready for us. I have a feeling they've figured out you're in the cab."

She reached over and grabbed the shoulder belt next to him, pulling it across his flat stomach. Her knuckles grazed the cloth of his shirt and as she sat back to buckle her own belt, her eyes briefly met his. The tiniest of smiles played at one corner of his lips.

She quickly glanced down, concentrating on tightening her own belt. The exchange had been brief, but it had warmed her, sending a delightful thrill of excitement surging through her. Less than two hours ago she wouldn't have trusted Ryan Donovan to drive her to the supermarket and now she trusted him with her life.

"Get down," he ordered, the tenseness in his voice conveying his concern.

Up ahead stood the main gate, the thick mesh locked down tight. The guards had driven two security vehicles, heavy-duty Hummers, back to back in front of the gates. Tess knew they were there to act as extra stopping power.

She shifted forward in her seat and peered through the windshield. "I see four—no make that five guards."

"Their weapons are drawn so they're aren't standing out there to wave goodbye," Ryan said over the roar of the engine.

He stomped on the clutch and shifted, hitting the gas and bringing the rig up to a teeth-rattling sixty-five miles per hour.

"If I had a ten-ton truck bearing down on me," Tess said through clenched teeth. "I might be holding a rifle, too."

She braced her palms against the dashboard and jammed her feet against the floorboards. Ryan's knuckles whitened on the steering wheel, but he didn't take his foot off the gas.

The speedometer kicked up to seventy. The roar of the engine rattled inside the cab, setting off an odd buzz in Tess's ears. As they closed in on the gate, the guards ditched the guardhouse, jumping out of the way. The truck hit the Hummers with a bone-jarring crash, and the cab shuddered as the two security vehicles hurled backward out of its path.

The front end of the truck hit the gates full on with the high, eardrum-splitting whine of metal against metal. The gate held for less than a second as the truck strained at full throttle to get through.

Finally the hinges snapped and the gates flew off their

posts. They hurtled past the windows of the cab, and the truck plunged through the opening.

Tess glanced into the rearview mirror as the five guards ran into the middle of the road. Three of them dropped down into firing stances and let go. She ducked as the glass on the side mirror disintegrated into flying shards. Other bullets pinged off the side of the truck.

She sat back and threw a triumphant glance in Ryan's direction. "That was damn good driving. You've got a real knack for this escaping business."

"Thanks." His expression hardened as he used both hands to keep the careening rig on the narrow road leading into town. "We need to get rid of the truck. It's too big to continue using. They're bound to be after us in a matter of minutes."

Tess nodded her agreement, but she was at a loss as to where they could hide. And at the same time, Tess realized that even though they had escaped, she still had no idea who she was or why Flynn was determined to keep her captive.

A SHORT TIME LATER, Ryan slowed and pulled the rig onto a small side road. It was rough going as the road was hard-packed dirt with a good number of potholes. The trees on either side grew close to the road and hung in the way, scraping and snapping off on the sides of the truck.

When the vegetation got too thick to drive any farther, Ryan stopped, shifting the gears into Park. He nodded to Tess, and she slid across the seat, showing a flash of white thigh as the nurse's dress rode up even higher. She piled out of the passenger's side without a word.

Ryan climbed from the other side and threw the keys in a high arch. They glittered silver for a moment when hit by the rays of the low-hanging sun but then disappeared into the surrounding brush.

The guards probably wouldn't have any trouble hot-wiring the truck when they found it, but Ryan didn't intend to make it easy for them.

"What now?" Tess asked, coming up to stand beside him.

"About half a mile down this road there's a path that cuts across the field and heads back toward town. I used to come out here on my bike with my friends when I was kid." He glanced up. "It'll stay daylight for another couple of hours so we won't have any trouble finding our way."

"But it will make it easier for them to see us, too," she countered.

"In all likelihood, they'll figure we headed for the interstate. I'm counting on them going there first. It'll be a while before they realize we didn't take that route."

He started off, using the shadows of the overhanging trees to shoot a covert glance in Tess's direction. He needed to know if she was physically up for a fast pace. She caught him taking stock of her condition and she scowled. She didn't appreciate him even considering her not being up to the challenge.

But in spite of her resentment, Ryan didn't miss the veil of fatigue that had settled over her features, the way she worked to hide it but couldn't.

He didn't need to ask to know that her energy reserve was low. She'd been fighting Flynn, Bloom and his research team both mentally and physically for God knows how long. But in spite of it all, Ryan was certain she'd rather collapse face first than admit to him that she was running on empty.

"Why is it exactly that we aren't heading for the interstate? Even though that's where they'd look first, wouldn't we make better time?" she asked, matching his stride with a determined set of her chin. "Aren't we trapping ourselves by ditching the truck?"

"They'd be on us before we had a chance to get off the on-ramp. We need to get ourselves a car and some cash."

"Don't even think about trying to pull any cash out of your account. As soon as you use your bank card, they'll know where we are."

"I know. I'm hoping my sister has some cash in her house." He reached up and brushed back a few strands of damp hair. There was a breeze, but the heat of the day still hugged the ground.

Off to the west, clouds were building, warning of an impending storm. They needed the rain—the humidity had gotten almost unbearable—but the thought of traipsing around in the woods in the rain wasn't pleasant.

"If we take my sister's car, we can sell it for cash and pick up a used car they can't trace."

"If we drag your sister into this, there's no telling what could happen. Better to stay away from her."

He nodded. "You're right. I can't risk anything happening to her or the boys. Any suggestions?"

"We take the first vehicle we can find, drive it to Des Moines and trade it for cash and a untraceable clunker."

He lifted an eyebrow. "Sounds like you've done this before."

Tess frowned and then shrugged. "I don't know. It just sounds right. But I can't be that good if the first time you found me, I was wandering around in the cornfield butt naked." She glanced down at herself. "At least this time I managed to escape fully clothed."

"And that fact is one of my greatest disappointments."

She laughed and then grew serious again. "I notice you haven't suggested we go to the police."

Ryan trudged across the field, reaching out now and then to steady Tess when a rock or tuff of high grass made her unsteady. "If Flynn is able to fabricate such an elaborate psychiatric file and such an official-looking court order, I have no doubt that he could convince any police department that we're making this up.''

Tess paused, her shoulder brushing his arm, and gazed at him appreciatively. ''I think you're actually getting the hang of this.''

Ryan vaulted over a half-hidden stone fence and then reached back to give her a hand as she scrambled over. The lines of fatigue on her face had deepened a bit over the half mile or so they'd traveled, but she didn't complain.

''Any ideas on a car?'' she asked.

''Ida Relations lives about a half mile from here. She always leaves her car out of the garage with the keys in it. She's been a volunteer firefighter for thirty years and prides herself on being the first one on a scene.'' He held back a branch, keeping it from smacking Tess across the cheek. ''We'll borrow hers. She'll never forgive me if there's a fire tonight and she can't get there. But we'll deal with that at a later date.''

TWENTY MINUTES LATER, they reached the hedge surrounding a large Victorian-style house. There were a few other houses farther off in the distance, but the huge rambling Victorian was the only one with lights on.

Ryan motioned to a soft spot near the hedge. ''Wait here while I take a look around.''

Tess didn't argue. She was so tired she could barely see straight. She sank onto the grass and waited while Ryan headed off to scout out the area.

She tried to ignore the persistent ache in her muscles, but she could feel her brain shutting down. She needed to get some rest or she wouldn't be able to walk, let alone talk.

A few minutes later, Ryan was back. He crouched down next to her, his broad shoulders shifting and bunching beneath his shirt. His smell, an intriguing combination of masculine sweat and strong soap, wafted up and touched the end of her nose. She had an overwhelming urge to curl up against him and fall into a deep, dreamless sleep. But then she realized it wouldn't be a dreamless sleep. Too many nightmares lately for that to happen. She snapped awake.

Ryan gently smoothed the hair back away from her forehead. His eyes, contemplative and gentle, told her that he knew she was almost done in. She hated seeing the concern on his face, but she knew there was nothing she could do to reassure him. She just needed to prove herself by keeping up.

"Can we get to the car?" she asked.

Ryan nodded. "The TV is on in the living room, and Ida's got the sound turned up pretty loud because she's in the kitchen making dinner. She probably won't hear a thing. As I expected, the key is in the ignition."

Tess grinned. "Would you think less of me if I told you I could have hot-wired that car in under thirty seconds?"

"And you picked up this little skill where exactly?"

"When I—" Tess stopped, confusion immediately clouding her brain. She bit her lower lip, angry again at the untimely intrusion of her memory loss. "I—I'm not sure exactly."

Ryan reached out and gently caressed the line of her jaw, the heat of his touch reassuring. "Relax. It doesn't really matter. I say we're just lucky you remember how to do it." He laughed. "But be assured, you and I *will* be discussing where you picked up that skill at some later date."

"You do realize that means you're stuck waiting around until that little issue of my failed memory is solved, don't you?"

Ryan hit her with that devastatingly sexy grin, the one that had the ability to shoot something hot and liquidy into her lower belly. "Oh, I've got time. In fact, I have no plans to be anywhere else but right here next to you until that memory of yours returns."

Tess ducked her head, knowing she didn't want him to see the sudden surge of gratitude that rushed through her. His willingness to verbally commit to staying with her throughout this ordeal meant more to her than even she realized. But she knew she didn't want to scare him off or make him think she'd become a quivering ball of pathetic appreciation.

After all, he'd already set the boundaries of their relationship once. He'd warned her that there could never be anything personal between them. She had to respect that.

He touched her shoulder as if checking to see whether she was ready to move. She nodded and slipped her hands in his, pulling herself up. They made their way across the yard, and the late-model Town Car's engine was purring in less than thirty seconds.

Somewhere inside the house, a little dog yipped, but no faces appeared at the tall windows. Ryan backed the car out of the driveway and then took off. They avoided the interstate and traveled the back roads, heading northeast. Neither of them was sure where in the East they wanted to go, but they knew they wanted to put as much distance as possible between themselves and the Bloom Research Center.

They kept moving through the night and well into the next day. Ryan insisted on driving, telling her that she needed to sleep off the effects of the drugs. Although Tess didn't argue, as she knew her body was crying for rest, she found sleep impossible. She had reached the point of running on pure adrenaline.

Several times, she tried closing her eyes and resting her head against the back of the seat. Nothing. She tried curling her legs up onto the seat and wedging a shoulder into the corner with her head against the window. Still nothing. Her brain refused to let her sleep.

Wild thoughts filled her brain, racing across her consciousness at breakneck speeds. Every car that roared up behind them on the lonely country roads brought Tess's heart into the back of her throat. She knew that any one of them could be Flynn and his men.

She knew Flynn would never give up. He'd follow her until she was recaptured and returned to the center. He needed her. For whatever reason, he couldn't let her walk away.

But the thing that made her knees weak with fear and her heart shudder with dread was the knowledge that if Ryan was caught, his fate would be different than hers. He wouldn't be returned to the center. Flynn would silence him. Permanently.

Chapter Eleven

Tess lifted her head and stretched. The map sitting in her lap slid off and curled down around her feet. She left it there, no longer even having the energy to lean down and pick it up.

It was dark outside and the clock on the dash blinked 10:00 p.m. A light drizzle started, hitting the windshield and sliding down the gritty glass in gray streaks. Ryan reached down and turned on the wipers. The blade on the driver's side limped across the glass, barely cleaning it.

"Guess that's a signal we need to find somewhere to hole up for a while," he said. "We need a few hours' sleep anyway and it'll give us a chance to figure out what we're going to do next."

"I had the same thought," Tess said. She was worried about the fatigue that weighed on Ryan's shoulders. He hadn't complained once, but she knew he must be exhausted. She might not be able to sleep, but she was pretty sure he would collapse as soon as his head hit a pillow.

The small town they were driving through had the usual recognizable motel chains, but Ryan bypassed them all, heading into the seedier section of town. Tess didn't argue. She knew without asking that he was looking for a place that was a little less high profile. A bit less touristy.

Finally he hit the turn signal and turned into the parking

lot of a run-down motel. As he pulled into a parking slot in front of the office, he glanced at her. ''Out of the way enough for you?''

''Perfect,'' Tess said, climbing out and surveying the pot-hole-riddled parking lot. She nodded at the tiny sub shop across the street. ''We even have gourmet dining within walking distance of our front door.''

Ryan laughed and walked over to the door to the motel office. He held it open for her. Tess stepped inside and took in the rather startling ugliness of the place. Dust-coated blinds shaded two grimy windows facing the parking lot, and a threadbare rug, with more than a few suspicious-looking stains, covered the worn floorboards.

A lamp sat perched on a high counter, its bulb casting a dim yellowish light through the room. Tess figured that the weak lighting was a blessing. From the looks of things, she was fairly positive that she didn't want to see any more of the place than was absolutely necessary.

A buzzing neon sign blinked on and off in the window, announcing to the cars passing outside that there were va-cancies. No big surprise there. From the looks of things, the Center City Motel wasn't exactly the kind of place that at-tracted weary travelers. Which in Tess's mind was a good thing. It made the place ideal for a few hours of much-needed rest.

In a small sitting area off to the side, a middle-aged woman, in a short leather skirt and tank top stretched over two abnormally large and perky breasts, sat filing her nails. She glanced up at the two of them, her gaze bored. She snapped her gum and nodded a silent hello.

''We'd like a room,'' Ryan said.

She grinned, red-glossed lips widening over tobacco-stained teeth, and pointed at the desk with her nail file. ''Just hit the bell there and Tony will be along to get you one.''

She went back to filing her nails.

Ryan hit the bell twice.

"Hold your damn horses," a man yelled, his voice filtering through the door directly behind the desk. "I'll be out in a freakin' minute."

Tess propped an elbow up on the counter and rested her chin on the heel of her hand. Every muscle in her body cried out in protest. The drugs still in her system were affecting her ability to think and see straight. If she didn't close her eyes and shut off her brain for at least a few hours, she knew she'd be flat on her face in a matter of minutes.

A quick glance in Ryan's direction told her that he wasn't in much better shape. His hair was rumpled and hung down over his forehead, trailing in his blue eyes. His usually clean-shaven face was heavily shadowed, giving him a dark, edgy look. Tess hid a smile. The two of them probably looked as though they belonged in the place.

The sound of water rushing through pipes sounded and the door behind the desk swung open. A rail-thin man stepped out, tucking the shirttails of a dingy cotton shirt into his polyester pants. He yanked them up so high they came halfway up his chest.

"Gets so a person can't even take care of business without someone ringing the damn bell." He shuffled over to the desk in a pair of matted-lamb's-wool slippers that had seen better days. He eyed the two of them from behind thick lenses. "How long do you want the room for?"

"One night," Ryan said.

"The whole night?" the clerk asked.

Ryan nodded.

The clerk glanced over at the woman seated in the corner. "Looks like we've got ourselves a couple of marathoners, Stacy."

The woman laughed and pointed her nail file in Tess's direction. "Well, if he tires you out, honey, you be sure to give me a yell." Her gaze traveled up and down Ryan's muscular frame with frank appreciation. "You got yourself a prime specimen of man there and I'd be more than happy to finish things up for you."

"Gee, I'll definitely keep that offer in mind," Tess said dryly.

Once the registration card was filled out, Ryan reached into his pocket and pulled out the cash to pay. Tess's suggestion that they hock his ring and Rolex at a pawn shop earlier in the day had been a smart one. It gave them enough money to function without having to use his credit cards.

As he slid the bills across the desk, he peeled off an extra fifty and handed it to the clerk. "We're not expecting any visitors, but if anyone should show up, we'd appreciate a phone call."

The man fingered the corner of the extra bills as his beady-eyed gaze jumped back and forth between the two of them, studying them with an air of suspicion. "I ain't lookin' for no trouble here, mister." His gaze shifted over to the woman in the corner and then came back. "I don't like the cops nosing around, here, if you get my drift."

"Not a problem," Ryan said quietly. "It won't be the cops looking for us if anyone shows up. Believe me, they aren't interested in talking to the cops any more than you are. All you have to do is give us a call if anyone shows up looking for us and we'll be gone."

The clerk stuffed the bills in his pocket and nodded. He shoved a key across the desk. "Take room fifteen on the end. Park your car around back. There's a small driveway that will take you out to a side street. If anyone comes nosing around, I'll ring your room three times and hang up." He ripped up their registration card and dropped it in the trash can. "Just make sure you lock up when you leave."

Ryan picked up the key. "Appreciate the help." He nodded to Stacy and pressed his hand against the small of Tess's back. They exited quickly.

"That was smooth," Tess said, as Ryan pulled the door shut.

"I thought so, too."

"You've got real potential for this business." Tess climbed into the car.

"Really? And what kind of business would that be?" Ryan asked as he slipped into the driver's side and started up the car.

Tess bent down and grabbed the map crumpled on the floor. She sat up and carefully folded it. "Spook business, of course."

"Spook stuff, huh? Are we talking ghost spook or the spy kind of spook?"

Tess laughed and shot him a glance that told him she appreciated his humor. "Spy naturally. You've got all the necessary qualities, Dr. Donovan. Something tells me that you missed your true calling. You don't lose your cool and you think ahead. But most important, you show a solid understanding of the need to grease the wheels of cooperation. All critically important skills of a well-seasoned spook."

"I think all those skills come from years of dealing with patients who show an uncanny ability to manipulate the system. No spook lessons needed."

She shrugged. "You still show potential."

Ryan drove past the row of cars lining the front of the motel and took a left at the end of the building. He braked at the end of the alley and shoved the gears into Park. The car engine rattled a little when he turned off the ignition but finally shuddered to a stop.

As he unbuckled his seat belt, he turned to her. "Any idea where you learned what a spook needs to do in order to function successfully?"

Tess paused and her eyes met his across the length of the

front seat. "I—I'm not sure. You don't think—" Annoyance flashed across her face and she glanced away. "Jeez! Will you stop with the questions already. You're like some kind of relentless head doctor."

He pocketed the keys.

Tess laughed bitterly. "Oh that's right, I forgot. You *are* a shrink."

He waited her out, allowing the heavy silence to build until she lifted her head and met his gaze. Both regret and sadness were visible in her eyes. "I'm sorry. I didn't mean to snap. I know you're just trying to help."

He shrugged. "Every little statement—every off-the-cuff remark—is a clue."

"Not everything. Sometimes a comment is just a comment. People read spy novels and watch the latest blockbuster movie about espionage. What red-blooded American wouldn't know what a spy needs in order to be successful?"

She yanked open the door, grabbed her knapsack and climbed out. Ryan pocketed the keys but stayed in the car, contemplating what Tess had said. Why was she angry? His training told him he was getting closer, and the closer he got to the truth, the more frightened she became. It wasn't that she didn't want to regain her memory. Consciously she did. But unconsciously her brain was fighting her, trying to keep her safe from the knowledge.

He knew that what she'd just revealed was something much deeper and more meaningful than the simple fact that she might have read the latest Tom Clancy novel. There was a confidence, a feeling of self-assurance, when she talked about government spooks.

Was it possible she really was some type of government spy? He knew some of Sidney Bloom's funding came from government grants. Could the government—the CIA or the Secret Service—be involved in some kind of hush-hush research project involving brainwashing techniques?

He reached over the back seat and grabbed his duffel bag. Human experimentation with an unknown, experimental drug wasn't something that would be sanctioned by the FDA. Experimentation was always possible, just not with human subjects. But people had been known to test that restriction before. Was it possible that Bloom was doing just that?

He sat behind the wheel and studied Tess. She didn't go straight to their room but, instead, walked down the alley-way to the back of the motel. He knew without asking what she was doing. She was scoping out what would be their getaway route should they need it.

If Tess was involved in some sort of government research project, why wouldn't she know that? And why all the secrecy surrounding the project? Was it possible that the project wasn't sanctioned by the government, that it was some kind of renegade group, conducting the research without the government's knowledge?

"Are you coming?"

Ryan glanced up to see Tess standing by the room door. He nodded and climbed out. The possibility of the research being something other than government sanctioned intrigued him. It might explain the excessive secrecy surrounding the project, the almost deadly take-no-prisoners attitude of General Flynn.

Ryan locked the car and followed Tess inside.

THE ROOM WAS IN WORSE SHAPE than the lobby. Tess pulled the drapes as Ryan bolted the door. The smell of cigarettes and another unidentified musky smell rose up off the cloth, threatening to suffocate her. Tess coughed and turned away to survey the rest of the room.

"I can see why the guy wanted to know how long we wanted the room for. My guess is that he rents them by the hour," Ryan said as he walked over to sit on the edge of the bed. He bounced up and down a few times and then winked at her. "This thing has seen a lot of action."

"Don't remind me," Tess said, kicking off her shoes and bending down to take off her socks. One look at the condition of the matted carpet and she rethought that decision. Better to sleep with her socks on.

"I'll go across the street and get us something to eat," Ryan said, getting up. "You haven't eaten in over twelve hours—with the exception of those four candy bars and two packages of M&Ms we got at the gas station. I'm betting you're ready to swoon."

"I wouldn't swoon," she grumbled. "Southern ladies swoon. I'm a Yankee."

"Really? Where in the north are you from?"

"Well, not that far north, but from the D.C. area." She carried her shoes over to the bed and then stopped dead. She met his eyes from across the room. "Holy cow! I just remembered where I lived."

Ryan nodded.

Tess sat on the side of the bed, her mind racing. "I live in a house, not far from…" She hit the top of her thigh with her fist. "Damn, it slipped away again."

"Take it easy," Ryan said. "It's coming back at a faster rate now. That's a good sign. But don't force it. Let the memories flow back on their own." He opened the door. "I'll be back in a few minutes. Ham-and-cheese sub okay with you?"

Tess nodded absently. "Yeah, sure, that's fine. I'm going to take a shower."

When she stepped out of the bathroom, clean and refreshed, she found Ryan already eating, his body hunched over a small café-style table in the corner of the room. She was wearing the stiff new jeans and tight T-shirt Ryan had bought earlier from the feed and farm store they had stopped at for gas.

A ham-and-cheese sub was halfway to his mouth when he spotted her. He paused, and one corner of his mouth quirked upward in a familiar devilish grin. "Guess I got the shirt a few sizes too small, huh?"

Tess pulled at the hem. "Gee, ya think?"

He laughed and tore off a bite, chewing contemplatively. He swallowed and added, "Personally, I think it fits just fine."

From across the room, she watched as his eyes darkened with something wild and dangerous, and she forgot all about trying to pull at the hem of the shirt. A delicious warmth flashed up the sides of her neck and infused her cheeks. But just as quickly as the look was there, it was gone again. As if he forced it down, made it disappear. His mouth tightened and the sexy playfulness in his expression changed.

He reached around and grabbed his suit jacket hanging over the back of the chair. He threw it to her. "Sorry, I should have paid more attention when I bought the shirt. You can use my coat to cover up."

Slightly confused, Tess shrugged her shoulders into his jacket. She bent her head and rolled up the sleeves to keep them from flopping over her hands. His scent, now so familiar that it felt a part of her, clung to his jacket and surrounded her with his presence. She inhaled deeply.

But even as she wrapped the front around her and crossed her arms to keep it closed, Tess knew she didn't want to cover up. Didn't want to hide herself from him.

She'd liked it when his gaze rolled over her length with a smoky seductiveness. It created a delicious flutter deep inside her belly, and Tess knew she longed to indulge in that sensation. But Ryan had turned off the warmth and seductiveness as if he was shutting off a switch. All of sudden, he seemed closed off and locked down.

Disappointed, she grabbed the other sub and slipped into the chair across from him.

He twisted off the top of one of the colas and held it out to her. "Do you want a glass?"

Tess shook her head. "No, thanks. From the looks of this room, I'd rather take my chances with the bottle."

She took the cola, purposely allowing her fingers to trail across the back of his hand, her palm caressing his knuckles and the light dusting of dark hair.

His gaze met hers for the briefest of moments and she saw the sparks of need flare in the depths of his eyes. She wet her lips, waiting. But his dark lashes lowered, shielding his eyes from her and he let go of the bottle. Before she could speak, he leaned down and picked up the remote sitting on the bed.

He clicked on the TV. "Let's watch the news. I'm curious to see if there's anything about our escape from the center. It's not every day that a truck crashes through the gates of a research center."

Swallowing against the lump of disappointment that rose in her throat, Tess nodded. "I doubt Flynn would let anything leak, but it's worth a look."

They were already several bites into their subs by the time the late news started. The newscaster launched into a quick clip of local interest, a story about a possible break in the downtown water main and then shifted to the national news.

Tess had her bottle of soda halfway to her mouth when the woman's voice filtered into her awareness. "In an interview today, Vice President Starling revealed that he would be making a major announcement at a reception being held in his honor Thursday night."

A sense of heightened excitement seemed to infuse the anchorwoman's voice. "Insiders speculate that the vice president will announce that he will *not* be President Rone's running mate for the upcoming election. This move is unprecedented in American politics. Although history shows that vice presidential running mates have been dumped before, most running mates who have been taken off the ticket were dumped due to their liability. This is definitely *not* the case for Vice President Starling.''

The scene behind the news anchor changed to show a youthful and enthusiastic Starling waving to a crowd at a fund-raising party. The faces of the people in the crowd held a certain rapture—not much different than the rapture seen in teenagers at their favorite pop star's concert.

An ugly buzzing sound droned in Tess's ear, and the vice president's image on the screen wavered and then blurred. She blinked, trying to clear her vision. Oh God, what now? She felt as though she were slipping into a waking nightmare.

Helpless, Tess clung to the newswoman's soothing tones.

"Enjoying unprecedented popularity—a popularity never before experienced by a sitting vice president—Starling can only be labeled a valuable asset when it comes to President Rone's reelection. Rone, who is viewed by many Americans as morose, brooding and horribly out of touch with the people, has little chance of being reelected without Starling on the ticket. If Starling deserts the ticket, many insiders predict that President Rone will be in for the fight of his life and that reelection will no longer be within his reach.''

The screen behind the anchorwoman changed again, showing a crowd of longshoremen gathered around a tieless Starling. The men surrounding him were clapping him on the back and vying to shake his hand. A breeze off the water behind them ruffled Starling's wheat-colored hair, giving him a youthful and movie-starish quality.

"The vice president's chief advisor, Eli Morgan, refused to comment on the validity of any of these rumors. He has asked that people wait until the vice president is ready to make an official announcement before speculating as to what this is all about. In spite of the rumblings rocketing through the power brokers in Washington, Vice President

Starling has stayed above the hoopla by concentrating on his goodwill trip to South America. He is expected to return to the United States later today.''

"Are you okay, Tess?" Ryan asked.

Startled, Tess looked up, the bottle of cola falling from her nerveless fingers and hitting the table with a thud.

From what seemed like a great distance away, she watched as Ryan jumped up, dodging the stream of liquid that spread out rapidly across the table. He grabbed a handful of napkins and quickly blotted up the spill, his eyes watching her with concern. But he didn't speak or try to intervene. She knew that by now he'd recognized her pattern and was waiting her out to see if a new flashback would be brought to her consciousness.

But even as this thought flashed through her brain, an excruciating jolt of pain shot through her head and Tess cried out, and her body jerked, sending her shoulders slamming back against the chair.

She clamped both hands to her head and rubbed, desperately trying to soothe away the pain shooting up from between her eyes.

"Easy, Tess? Just let it come. Don't fight it. Talk to me, tell me what you're feeling."

She opened her mouth, but nothing came out, and then suddenly he was beside her. His warmth and concern seemed to surround and enclose her even as her body shook with waves of pain. His voice, smooth and caressing, seemed to wrap her in a cocoon of safety. God, she loved that voice. It was her anchor. Her salvation. And in the darkness surrounding her, Tess struggled to reach out for it, to hold on to it before she slipped away into whatever ugliness hugged the surface below.

He knelt next to her, his hands on hers as he tried to draw them away from her face.

Tess lifted her head, dazed. Confused. Her vision was

blurred and Ryan's face disappeared into a brilliant kaleidoscope of color. She blinked trying to see through the shifting colors.

But instead of the motel room, the frightening image of the man lying in a spreading pool of red was back. The people around him cried and screamed. And as she watched, the pool widened and grew at an alarming rate. Slowly the crowd seemed to step back and she could see the man's face. She jumped, a small whimper slipping from her lips. The man was Vice President Starling.

Her legs trembled, and her fingers tightened on the arm of the chair, but she didn't fight the image. She allowed herself to totally immerse herself in it. As she watched the reel play out in her head, the pool of blood widened and soaked the trademark wheat-colored hair. Starling's eyes were open, staring vacantly up at her.

Tess shuddered and gasped for breath. Bile rose in her throat and threatened to drown her. She sucked hot air, her entire body shaking with shock and rage.

"Tess, open your eyes. Talk to me. Tell me what you see so I can help you." Ryan's voice cut through the image and she struggled to concentrate on it, to hold on to the calm, deep tones like a drowning victim clung to a life ring. If she ever needed Ryan Donovan it was now.

"I—I can't breathe," she gasped. Another shock of excruciating pain washed over her and she whimpered. "Hea-head hurts."

Ryan's hand stroked the center of her back, directly between her shoulder blades, and the soft timber of his voice reached down through the pain and calmed her. "Don't panic, Tess. Slow, deep breaths. You're okay. You're going to be fine."

But his words were no sooner out of his mouth than the pain shifted, hitting the pit of her stomach and doubling her over. I'm not going to make it, she thought. I'm going to lose it right here.

Jumping up, she ran for the bathroom, slamming the door after her.

She barely had time to register the fact that the place was surprisingly clean considering the condition of the rest of the motel room before she hit her knees and lost what little food was in her stomach.

As she retched, she heard Ryan's voice through the door, "Open the door, Tess."

"Go away," she said weakly, barely able to lift her head. "I'm okay. Just a little nauseous."

She leaned her forehead against the cold tiles lining the wall. They felt like a cool cloth on her hot forehead.

Ryan rattled the doorknob. "Open the door."

She closed her eyes and commenced to shake, the chills taking over her body with a vengeance. "I'm okay. Just give me a minute alone."

She didn't want him to see her this way—retching and sweaty, her hair in her face and her body racked with tremors. She hated this feeling of being out of control. Weak and shivering. It diminished her and made her seem less than she was. And if there was one thing Tess hated more than anything, it was being seen as weak.

She retched again, and Ryan jiggled the doorknob harder. "Open the door, Tess. *Now.*" His tone held none of its familiar calm, signaling a loss of patience. Tess figured that he was about ready to come through the door, lock or no lock.

Reaching up, Tess undid the bolt and Ryan stepped inside. He crouched down beside her, one hand coming out to cup her chin and turning her head toward him.

His warmth seeped into the clammy coolness of her skin and a flush of warmth shot through her. Tess blinked and stared up into the infinite compassion in his eyes. How did he have so much to give?

For the first time since they'd started their run, Tess noticed the dark smudges under his exquisite eyes. Fatigue seemed to infuse the muscle of his solid frame, and short strands of black hair lay in disarray across his forehead. She reached up and gently pushed them back, her fingers tangling in the threads for a moment before he shifted slightly.

Her heart wondered if he'd ever allow himself to take rather than receive. He'd been up for over twenty-four hours, taking care of her, watching over her every minute. Not once had he thought of his own needs. Even now, his only thought was of taking care of her.

"Tell me what you saw and be specific," he ordered.

She dipped her lashes, breaking eye contact. "I just ate too fast."

"Don't lie, Tess. You had another flashback. I can't help you if you don't talk to me."

Tess knew he needed his rest. He didn't need to spend the rest of the night giving her therapy and working out her stupid flashbacks, her disjointed dribble that meant nothing other than the fact that she was going quietly insane.

She pushed his hand away and stood up. Moving to the sink, she avoided his eyes in the mirror. Something told Tess that if she looked into those eyes too much longer, she'd become a whimpering, quivering pile of mush. And she refused to do that.

What if she did tell him what she'd seen? He'd lock her up, that's what he'd do. People didn't see the vice president of the United States dead with a bullet to his head without being seen as crazy. Hell, if someone confessed such a thing to her, Tess knew she'd be the first to vote that the men in white coats come and cart the person off.

She turned on the faucet, bent down and splashed cold water on her face and into her mouth. She rinsed out her mouth and tried to ignore the fact that he was standing right over her, watching her every move.

She glanced at him out of the corner of her eye. The concerned look hadn't changed one iota. "I swear to you. I'm fine. Just ate too fast."

She brushed past him, pushing aside the fact that her knees were the same consistency as undercooked chocolate pudding, and made her way over to her knapsack. She rummaged through it until she found her toothbrush. She needed to do something. To be busy. Otherwise she was going to melt into his arms like a big, whiny baby.

As she moved past him again, he caught her arm. "Will you slow down? You're the color of rice paper and getting whiter by the minute."

She shook his hand off and made her way back to the sink. "Funny about that—I didn't get much chance to tan inside that prison they kept me in."

As she squeezed the toothpaste out onto her brush, she glanced in the mirror. Sure enough, he hadn't moved, one shoulder jammed up against the doorjamb, his corded arms folded expectantly across the broad expanse of his chest. He didn't budge. Apparently he got off on watching women brush their teeth.

She shrugged and shoved the toothbrush into her mouth. So let him watch. No skin off her back.

"You're probably experiencing some side effects of the medication they gave you."

Tess didn't bother answering. She simply scrubbed harder, trying to ignore the fine tremor in her hand.

"Why don't you let me check you out. I could give you something to take the edge off. Something that would put a stop to the nausea and shakes."

Tess dropped her hand to the edge of the sink, leaving the toothbrush wedged up against her cheek. She was barely aware of the fact that her mouth was filled with foaming toothpaste.

She stared at his refection in the mirror. "Are you insane? Do I really look like someone who wants more *junk* pumped into her bloodstream?"

He didn't answer, his eyes softening; a hint of deep sympathy lurking in their depths. The sympathy angered her. She didn't want him feeling sorry for her or feeling as though he had to take care of her. She had to take care of herself. Stand on her own two feet.

He wasn't always going to be there. She couldn't rely on him. He had a life, a job. She couldn't confuse his caring attitude for something it wasn't. Hadn't she done that once already? He'd backed away from her, refusing to step over the line he'd drawn between them. No matter how much she wanted him, she had to respect the boundaries he'd drawn.

His confidence and powerful presence made her feel vulnerable. Naked almost. She squeezed her eyes shut. God help her, but all she wanted was to sink back into those big, capable arms and let him hold her. To comfort her and soothe her.

"If you really want to help me, just leave me alone," she said. "I need to work through this on my own. It's safer that way." Safer for you, she thought.

His expression didn't alter, the serene blue of his eyes stared steadily back at her. Damn him, didn't he ever get mad? Was he always so infuriatingly patient? So willing to take on the troubles of the world?

She gritted her teeth. Why didn't he just leave her ungrateful butt in this seedy hotel room and go back to his comfortable life in Half Moon?

Instead, he came back at her with the same reassuring approach she'd come to expect. "Look, Tess, I know what you're doing. You're trying to push me away, but it isn't going to work. I'm not going anywhere. I'm here for the duration.''

He paused and waited, as if expecting her to answer. But she didn't. She gripped the inside edge of her bottom lip and held on tight, as if somehow she could freeze him out with her silence.

He sighed. ''When are you going to learn that you can trust me?''

Tess leaned forward and spit out the paste. Cupping one hand under the faucet, she fed herself a quick mouthful of water and rinsed out her mouth. She reached over and swiped a threadbare towel across her mouth.

''Never.'' She straightened up and pushed past him to reenter the room. Ignoring him, she yanked the bedspread back and climbed beneath the blankets. She turned on her side and pulled the covers up to her neck, gathering the sheet until she was wrapped up tight. ''Shut off the lights when you come to bed,'' she snapped, closing her eyes and heart to any more talk.

''I'm not giving up on you, Tess. Try to shut me out all you want, but I'm not leaving.''

She opened her eyes a crack to see him sitting in the chair directly across from her. She closed them again. ''Suit yourself. But you're going to get sore sitting there all night.''

''I've done it before.''

And she figured he had. She just didn't want to think about how much he'd done for her. How hard he'd worked to win her trust and confidence. Because if she thought about it too hard, she'd lose the battle. The battle that meant she'd let down her guard and ask him into her heart. She knew she couldn't risk that, couldn't allow him to be put in that kind of danger.

She pulled the blanket over her face, trying desperately to shut him out.

Chapter Twelve

Tess opened her eyes. Wherever she was it was nearly black. The only visible source of light came from a flickering table lamp across the room. A strange twist of fear gnawed on the fringe of her nerves.

Somewhere in the near-darkness, an ancient air conditioner wheezed, sounding as if it was on its last legs. The strong smell of onions drifted on the air and teased her nose.

She lifted her head, wondering where she was and how long she'd been asleep. There were no restraints on her arms and legs and the realization that she wasn't in her cell deep inside the center settled over her. The motel room. She was inside the motel room. Ryan had helped her escape.

Confused, she rolled over and bumped up against something solid. Someone slept next to her.

Ryan, of course. There was only one bed in the room, and he really wasn't about to sit up all night. After she'd fallen asleep, he'd obviously crawled into bed next to her and conked out.

He was rolled up on his side, his back to her. Through the soft glow of the lamp, she could see the broad expanse of his shoulders beneath his T-shirt and the fringe of dark hair lying along the back of his neck.

She reached out, her fingers lightly skimming the fringe of hair. The strands were soft and fine, like silk feathers of a tiny bird. The ends curled slightly around her knuckle and she smiled. He needed a haircut.

He didn't have much time for himself since she'd come into his life. Everything had been turned upside down, turned on end. But he hadn't balked. Hadn't run off or booted her ungrateful butt out of his life. Even when she'd told him to push off and leave her alone. He'd stuck by her, just as he said he would. Patiently waiting her out. Determined to help her no matter what.

She could feel the warmth of his body radiate upward, heating her face. Both shoulder blades were hard and pronounced beneath his T-shirt. Feeling like a voyeur, as if she was somehow taking advantage but unable to stop herself, Tess lifted the sheet and allowed her gaze to skim lightly, greedily over his body. The jangled hum of her nerves quieted, flooding her instead with a sweet liquid warmth.

His hard butt and lean hips dented the sagging mattress, and she reached out and lightly traced the deep indentation above his hipbone, just above the elastic of his boxers. His skin was dark and tanned against her white skin. The contrast was startling. Delicious. She slid her hand down over the cloth of his shorts to the top of his thigh.

She lifted the sheet a little higher, her eyes devouring him. He had long muscular legs, corded and covered with dark hair, so long they almost hung off the end of the mattress. She was pretty sure she'd never felt small next to a man before, but Ryan's body seemed built to do just that.

Without thinking of the consequences, she slid closer, pressing her body up against him, molding herself to him, savoring the feel of his firm butt against her soft belly. He mumbled something in his sleep, and Tess paused, holding her breath.

She didn't want him to wake up. Not yet. She didn't want him to stop her investigation, and she knew she couldn't handle his rejection. His caution. She wanted, no she *needed,* to explore more.

She slid a hand up beneath his shirt, pushing it out of the way, and she pressed her lips to the indentation of his spine, gently kissing and inhaling his clean, masculine scent.

His skin was smooth and he had a small birthmark, a tiny brown freckle directly below his left shoulder blade. She kissed it and then gently touched it with the tip of her tongue. Tasting. Memorizing. She pressed her lips to it again, marking it as her own.

She slipped an arm around him and his shirt whispered beneath her hand. Her fingertips brushed across the hair on his chest, and he shifted, his hips moving backward until they pressed tight against her belly, sending another burst of warmth shooting through her.

Her hand slipped lower, sliding across the firm muscles of his flat stomach and coming to rest directly below the waistband of his boxers.

''Keep that up and we're both going to be in for a big surprise.'' His voice sweetened the stillness of the room, like smooth honey.

She moved her hand lower. "How big are we talking? Big? Or *really really* big?''

He laughed, and she felt the shake of his long body against hers. But even as he laughed, he shifted his body a bit and moved as if to sit up. And in that single instant, her body mourned his coming desertion.

She tightened her arms around him, holding him to her and wishing with all her heart that she could capture and hold the essence of him inside her soul—all his power, warmth and goodness.

She pressed her cheek against the center of his back and savored the steady beat of his heart through his skin and the reassuring rhythm of his breath. He reached down and gently pulled at her hands. "Tess, you know this isn't right. Let—"

If he deserted her now, Tess wasn't sure she'd bounce back. Somehow she had to make him understand, make him realize how much she needed him. "Please," she whispered, a small sob catching in her voice. "Please, don't push me away."

He froze, every nerve in his body seeming to still at once.

"I really need you right now," she said.

"Tess, we can't—"

She tightened her hands and braced her body against the rejection in his voice. Her lips moved against his skin, "Please, Ryan, just hold me. Hold me and make love to me. I promise you no regrets. No guilt."

He shifted, turning to face her, and Tess immediately slid closer, pressing the length of her body to his and wrapping a bare leg around his. She shuddered with pleasure as his hand slid down her side and came to rest on her left hip, his fingers curled to fit the curve of her body.

"Whatever it is you need, I'm here for you," he said. "You only need to ask."

He bent his head and touched his lips to the pulse beating frantically in her neck. It quickened with the slow erotic brush of his lips over her skin. She moaned softly, asking for more. He moved his lips slowly down the length of her neck to the hollow of her throat. His tongue gently teased her and encouraged her, and he only stopped to slide off her shirt.

And then he was back, gently gliding his mouth over her skin to the tips of her breasts. His tongue teased and taunted, and she tangled her fingers in his hair, holding him to her and urging him not to stop.

He set her heart racing and her mind spinning. How did he manage to reduce her to this tangle of hot emotion so quickly, so easily? What was it about the man that confused and excited her all at the same time? Whatever it was, she didn't want to question it. Didn't want it to ever stop.

She didn't care that he made her feel vulnerable and open. She didn't care that being with him meant something dangerous and forbidden. All that mattered was his scent. His feel. His caress. And they all surrounded her and overwhelmed her and made her head whirl and dip with anticipation.

She stretched her hands over her head and arched her spine. He sank lower, using his skilled tongue and hands to make her body hum with expectancy, and when he rose up over her, sinking the length of his hardness into her warmth and moistness, she cried out his name and went with him over the edge into another kind of glorious oblivion.

RYAN'S BODY SHUDDERED and rocked with his release, and he buried his face against the side of Tess's neck, inhaling her sweetness, an intoxicating blend of soap, toothpaste and something uniquely Tess, a citrusy scent that reminded him vaguely of oranges.

He held her against him with a fierceness that surprised even him. "You're incredible," he whispered, shifting his body to lie next to her, worried his weight might crush her beneath him.

How was it that one minute she seemed so indestructible, so damned capable and the next she seemed vulnerable, almost fragile?

He slid an arm around her and drew her to him, fitting her up against his length and allowing their sweaty skin to touch. It sent a new jolt of need trembling through him.

Tess reached out and pressed her palm against the center of his chest. "You aren't so bad yourself."

Her fingers made tiny circles around his nipple, curling his chest hairs with the tip of one finger and sending tiny flashes of warmth down the center of his stomach directly to his groin. He bit his bottom lip in an effort to keep from moaning aloud. The woman had him under her spell, totally at her mercy.

She leaned in and kissed him hard, a savage kiss filled with passion and open need. He could feel her melting against him, her skin burning with a heat so hot that she seemed about to burst into flame. Her hands touched and caressed, seeming to be everywhere at once.

But as Ryan lay there, soaking the sensations in, he felt the first nagging pull of guilt hit his gut. The weight of it was so heavy he thought he might surely crumble beneath it.

He closed his eyes, allowing it to roll over him, and he waited, knowing the voice of reason would speak, telling him he had used her. Taken advantage by satisfying his own selfish needs.

Sure, she'd asked him to make love to her. No, begged him to. But Ryan knew better. He'd allowed himself to step over the line, a line he had sworn he wouldn't cross. He'd taken something from her that shouldn't have been his to take, and at that moment, he hated himself.

He gently drew away. How could he have forgotten his promise to himself? Was he so depraved that he couldn't control his own emotions? His own needs? Was he really that far gone?

Tess's hands stilled and she tilted her head back. She studied him with questioning eyes. "I thought we agreed there wouldn't be any guilt?"

He managed a small laugh but then quickly disengaged his legs from her smooth limbs. He moved to sit on the edge of the bed. "No guilt here."

He drew a shaky hand through his hair. Great, now he was lying to her. But couldn't he not lie? It wasn't easy to explain away guilt that weighed so heavy it was hard to breathe.

This was something he needed to deal with all on his own. It wasn't her problem. She had enough to deal with without him adding to it.

He heard her move, the sheets whispering as she slid across the bed. She pressed her body against his back and propped her chin on his shoulder. She reached around to hold him, embracing him with her warmth.

"Tell me what are you thinking," she demanded.

"Nothing."

"You owe me the truth."

He sighed. He owed her something. "I'm thinking that I have a tendency to take unfair advantage of my patients."

Tess pressed her lips to the taut tendons in his neck. She kissed them gently, as if the softness of her lips would release the pent-up tension.

"Haven't I told you enough times that I'm not interested in you taking care of me? How many other ways can I say it?"

He slipped from her grasp and stood up. He reached out and yanked his pants off the chair, pulling them on.

He met her gaze as he zipped up, trying not to see the hurt in her eyes. "I should have never climbed into bed with you, Tess. You don't need me adding to your confusion."

She sat down and crossed her legs. Her hair fell over her shoulders and draped artfully across her high, firm breasts. She wasn't in the least inhibited by her nakedness.

"Who said I was confused?"

He didn't answer and she cocked her head, grinning playfully up at him. "Are you psychiatrists all this sexually repressed or are you just personally really good at it?"

"Look, you don't understand. I stepped over the line when I made love to you."

She shook her head. "In case you didn't catch on—I've wanted you from the moment I met you. And I'm pretty sure you wanted me, too.'' She spread her hands, her face questioning him. Challenging him. ''So how exactly is it wrong for two people who want each other to act on that?''

''It's a problem because you're my patient. I took advantage of your trust by sleeping with you.''

Tess snorted, one hand reaching up to fling her hair back. ''Ridiculous. I was *never* your patient, Ryan. I told you that first day I met you that I hated doctors and I didn't need one to take care of me. It isn't what our relationship is about.''

She stopped and searched his face, her expression intense. ''Wait a minute, this isn't about us making love, is it? It's about something else. What's wrong?''

He dropped into the chair across from her. How did he make her understand? How could he explain his failures to a woman who didn't accept failure? A woman who kept pushing until she got what she wanted.

He lifted his head. ''I used to be a pretty good clinician. Or at least I thought I was. But then I got a dose of reality. I failed a patient and ended up quitting clinical work in favor of research.''

''So tell me what happened.''

He stood up and paced the floor next to the bed. ''I was treating a young woman for a pretty serious case of depression. She started making progress, getting better. I thought we were out of the woods, but then she started obsessing about me.'' He glanced up, pausing a moment to meet Tess's eyes. ''Her obsession became unhealthy. Excessive. She stalked me. Called my personal line forty, fifty, a hundred times a day. She'd show up at my office and then at my apartment. She'd threaten suicide if I didn't see her.''

''What did you do?''

He was back to pacing. ''I talked with my clinical supervisor. We discussed a variety of strategies. None of them worked. Finally, I wanted out. I felt as though I wasn't doing

her any good. I thought it would be better if I transferred
her case to another physician, a female psychiatrist on staff.
I talked with the woman and she agreed to take the case,
but my supervisor refused. He felt it was important that I
deal with the transference issues. He said it would make me
a stronger clinician.''

"But he was wrong, wasn't he?''

Ryan nodded, swallowing against the guilt that rose up
in his throat, threatening to choke him. "Things got worse.
I tried several times to have her committed, but she fought
it every time. She was smart. Articulate. And she knew the
law. She knew how to present a rational face when she
needed to.'' He glanced up again. "Even my supervisor
thought I was blowing things out of proportion. He met with
her several times and *every time* he came away convinced
I was overreacting. He refused to sign the commitment papers.''

"What happened?'' Tess asked softly.

"In late spring, she came to my office unannounced. She
didn't have an appointment, but she told my secretary that
she was leaving town, that she wouldn't be back and had
come to say goodbye. My secretary buzzed me. I was in a
session, but I went out to talk to her, concerned something
was wrong. But before I went out, I called security and my
supervisor, told them to get up to my office.''

He slumped in the chair and tilted his head back, staring
at the ceiling tiles. This was harder to tell than he'd even
thought. That's why he hadn't talked about it with anyone
since it happened, not even his sister. Oh, he'd hashed it out
with the police and the hospital ethics board when an investigation was done. But he hadn't talked about it on a
more personal level.

Instead, he'd bottled it up inside and kept it churning
around inside him, creating self doubts. Doubts that threatened to cripple him as a therapist and as a man.

"What happened when you went out to meet her?"

"She was waiting for me. All dressed up, her hair done, makeup on. She had a suitcase and I thought maybe, just maybe, she really had decided to leave town, to start new." He shook his head, the cushion behind his head rubbing the back of his neck. It was hard to speak, his words almost muffled by the emotion. "But she fooled me. She'd come for her final say in the whole matter. She didn't even give me a chance to talk to her. She just stood up and pulled a gun out of her purse."

Tess gasped.

He continued on in a monotone, trying desperately to keep the emotions at bay. "Before I could stop her, she stuck the gun in her mouth and pulled the trigger."

He choked, anger flooding his throat and closing it off. He hunched forward, his elbows jammed against his knees as he rubbed his face roughly with his palms, as if he could wash away the feelings of guilt and despair.

Tess was up and crouched in front of him, her hands on his knees. "You have to know somewhere inside you that it wasn't your fault. You tried to get her help. She refused. What more could you have done?"

"I could have tried harder."

"How? Tell me exactly what you could have done differently?"

"I—I could have made my supervisor see how desperate she was. Forced him to recognize that she was teetering on the edge."

Tess shook her head. "And how can you force someone to see something they refuse to see?" She took his hands and held them in hers. "Don't you see that you did everything you knew how to do? Don't you see that she couldn't accept the help? She failed all on her own, even with you at her side, trying to rescue her and bring her back from the edge."

He laughed bitterly. "Obviously I didn't try hard enough. She's dead." He lifted her head and stared at her, angry that he'd lash out at her but unable to help himself.

"No, you spent a hell of a lot of time trying to convince yourself that it was your *fault*. You're a perfectionist, Dr. Donovan. And perfectionism like that can lead to guilt. Didn't you realize you can't rescue the world?"

He reached out and wrapped several strands of her hair around his hand, feeling them slide effortlessly through his fingers. Unable to resist, he dipped his head and tasted her, savoring the yielding, giving quality of her mouth. Her hands encircled his neck, holding him to her. Her gentleness and compassion surrounded and filled him, and the first wave of inner peace he'd felt in months washed over him.

"Thanks for listening," he said softly. "I don't think—"

The phone rang, interrupting him.

"They're on to us," Tess said urgently.

The phone stopped ringing. Three rings and then nothing. The silence was deafening.

"We need to get out. Now!" Tess scooted across the bed, pulling on her clothes. "Hurry, we don't have much time. They're probably already on their way down here."

He jammed his feet into his shoes as Tess moved to the window, opening a small slit between the drapes. "See anything?" he asked.

"There are three cars and a van parked up near the office with their lights on. Six men standing around the outside. I don't recognize any of them—must be the gorilla squad. The others must still be in the office."

She let the curtain drop back in place and turned toward him. Her gaze met his. He couldn't help but notice the startling calm in her eyes, the complete lack of fear.

Ryan zipped up his bag and stood. "We don't have a lot of options, Tess. If we leave, they're bound to see us. If we stay, they're going to search this room at some point."

She nodded in agreement and whirled around, headed for the bathroom. Ryan followed.

She pushed aside the shower curtain and climbed up on the side of the tub. He stared at the tiny window and then back at Tess, making no effort to hide his disbelief.

"You're kidding, right? There's no way I'm going to fit through that thing," he said.

"I'll go first. I'll pull on the other side. We'll get you through." Tess pushed up the window and snapped out the aluminum screen.

"There's no way, Tess."

"We don't have a choice, Ryan. I checked this out when we first arrived. You'll fit. It'll be a tight squeeze, but you'll fit. Now give me a boost. We don't have time to argue."

He watched her slither through the window frame as effortlessly as a snake slips through the water. Wedging the toes of one foot on the opposite side of the tub, Ryan lifted himself up to the window and looked out. His shoulders rubbed up against the side of the window.

Tess waited below, darting glances in the direction of the side of the motel, checking for any sign of Flynn's men. "Go through the window sideways, Ryan—hands out in front and I'll pull you through."

He boosted himself up and slipped his upper body out the window. It was more than a tight squeeze, but not impossible. Suddenly he froze. From inside the room, he heard the loud knock of someone pounding on the motel-room door. They had arrived.

"Come on," Tess urged from below. "Give me your hand."

Ryan slid back through, ignoring Tess's frantic questioning of what the hell he thought he was doing.

He dug into his pocket and pulled out the car keys. Leaning back over to the window, he threw them out. Tess caught them with one hand.

"Get out of here. Now!" he ordered.

For the first time since they'd gotten up, the intense expression of determination on her face disappeared. She stared up at him with a touch of confusion, panic almost. The green of her eyes sparked in the early dawn. "What are you doing?" she demanded. "I'm not going anywhere without you."

"They want you, not me. Go! I'll stall them for as long as I can."

"I'm not leaving you, Ryan. Now get your butt out here." Her voice was gruff, but he didn't miss the underlying quiver of fear and the sound wasn't something he'd come to expect from Tess. She knew he was serious, and she wasn't liking his decision one bit.

"I'm not arguing with you, Tess. They're here, and there's no time to argue. Now get going."

He pulled down the window, but not before she whispered, "I'm not leaving you, Ryan. I'll be back."

He rearranged the curtain, brushed their shoe prints off the side of the tub and then flushed the toilet. As he opened the bathroom door, the outer door crashed open and three oversize men pushed through, followed by a familiar face— General Flynn.

Ryan affected an expression of surprise as he casually tucked in his shirt. "What are you doing here, Flynn?"

Flynn didn't answer but instead snapped his fingers at the two men standing on either side of him. They immediately grabbed Ryan, and when he tried to shake them off, they stepped in closer and pinned his arms back. A third man drew a gun and cautiously made his way over to the bathroom.

"I'm in no mood to play games, Doctor. In fact, I'm feeling more than a little irritable. So—" Flynn flicked on the overhead light "—let's cut to the chase. Where is she?"

"She? I'm not sure who you're referring to, General. I'm

alone. Took off for a little trip north to see the sights.'' Ryan grinned. "But if you're looking for some female companionship, I think the clerk out at the front desk would be more than happy to fix you up with some lovely lady.''

The general's eyes burned hot, but he didn't bother responding. He nodded his head at a third man. "Check the bathroom.''

The man was gone for a minute and then stepped back out. "Empty. But there's a small window in there. Locked, but she might have squeezed through.''

"Go!'' Flynn jerked his head toward the door. "Find her.''

Ryan tried to push himself in front of the door, but the two men muscled him to his knees. He watched in frustration as the third man skirted around him and headed for the alley behind the motel.

Chapter Thirteen

"You need to understand something, Doctor."

General Flynn settled into the chair directly across from Ryan, his voice pleasant. Reasonable. "I'm not what you'd call a very nice person. Especially when I'm impatient. And at the moment, I'm feeling impatient."

"Perhaps you should consider taking a seminar on anger management, General," Ryan said, allowing his own tone to match Flynn's. But even as he spoke, his mind raced. Somehow he needed to stall them, keep them occupied until Tess got far enough away.

"How'd you find us?"

"I have one of the best trackers in the business working for me. You'll meet him soon enough." Flynn nodded to the two hired thugs, and Ryan found his arms yanked behind his back. Pain radiated up the length of his arms into his shoulders.

Flynn smiled. "Now that I have your attention, I need to know where Tess is headed and how much of the project the two of you were able to piece together."

Ryan kept his facial expression blank. No way would he give the man the satisfaction of seeing anything he was feeling. "Tess left. That's all I know."

"We don't have time for this." Flynn nodded to the man at the door. "Get McCaffrey in here."

The door swung open, and a tall and powerfully built man sauntered in. Ryan figured Flynn's enforcer had arrived.

The man's hair, the color of January ice, had an almost bluish undersheen to it, and the strands, close cropped and bristly, crowned his perfectly shaped head with military precision.

But it was the man's eyes that were the most disturbing. He leaned against the doorframe and studied Ryan with oddly empty eyes, the color of washed-out denim. Ryan's internal radar went off with a deafening roar. This was someone dangerous. The kind of person Ryan had met on more than one occasion when doing court-ordered forensic evaluations.

If this was the person Flynn was using to track Tess down, Ryan knew he'd have to buy her more than a few minutes head start. This man had the look of the streamlined bloodhound, a true killer.

"Have we met?" Ryan asked.

The hired tracker lifted himself off the doorframe and stepped into the room. His gait was loose and rolling.

"Actually, Doctor, we've never met. But like you, I'm a great admirer of Tess." He smiled, a smooth stretch of lips that gilded over shark-white teeth. "Tess and I are *soul mates* of a sort. Two parts of a whole." He held out a hand. "The name's McCaffrey. Ian McCaffrey."

Ryan simply stared at McCaffrey's hand. "Sorry, I seem to be indisposed at the moment."

McCaffrey's smile widened and his cold eyes flicked up toward the two thugs holding Ryan. "Ease up, gentlemen. Dr. Donovan is our guest."

The two guards laughed but their holds didn't loosen.

"And how is the lovely and talented Tess?" McCaffrey asked.

"She's just fine." Ryan decided to push the man's buttons a little. "It's strange though. She's never mentioned you, McCaffrey. I'm guessing the two of you aren't as close as you thought, huh?''

Something dark and ugly flashed across the surface of McCaffrey's eyes. One minute it was there and the next it vanished. But it told Ryan something important. McCaffrey felt something for Tess, and he didn't like the idea that his feelings might not be reciprocated.

"The general asked you very politely where Tess was headed. Now I'm asking and I'm not asking in such a nice and polite way."

Ryan shrugged, and it was then that McCaffrey lifted his right knee. He moved so fast that Ryan only saw an explosion of white. It wasn't until the pain ripped through his gut that he realized McCaffrey had kicked him.

His head dropped onto his chest and a trickle of sweat slid down the center of his back. He sucked hot air, waiting for the pain to subside.

"I have it on good authority that you're an intelligent man," McCaffrey said. "Don't force me to break you down."

"Do what you need to do," Ryan said, lifting his head, his gaze defiant. "But I have nothing to tell you."

Ryan braced himself and McCaffrey nodded a command. One of the thugs hit Ryan behind his left ear. He grunted and hot shards of pain shot up the back of his head.

McCaffrey leaned in and spoke softly in his ear. "Don't play hero with me, Doctor. We both know you don't have what it takes. You can't hope to withstand the punishment I've been trained to inflict."

"Then I guess we're in for a long evening, because I have no intention of telling you anything."

The words were no sooner out of his mouth than McCaffrey's knee came up again and hit Ryan under the chin. His head snapped back and lights danced in front of his eyes. One of the men behind him double-punched his left kidney and the word *pain* took on a whole new meaning.

Ryan grunted and coughed. A string of blood and saliva slipped from between his lips and spilled onto the carpet, staining it a dark crimson. ''Go to hell, you bastard,'' he managed from between swollen lips.

From what seemed like a great distance away, Ryan heard Flynn's voice. ''All right, that's enough. He isn't going to tell us anything, and I don't want him bruised up.''

Panting, Ryan rested his chin on his chest. He needed to stay conscious. He needed to stall them. The longer they were with him, the less chance there was that they'd find Tess.

''Get him in the chair,'' Flynn ordered.

They dragged him over and dropped him into the chair. When he tried to get up, two of the men slammed him back down.

Flynn crouched down to eye level. ''Listen to me, Doctor. Tell me now what I want to know and you can go home.''

''Go to hell.''

Flynn stood up. ''This is a waste of my time. Tess will follow her programming. McCaffrey and I will go on ahead. You two get these down him.'' He slammed two bottles of pills on the table beside Ryan. ''But do it slowly. I don't want him puking them back up.''

He checked the label on the bottles. Valium and pheno-barbital. Damn. Enough in both bottles to kill three of him.

''Once the pills are in, get him on the bed. I want him found with a suicide note.'' Flynn pulled a note out of his pocket and set it on the stand. He glanced at Ryan. ''I added a section regarding the woman in Boston. It's a rather nice touch, I thought.'' He chuckled and patted Ryan's cheek. ''Everyone will think you found it impossible to live with your guilt.''

He turned back to the two men. "Make sure you go through the entire room and wipe it down for prints."

"How are we gonna get him to swallow them?"

"Be creative. Just don't bruise him up any more than he already is. Get the whiskey out of the car. Use that to wash the pills down," Flynn said.

"I'm not swallowing anything," Ryan mumbled.

Flynn reached out and patted his cheek. "Of course you will, son."

Ryan heard the door slam as the two left. He clamped his mouth shut as one of the thugs yanked his head back and tried to stuff a few of the pills in his mouth.

Snorting with frustration, the other one pinched his nose shut, cutting off his air. A few minutes later, when he gasped for air, he shoved four pills into Ryan's mouth. The neck of a liquor bottle followed, the tip clanking against his front teeth.

Ryan tried sticking his tongue into the end of the bottle, desperate to stop the booze. But he wasn't fast enough. Raw liquor poured into his throat. He gagged and then swallowed, the pills floating down the back of his throat, riding a stinging wave of booze directly to his stomach.

As they tried to pry his mouth open for another handful of pills, Ryan wondered if he had managed to buy Tess enough time. Had she put enough distance between them? Was she out of McCaffrey's reach?

The thought of McCaffrey touching Tess or caressing her with those cold, vacant eyes made Ryan wild. He bucked and thrashed, and the two men grunted, trying desperately to hold him still.

Ryan clamped his teeth down hard, biting one of the thugs. The man yelped and pulled back. Two pills slipped out.

As the thugs renewed their efforts, Ryan wondered if Tess knew how much he cared for her. If she realized how much he loved her. His head reeled. Why hadn't he realized it before? Now he'd never have the chance to tell her how he felt or hold her again.

CIRCLING BACK, Tess entered the motel parking lot from the opposite end, near the office. She crouched behind a lattice wall hiding the oversize trash bin.

The green paint on the bin was flaking off and the stench was overpowering. A light was still on in the office, and she could see the clerk sitting behind the desk dozing. Stacy was still filing her nails.

The van was gone from in front of their room, but their car was still there. She hoped that meant Ryan was still in the room, still within her reach. She could only hope they left him alive.

Keeping to the shadows, she ran to the office and pushed open the door. The clerk and Stacy looked up in unison.

"Didn't expect you back," the old man grumbled.

Tess ignored him and focused her attention on the woman. "I need help."

Stacy nodded. "I figured you weren't expecting that little invasion. That's why I told the old man to ring your room." She laughed. "Hope they didn't interrupt anything serious."

The thought of Ryan rising up over her, his skilled touch and beautiful hands making her body sing with sweet fulfillment tore at her. But Tess shoved them aside. Not now. Later they'd talk and she'd be able to tell him what he meant to her. How she craved him like something sweet and forbidden.

She moved away from the window. "Will you help me?"

The woman blew a bubble with her pink gum and then sucked it back between her lips. "What did you have in mind, sugar?"

Tess pulled at her shirt. "A change of clothes for starters. Then we go trolling for a few boys down in room 36."

"What's in it for me?"

"My undying gratitude."

Stacy laughed again. "Much less than my usual fee, but tonight's your lucky night. I'm intrigued." She stood up and nodded toward the back room. "Follow me. We'll have you fixed up in no time."

RYAN'S HEAD LOLLED forward and his chin hit his chest. Someone grabbed a handful of his hair and yanked his head back.

He tried to focus, but everything shifted and turned upside down. Nothing seemed to want to stay still. From somewhere in the back of his brain, a voice shouted at him to wake up. But none of his muscles wanted to cooperate.

Someone shoved three more pills into his mouth and followed it up with a healthy swig of booze. But Ryan coughed and everything shot out of his mouth and across the room.

He laughed and someone swore. But before they could start all over again, there was a sharp rap on the door.

"Help me get him on the bed," one of the thugs said.

Two arms slipped under his and pulled him roughly to his feet. They threw him onto the bed, and he landed on his back. He tried to kick out but missed. He watched one of the men walk through a white haze to open the door. Ryan wondered if it was actually hazy in the room or if his vision was going.

The door opened to admit a redhead with a pair of knockers the size of party balloons. But it was the other woman, the one with the straight black hair and an overabundance of blue eye shadow who was the real knockout. A combination of beauty and kick-ass arrogance. He tried to lift his head to tell them to watch out, but his tongue wouldn't work.

"You boys the ones who called for a party?" the redhead asked. She spotted Ryan on the bed and shot him a purplelipsticked smile. "Looks like you boys got started without us."

_ "You've got the wrong room," the man growled, starting to close the door.

The dark-haired one jammed her three-inch-heel pump between the door and stuck out her hand. "Not so fast. We didn't come all the way out here to get turned away. It's fine by us if you changed your minds. But we need to make a living."

Ryan thought the two women looked vaguely familiar, especially the dark-haired one. But he couldn't get his head wrapped around who they were. He lifted his head and stared, spying the dark-haired beauty's long legs in the leather short shorts. Damn, they were fine, and the fishnets were a nice touch. He'd have to tell Tess to hang on to the shorts and nylons. His eyes snapped open. Tess?

He caught the warning glance she directed toward him. Brilliant green. Yep, it was Tess in a wig and dressed for business. He opened his mouth to tell her that the guy at the door had a gun, but nothing came out.

"Shove off," the goon said, starting to close the door again.

When he leaned forward to kick Tess's foot out of the way, she came up with a nice right. Her fist connected with his chin and his head snapped back. He dropped like a stone, and his gun flew across the room.

Stacy screamed and Tess pushed her out of the way as she dived for the loose gun. Next to Ryan, the other thug tried to run, but Ryan stuck out his foot and the guy tripped. The thug scrambled on hands and knees for the bathroom and from the doorway, he got off two shots. Pieces of bedding and mattress flew up around Ryan's ears.

Ryan drew up his knees and rolled backward off the bed, hitting the floor with a thud. Several more slugs hit the wall over his head and the plaster rained down on him. But then he heard the retort of another gun and knew Tess had located the revolver.

A few minutes later, there was a grunt and the guy in the bathroom fell out the doorway onto the worn carpet. Even with his blurry vision, Ryan could tell the guy wouldn't be shoving any more pills down his throat.

"Are you okay?" Tess bent down next to him, her hands on his face, her eyes misted with tears.

"I'm juss fine," he managed.

She leaned down and kissed him. "You also reek of booze."

"Yuss, I do."

"Help me get him up," she said to Stacy.

They bent over him and pulled him to his feet. Ryan staggered against them. "Did yu know you're both mighty fine lookin' women."

"And you're loaded," Tess said, turning her head to avoid the fumes of his breath. "Help me get him into the car. He can sleep it off in the back seat. We need to get out of here before the police come."

They loaded him into the back seat, and he lifted his head, grabbing Stacy's arm. "Dohn't let her give you those leather shorts back. I've got plans for them."

Stacy patted his cheek. "Don't you fret, baby. Stacy will make sure she takes them with her."

"Obviously he's going to be fine if all he's thinking about is the shorts," Tess said dryly.

"He's a man, sugar. It's always about the shorts."

The two women laughed again and the car door slammed.

Ryan smiled and let his head drop back against the seat. The world went softly dark around him.

BY THE TIME Ryan had slept off the drugs and alcohol, it was morning and they had arrived on the outskirts of D.C. His deep groan from the back seat told Tess he was awake, but she barely had to time to glance up to greet him as the traffic surrounding them was whipping past at a dizzying speed.

"There's some orange juice in the cup holder and a semi-warm sausage biscuit in the bag." She used one hand to steady the wheel and the other to throw a fast food bag over the seat to him. "There might be some hash browns in there, too, but I wouldn't bank on it. They were pretty tasty and I was hungry a few miles back."

He sat up and rubbed his face, his appearance endearingly grungie in her rearview mirror.

"How long was I out?" he asked, opening the bag and taking a whiff. His color turned a little greener, but she gave him credit—he didn't lose anything.

"Long enough to have me worried. I pulled over a couple of times just to make sure you were still breathing. But you were snoring away peacefully every time." She grinned at him in the mirror. "You're cute when you're drunk."

"I don't feel so cute," he grumbled. "My mouth tastes like a five-day-old diaper pail."

Tess shuddered. "Well, that's romantic. Not to mention my concern about why you'd know how a five-day-old diaper pail actually tastes." She passed another cup over the seat with one hand. "Here, drink this. Black coffee. It'll take the edge off the headache."

He took a sip and grimaced. "Or the enamel off my teeth." He looked up again. "Where are we?"

"D.C."

"Do you know where in D.C. we're headed?" He took another bigger sip and some color came back into his face.

She shook her head. "No, I'm just going with the flow."

She truly didn't know their destination. She only knew that she'd recognize it when she saw it. Ryan didn't question her. He simply leaned against the seat and sipped his coffee.

At one point, when they slowed to a crawl in the heavy

traffic, he passed her his cup of coffee, climbed over the front seat and settled into the passenger's side.

They came down Massachusetts Ave., driving deeper into the heart of Washington. "Where are we?" Ryan asked, leaning forward to look for street signs.

"I have no idea, but wherever it is, it's beginning to feel right." She pointed to a sign.

Dupont Circle.

The lush greenery and people crowding the sidewalks and benches told her they'd reached the park. They started around the circle with the rest of the traffic when she caught a sign for P Street out of the corner of her eye.

Without thinking, she snapped on her signal and turned onto the street. Spying a parking slot, she whipped the car into the empty spot. From the level of activity on the street, she was certain parking spots were a fairly rare occurrence. She realized just how rare when the driver of the SUV double-parked in front of them laid hard on the horn.

Ignoring the driver, Tess turned off the engine and they exited the car. She studied the historic buildings lining both sides of the street. Nothing struck a chord. None of it looked familiar.

She kept walking, paying attention to the relentless little itch at the back of her neck that told her to stay with it. To keep looking. Then, suddenly, it appeared. An elegant brownstone tucked neatly in between two other less impressive ones. A flood of emotions ripped through Tess and she stopped dead.

She sensed Ryan moving closer and she put her hand out, asking him to give her a minute. Instinctively he seemed to know what she wanted, because he didn't speak. He waited, giving her the space she needed to reach for the memories on her own.

She walked up to the cast-iron gate surrounding the post-age-stamp yard and wrapped her fingers around the sun-warmed metal. Her gaze rolled over the reddish stone steps leading to the double oak front door.

The main floor of the building had floor-to-ceiling windows, each with window boxes sporting red-and-white geraniums. Affixed to the right of the front door were the polished brass numbers: *5687*.

Tess's pulse kicked up a beat, and her fingers tightened around the metal spikes of the gate. "I know this place."

"Let it come," Ryan said softly. He shifted and the warmth of his big frame pressed in on her, lending his support and encouragement. She leaned into the gate, straining to capture the memory that danced in the background. She closed her eyes and let the images come.

Light. Laughter. A child's giggle.

Glass library doors opened to a large room with hardwood floors covered with elegant rugs in bright, rich colors. Huge couches and tapestry chairs with carved wooden backs and arms clustered around an oversize brick fireplace. A welcoming fire burned behind the gate.

Tess got the sensation of cold pressing in on the windows glowing with the warmth from inside. It was winter.

She allowed her gaze to shift, to take in the entire room.

The main focus of the room was a grand piano. Rich mahogany wood polished to a high gloss. Someone was playing the piano, the notes crisp and sweet.

Tess pressed her body against the gate, trying to see more, and as she strained to see, she heard again the giggle of a young child. She blinked and the images wavered. Frightened of everything shutting down again, she tightened her grip on the gate.

Don't stop, she begged silently. *Don't leave me here.*

The images sharpened and she saw a child, a young girl with white-blond hair, run into the room. She was about seven or eight, dressed in a flannel nightgown and a battered rag doll clutched close to her chest. The sight of the doll sent a shock through Tess. She fought to breathe.

"Emmie," she whispered, the words catching and rasping in her throat. "My doll, Emmie."

Ryan's hands lightly touched her shoulders, and her breathing calmed. The little girl ran across the room, her bare feet slapping softly on the hardwood floor, and suddenly Tess could feel the cool wood of the floor beneath the soles of her feet.

A bolt of surprise ripped through her. She *was* the little girl! She concentrated, straining to push aside the fog.

She reached the piano, her small childlike fingers reaching up to touch the smooth surface of the ivory keys. And then, as quickly as the mist had appeared, it parted and she could see the man at the piano. He had deep brown eyes and a broad, strikingly handsome face. He continued to play, his large hands moving effortlessly over the keys.

He turned his head and his mouth stretched into a welcoming, loving smile. "Hello, Pumpkin." The voice was soft, melodious and so familiar to her ears that she felt tears prick the corners of her eyes.

"Daddy." She basked in the warmth of the man's smile, and her fingertips ached from their grip on the gate. She sagged, and a headache of monumental proportions stabbed the top of her head.

Ryan caught her and pulled her against him, wrapping her in his strong arms. "Easy, Tess. Slow, deep breaths."

Tess fought the overwhelming urge to slip away, to succumb to the strange heaviness that pulled at her. But instead, she straightened up and turned to face Ryan. He steadied her, his eyes searching her with a thousand unanswered questions.

"I saw him. I saw my real father," she said.

"Your real father?"

"Flynn lied. He's not my father." She fought a wave of

dizziness. "Flynn's my stepfather." She laid her forehead against Ryan's chest, and her arms slipped up to encircle his neck. An unbelievable sense of peace and contentment washed over her. "Do you have any idea how good that feels? How comforting it is to know that someone truly loves you?"

Ryan grinned and brushed away a strand of hair that had caught against the corner of her mouth. His touch was gentle. Loving. Familiar. "What do you remember about him?"

"He loved to play the piano. He was a wonderful musician." She smiled slightly as the faint strains of music whispered again in her ear. "He could have been a concert pianist if he'd wanted. But he loved politics more." She stared at Ryan with a sense of awe. "My name is Tess Ross and my father was a United States senator. He used to say, 'the words of the U.S. Constitution are just as perfect sounding as the notes of Mozart, Pumpkin.' H-he called me Pumpkin because I was born on Halloween."

"Pumpkin." Ryan held her close, his words whispering in her ear. "I like it."

Tess swallowed, a terrible sadness welling up inside her, making it difficult to speak. Ryan's arms tightened, cradling her and letting her know that it was okay to feel the emotions flooding her body. She wept, her tears soaking his shoulder.

Finally she lifted her head. "He died when I was twelve. A helicopter crash. He was traveling to—" She closed her eyes, digging down deep for the answer, and it came. "New York. A quick campaign trip in the fall right before my birthday. Momma stayed home with me because I couldn't miss school."

She turned to look back at the brownstone. "I lived here, right here in this house. With my mother and father. And my doll, Emmie."

"Here now, what do you two think you're doing over there?" a voice interrupted.

Tess turned to see a short, stocky man rounding the far corner of the brownstone. His chubby face held an expression of firm disapproval. He carried a gardening rake in one hand.

As he drew closer, he squinted and then stopped short. A wide smile of welcome stretched his tiny mouth. "Ms. Ross! I didn't recognize you." He hurried over to unlatch the gate, throwing it open. "Why didn't you call? I would have sent a car to the airport for you."

"Do I know you?" Tess asked.

Startled, the man's eyes widened and his bowlike mouth fell open. Without knowing why, Tess had the feeling that he was a man that wasn't often at a loss for words.

"Know you? Of course you know me." He glanced over at Ryan, his confusion splashed plainly across his face. Not recognizing Ryan, he turned back to Tess again. A frown had sprung up between his thick eyebrows. "I'm Pete, miss. Pete Waverly—your caretaker."

Tess shook her head. Nothing. Not even a fragment of memory. How could she have remembered so much a few minutes ago and now remember nothing?

Ryan pressed a reassuring hand to the small of her back. "Tess had an accident a few days ago, Mr. Waverly. She's having a little trouble with her memory. But it's coming back slowly."

Concern flickered in the elderly man's eyes and he immediately stepped forward to open the gate. "I'm so sorry. I didn't know. We didn't hear anything from you, so we thought all was going well with your trip."

Tess nodded silently, racking her brain for some indication she knew this man. "Is this still my house?"

The question seemed to startle the caretaker, but he

quickly recovered. "Of course it is, miss. Been yours ever since your mama passed on five years ago."

Tess nodded in Ryan's direction. "This is my good friend, Ryan Donovan."

Pete pumped Ryan's hand. "Welcome."

"Do I live here with anyone?" Tess's heart hammered against her rib cage as she waited for the answer. She dreaded the possibility that Pete would tell her that Flynn was also a resident of the brownstone.

The barest hint of a smile touched one corner of Pete's mouth. "Joan—" he glanced back and forth between the two of them "—that's my wife. She does the inside work and I take care of the outside. We have a small apartment in the basement. But other than that, you live here by yourself—been that way since you took over the house.

"Joan and I always held out the hope that you'd find a nice man and settle down. But you've been too busy for that."

His eyes seemed to lose focus and he got a faraway look. "Your daddy used to call you his greatest hope for the first woman president." He laughed. "Course, you'd have none of that. Told him you were going to be a newspaper reporter. But you always had your daddy's good instincts when it came to people. Knew how to tell the fakes and con artists, you did." His gaze sharpened again, taking on a hint of sadness. "Your mama wasn't so lucky."

"You're talking about my mother's second husband, General Thomas Flynn, aren't you?" Tess asked.

Ill-disguised resentment flashed across the caretaker's lined face. "How'd you guess? Course you knew what he was up to two seconds after he stepped foot in this house. You were only thirteen, but you were already speaking your mind. Let him know in no uncertain terms that he wasn't going to step into your daddy's shoes or use his name to advance any of his conservative causes."

"Ms. Ross's memories of those years are very sketchy, Pete. Do you have any knowledge of Ms. Ross suffering from any illnesses?" Ryan asked.

Tess tightened her hand on his, scared for the first time that someone might actually confirm what Flynn had reported as her history of mental illness.

The old man seemed to give the thought serious consideration for a moment, but then he shook his head. "Nope, can't say that I can. She was a pretty healthy kid. A broken leg when she was fifteen."

He looked at Tess. "You've always had a bit of the daredevil in you. Even independent when it came to picking schools. The general, he wanted you to go to George Washington University, but you insisted on R.I.T. And then you landed yourself a job working for a small magazine shortly after graduating—in Paris, France. Flynn tried to pressure you to take a job at a conservative paper he had some pull at. But you wouldn't hear of it. You were off to see the world. You really don't remember any of this, do you?"

Tess shook her head. "None of it."

"Well, come along then and I'll show you the house. No sense in us standing out here in the middle of the sidewalk entertaining the neighbors." He stepped back and waved them into the yard.

The three of them climbed the stone steps leading to the heavy oak doors to the brownstone. Pete lifted an oversize ring attached to his belt, carefully selected a key and inserted it into the lock. As the door swung open, he stepped aside, allowing them into the brownstone's entry hall first.

"Joan is up in Philly, visiting her mom." He glanced anxiously in Tess's direction. "Her mom is in a nursing home there. She'd have been here if we knew you were coming. She wouldn't have missed your homecoming for the world. But your last message said you wouldn't be back until the end of July—maybe even August."

"How did Ms. Ross get that message to you?" Ryan asked.

"She e-mails us every week with an update on her itinerary. She travels so much that one week she's in Greece and the next time we hear, she's in Moscow." He smiled. "You've never liked phone calls."

"Did you keep those e-mails by any chance?" Tess asked. At Ryan's questioning glance, she added, "Someone might be able to trace the e-mails back to the location they were sent from."

"Joan might have kept them. I'm not too good at using that dang computer so she prints the messages out for me and leaves them for me to read. I'll check."

"I'd appreciate that," Tess said.

"I'll let you get settled while I go down to the store and have a new key made." The map of wrinkles around the man's eyes crinkled with concern as he studied Tess's face. "You sure everything is going to be okay, Ms. Ross?"

Tess smiled at him, acknowledging the man's generosity. "I'm going to be fine. I just need some time to reacclimate myself to things around here." She didn't say it, but deep down she hoped that was all she needed. But the fact that she hadn't even recognized a man who obviously had been in her family's employ for years didn't do much to bolster her level of confidence.

Whatever Flynn and his cronies had done, it had taken a heavy toll on her brain, wiping it cleaner than a newly scrubbed floor. Getting those memories back wasn't going to be as easy as simply reintroducing her to her old life.

Pete left, pulling the door shut after him and sealing them in a heavy silence.

Tess looked around the hall, taking in the polished hardwood floor, the ornate cherry banister and staircase leading to the second floor. She didn't miss the antique umbrella stand occupying a corner next to a walnut wardrobe with leaded glass doors. "Apparently, I have very good taste."

"Or an excellent decorator and more than a little money."

"Don't tell me—you're the kind of guy who can't handle rich babes, right?"

"Oh, I'm rather partial to rich babes." He stepped in close, wrapping his arms around her and pulling her up against him. His hands slipped down to cup her behind and he lifted her, pressing her tight to his body. "I'll have you know that I'm an expert at *handling* rich babes."

She laughed, but Ryan cut her off by dipping his head and pressing his lips to hers, and in that single instant, the gentle but persistent pressure of his kiss wiped away her worries about forgotten memories.

She lost herself in the heat of his kiss, and it was then that she realized it didn't matter how long it took to regain her memory. Ryan was what mattered, the sweetness of what she felt for him. The wondrous sensations he created within her with each glance, with every word spoken. It was Ryan, not the memories, that made her life complete. She loved him.

Tess slid her hands up the length of his back, savoring the feel of him, the strength, the power of his muscles shifting and moving beneath the smooth cloth of his shirt.

She tilted her head back and stared up into those endless blue eyes. "I've forgotten to thank you, haven't I?"

"For what?" he asked absently, his mouth gently nibbling her bottom lip.

"For everything you've done. For sticking by me through this."

His lips moved to the side of her neck, the kisses and tiny nips scorching her skin and setting her insides on fire. He lifted his head long enough to say, "I'll consider this my thank-you."

"Oh, I'm sure I could do better."

"You have my permission to work on it."

"How long do you think it will take Pete to get a key made?"

"Why? What do you have in mind?"

He bent down and slid an arm under her legs, picking her up. "Do you think you could remember where the bedroom is in this monstrosity?" he teased.

Tess reached out and stroked the side of his face, her fingers touching the bristle of dark beard, smoothing the lines of fatigue in the corners of his eyes. "Have I mentioned how much I love you?"

He paused, his eyes widening slightly at her confession. "No, you haven't."

"Want to hear me say it again?"

He nodded.

"I love you. I love your mind. I love your body. I love the way you look at me. In short, I love everything about you, Ryan Donovan."

She leaned forward and kissed him and her hunger for him shifted and curled in her belly, allowing her to melt against him. This was where she wanted to be, in his arms.

Ryan pulled back a little and looked down at her. A small smile curled the corner of his mouth. "But the million-dollar question is, do you need me?"

She paused, sucking in air through a throat that felt as though it might close down on her. Damn. The need question. The thing that meant admitting that she depended on him, that she leaned on him and couldn't get by without him.

A part of her, a part so deep that it seemed almost buried, knew the truth. Knew what she'd already admitted to herself—that she couldn't get by without him. But to admit it openly? To confess that it was true? How could she? That meant surrender. Loss of herself. And if she surrendered, she'd never get back the person she was.

"Isn't love enough?" she asked.

A flicker of sadness flashed in the depths of his eyes, and he nodded. "For now it is."

He bent his head and pressed his lips to hers.

Chapter Fourteen

Ryan lifted his head, his lips leaving hers by degrees, as if even that much separation from her was hard. Tess knew how he felt. She was swimming in the same emotions, feeling as though she needed to stay in contact with him forever.

She touched her tongue to her bottom lip and savored the taste of him. "That was nice."

That wicked mischievous smile of his, the one that sent her heart south to her knees, appeared. "Now where's that bedroom?"

But before she could respond, the phone rang. Ryan's gaze met hers and they stood in silence for a moment. He set her down, and she felt a twinge of true regret.

"Should I answer it?" she asked.

Ryan shrugged. "Might as well. If it's Flynn, then we know for sure that he is on to us. If it's anyone else, it might help us figure out what the hell is going on."

Reluctantly Tess nodded and walked into the huge library to pick up the phone. "Hello?"

"Ms. Tessa Ross please," a woman said, her voice clipped and businesslike.

"This is she."

"Please hold for Mrs. Starling."

Tess covered the receiver and glanced up. Ryan was looking out from between the crack in the drapes. She snapped her fingers. "A Mrs. Starling," she hissed. "She asked for me by name."

"Starling?" Ryan frowned. "As in Mrs. Starling the vice president's wife?"

Tess gave him an exasperated look. "Of course it's not the vice president's wife. What would the vice president's wife want with me?"

Ryan shrugged. "It's possible. You had a pretty significant reaction to Starling's appearance on TV the other night."

Tess's fingers tightened on the receiver. Was he right? Was this the vice president's wife calling her? Why couldn't she remember if she knew her or not? Sweat broke out on the back of her neck and her fingers tingled, threatening to go numb.

Ryan moved to stand beside her, pressing his head next to hers so he could listen. The warmth of his closeness gave her comfort and she took a deep breath. She'd get through this with his help.

"Tess, it's me, Paige," a slightly breathless voice gushed over the phone line. "Where have you been, sweetie? Jacob and I have been worried sick about you."

Tess watched an expression of total surprise cross Ryan's face at the mention of Jacob Starling. She dropped down onto the hassock next to the telephone table, her knees slightly wobbly. Ryan followed her down, crouching next to her. "Hell-hello, Mrs. Starling," she managed.

The remarkably clear tones of amused laughter filtered across the phone's receiver. "Mrs. Starling? Heavens, Tess, you've been overseas way too long. When did you ever not call me Paige?"

"I—I'm sorry—Paige. You took me by surprise. How did you know I was home?"

"Don't ask me to divulge my sources. You should know by now that I have spies all over Washington—a person can't sneeze without me knowing about it.'' Paige Starling laughed again. ''Actually, Nancy Taylor saw you walking down the street with an absolutely adorable man. She called to ask me who you're dating now. Be careful, she'll try to steal him away. Who is he anyway?''

''Just an old friend.''

''Of course he is. They're all *old friends*. But enough about that. Jacob is beside himself with worry. He didn't think you'd make it home in time to attend the reception tonight. I, on the other hand, have harbored no such fears. I've told him repeatedly that you never go back on a promise.''

Tess heard several people speaking softly in the background.

''Hang on a moment, Tess.'' The voices were muffled for a moment and then the vice president's wife returned. ''I'm sorry, Tess, it's crazy here. This evening's plans have my entire staff spinning. Please put my poor husband out of his misery and reassure me that you're coming tonight.''

Tess shot a questioning look at Ryan. ''What should I say?'' she whispered.

''Say yes,'' he said. ''Whatever she's talking about might give us more clues as to what we're searching for.''

Tess nodded. ''I'm coming, Paige—wouldn't miss it for the world.''

Good Lord, what was she agreeing to? She looked into Ryan's eyes and took comfort in the composed, unruffled expression on his face. He flashed her a quick grin, his eyes telling her that he knew what she was feeling.

The single glance was enough to extinguish the squirt of anxiety that threatened to send her over the edge. The man was her rock, her anchor.

''Oh, Tess, that's wonderful. Jacob is going to be so pleased. This means so much to him. He talks constantly about how he wishes your father could be there, too. But he'll take comfort in having you there.'' She barely took a breath before prattling on. "I'm going to have a courier bring over a set of passes. You *are* still bringing a date, aren't you? What was that young man's name you put down in your e-mail as your escort..." Paige's voice trailed off and Tess could hear her shuffling through papers. "Oh! Here it is. McCaffrey. Ian McCaffrey, right?"

Tess gave Ryan another panicked look, but he nodded his head and mouthed the words, *Say yes.*

"Yes—that's right. Ian McCaffrey."

"Be sure to get there before eight. In fact, I'm making a note to myself to send a car for you and your date." Paige laughed softly. "You know how chronically late you are. The car will pick you up at seven-thirty sharp. I'm messaging the invitations over as we speak. Jacob makes his announcement at eight-thirty, so come right up to the dais as soon as you arrive. Okay?"

"I'll be there on time, Paige." In the background, Tess could again hear someone whispering to the vice president's wife.

She came back on, her words rushed and slightly harassed.

"Listen, I've got to run. Things are heating up here. We'll see you tonight. Don't you dare be late!"

The phone clicked off and Tess dropped the receiver into its cradle. "Well, that was totally bizarre. What do we do now?"

"We make a quick stop at a local drugstore for some supplies and then we go to a party."

"Supplies?"

He nodded. "Something tells me that we won't be able to bring any weapons to this shindig, but I don't intend to go unarmed." He smiled. "I'll be bringing a few professional tools of the trade."

She stared at him as a deep, undeniable feeling of dread

rolled over her. She knew without saying anything that going to the party was a mistake. A mistake they would both
pay for. A voice inside her head screamed at her to run, to
take Ryan and run as far and as fast as they could in the
opposite direction. She opened her mouth to say that, to tell
Ryan they needed to escape. To get out of Washington.

But no words came out. Her throat was frozen. Paralyzed.
Instead, she nodded in agreement. Yes, they'd go to the
party. She had a job to do. What that job was, she wasn't
sure, but something told her it was waiting for her.

The word *destiny* floated to the surface, hovering in front
of her eyes, and it was at that moment that Tess realized
there was no going back. Her path had been predetermined.
No matter how much she loved and trusted Ryan, even he
couldn't change things.

Oblivious to her feeling of impending doom, Ryan stood
up, his hand reaching out to lightly caress her cheek. She
leaned her head against his hand and closed her eyes, soaking in his strength and courage. And as she basked in the
radiance of his touch, she pushed back the dread. Somehow
she'd survive this night. Because of him, she had to.

SEVERAL HOURS LATER, Ryan and Tess arrived at the Washington Excel. Television crews and reporters jockeyed for
position behind carefully erected police barricades around
the posh hotel. Camera flashes lit up the darkness blanketing
the city.

Ryan stepped out of the limo and reached to offer a hand
to Tess. She slipped her hand into his and smiled up at him.
As she gracefully swung her legs out, her dress—an elegant
red sheath with a daring slit up one side—parted slightly,
giving him a clear view of one long leg. Fierce possessive-
ness flooded him, surprising him with its intensity. He
wished he could usher her back into the car and slam the
door against the crowds pressing in on them.

But something in her eyes, the grim determination, told Ryan that wasn't a possibility. They didn't have a choice. They had come to find answers and Tess wouldn't leave until she had them.

She took his arm, her smile confident. But he knew without question that she was frightened, worried about what they faced once they walked through the doors of the hotel.

The air around them held a charge of heightened expectation. Even the crowd seemed to sense this was a momentous occasion. At the entrance to the lobby, a uniformed employee and two men in suits checked their invitations and then directed them to a private elevator leading to the terrace reception.

They crowded into the elevator with six other couples. The mood was festive with everyone talking at once. They were dressed in formal attire, the men in crisp white shirts and immaculate tuxes, and the women in expensive gowns, their necks and ears dripping with precious gems.

When the doors opened on the top floor, the group surged out into the hall. People lined the corridor and at the opposite end of the hall leading to the rooftop terrace, Ryan spied the security detail. Five Marine guards stood at attention on either side of the four doors leading to the terrace. Through the doors filtered the sound of music, clinking glass and many voices engaged in animated conversation.

In front of the marines stood a group of men dressed in conservative dark suits and sporting tiny headphones in their ears. Ryan knew they were the Secret Service detail assigned to guard the vice president.

The Secret Service checked handbags and ran sophisticated metal detectors over everyone awaiting admittance to the gala. None of the people waiting seemed impatient or put off by the security routine. Ryan figured that all of them were seasoned Washington partygoers. They knew the routine. Knew what to expect.

As he and Tess got into line, waiting their turn, the elevator doors opened again, discharging another group. The group waiting in the hall swelled to approximately twenty-five people.

The group shifted and moved. Two couples jostled for position next to him, their voices loud and boisterous. The smell of liquor was strong. Apparently they had started their partying a little earlier than the rest.

Ryan moved aside as one of the men's elbows jabbed him in the rib. The man mumbled an apology. Ryan nodded and turned to say something to Tess. But she had gotten separated from him, moving farther up the line and closer to the security checkpoint.

He watched her hand one of the men her invitation and her beaded purse. The agent examined it carefully, comparing it to a list on his clipboard. Another of the Secret Service men ran a metal detector over her slender frame.

Eager to join her, Ryan tapped the person ahead of him, motioning that he needed to get by. But the man shot him an impatient look and closed ranks. Unless he wanted to do an end run around the group ahead of him, he was going to have to wait.

The agent waved Tess through, and Ryan was surprised when she didn't turn to find him in the crowd. But as he moved forward, he decided that her anxiety had gotten the better of her and she wasn't even aware that they had become separated.

"May I have your invitation, sir?" one of the Secret Service men asked politely.

Distracted, his eyes still on Tess standing in the huge doorway leading to the outside terrace, Ryan handed the agent the envelope with his invitation. The man slid it out and compared it to the names on his clipboard.

"I'm sorry, sir, but you'll have to wait here." Another

agent, not either of the two conducting the security check, stepped in front of Ryan, blocking his way.

Ryan's pulse rate hit a new high. "Is there a problem?"

"Just a slight irregularity with the invitation, sir. We'll have it all cleared up in no time. If you'll just follow me please."

The agent made a quick motion with one hand and two marine guards materialized, closing in on either side of Ryan. The people around him backed away, as if frightened to be associated with him. They stared and whispered.

The two guards didn't touch Ryan, but he knew without question that they wouldn't hesitate to take him down if he made any move to indicate he wasn't in a cooperative mood.

He glanced again in Tess's direction, hoping she'd noticed that he hadn't been able to get clear of the security detail. But she stood with her back to him, oblivious to his difficulties.

"Tess?" he called.

She turned and looked over her shoulder, and in that instant, their eyes met. A chill of fear overwhelmed Ryan. Her familiar green eyes looked right through him, her gaze vacant, devoid of expression.

He realized that she didn't see him, didn't recognize him. It was if he'd suddenly ceased to exist. Something drastic had happened.

He watched as two men in tuxes closed in on either side of her, one gently taking her arm and leading her back down the hall toward him. The man leaned down and whispered in her ear, speaking to her as if they were old friends. She listened, her face blank. They brushed past him and Tess glanced at him, but no recognition entered her eyes.

Fear clawed at Ryan's belly. Something was wrong. Terribly wrong. The two guards nudged him down the hall in the same direction. Their demeanor was polite, but their attitude didn't allow room for protest.

All avenues of escape were now effectively cut off. Ryan knew that, within minutes, the Secret Service would find out he wasn't who he pretended to be.

The only positive thing up to this point was they were taking him in the same direction as Tess. At least for now they weren't going to be separated.

When they reached the elevator, the agent turned to the guards. "We'll take it from here, gentlemen."

The marine guards nodded and waited until Ryan, Tess and the three agents were safely on the elevator before heading back down the hall to their post.

Tess stood between the two agents in total silence, staring straight ahead. When Ryan attempted to speak to her, the two agents closed ranks, blocking her from his view.

"Where are you taking us?" Ryan asked the man standing next to him.

"You'll find out soon enough."

"Are you Secret Service?"

The three men laughed.

"Who are you then?"

The man next to Ryan exchanged amused glances with the other two men. "Just good friends and supporters of the president."

The elevator doors slid open and he ushered Ryan across the empty hall to the door of one of two suites on the floor. The door was open a crack, and he pushed it wider, waving Ryan and Tess in ahead of him.

"How nice of you to join us, Dr. Donovan," a familiar voice greeted him.

Across the room, Ryan saw Flynn sitting in a comfortable leather chair. He didn't look terribly pleased to see him, but he didn't appear surprised, either.

Ryan stiffened when he noticed who stood directly behind the general. Ian McCaffrey. The big man nodded in Ryan's direction, the cold blue of his eyes slightly mocking.

Both men were dressed in formal dinner wear, McCaffrey in a tux and Flynn in a dress uniform. The two agents with Tess guided her to a chair off to the side. Ryan watched as she sat down and folded her hands in her lap. She stared calmly straight ahead, her eyes unfocused, dreamy.

Flynn motioned to a chair directly in front of him. "Please join us, Doctor. We've been expecting you. We have a bit of unfinished business to wrap up." He glanced in the direction of the men who had accompanied them to the suite. "You have the invitation?"

The man nodded and stepped forward to hand the general the pristine white envelope. Flynn took it and then waved the man off. "Wait outside until I need you."

The men let themselves out. They didn't appear in the least put off by the general's seemingly abrupt dismissal.

Flynn nodded again in the direction of the chair. "Sit down. We have things to discuss."

"Thanks, but I prefer to stand."

Flynn shrugged. "Suit yourself." He passed the envelope over his shoulder to McCaffrey. "I think it's time you and Tess joined the celebration."

McCaffrey accepted the envelope and nodded in Ryan's direction. "Thanks for making sure my date arrived on time."

He strolled across the room to Tess and bent down, offering his arm to her. She barely glanced at him, but obediently accepted his offer, wrapping her arm around his and standing up.

"Tess," Ryan said urgently. "Tess, look at me."

She turned slowly as if in a dream and stared across the room at him. It was as if she was frozen.

"Tess, please, baby, don't go with him. Fight it."

She stared at him blankly.

"Listen to me, Tess. Don't go. Don't listen to anything they're saying."

Nothing touched her face. No reaction. No flicker of recognition.

Ryan turned to Flynn. "What's wrong with her?"

Flynn raised an eyebrow. "You're a doctor, why don't you tell me?"

"If you've harmed her in some way, I'll—"

"You'll what, Doctor? I don't think you're in a position to do anything. Besides, does she look harmed?" Flynn waved a hand at Tess. "Personally, I think she looks like her stunning self. A little stiff, perhaps, but maybe that's her nervousness. Her anticipation of what's to come."

"What's to come? What did you do to her?"

Flynn steepled his hands, his expression amused. "I simply prepared her for her destiny." He nodded at McCaffrey. "Go ahead. I'll keep Donovan company. Give my regards to Starling."

Ryan took a step in Tess's direction, but Flynn stopped him. "Don't be foolish, Doctor. You'll be dead before you get halfway to her."

Ryan glanced back, not in the least surprised to see a gun trained on him. The muzzle of the gun waved slightly as Flynn motioned him toward the chair. "Now sit down and behave."

McCaffrey gave him a jaunty salute and then slipped out the door, Tess following compliantly.

"What destiny are you sending her to?" Ryan asked, not sure he really wanted to know, a terrible feeling of trepidation creeping through his system.

"As the daughter of Senator William Ross, the Don Quixote of leftist causes, it is only fitting that she be the one to take care of her father's crown prince, Jacob Starling. That she be the one to teach him the ultimate lesson in what happens to traitorous turncoats."

Dread crawled up Ryan's spine and he dropped into the chair across from Flynn. "You can't be serious?"

"Oh, but I am, Doctor," Flynn assured him. "Tonight, our darling Tess will calmly and purposefully assassinate the vice president of the United States as he announces his intention to resign from the Republican Party and run for president."

"Are you really so crazy that you'd believe that you can get away with assassinating the vice president of the United States?"

"Oh, not in the least crazy, Doctor, I assure you. In fact, I have every intention of succeeding." Flynn picked up the cigar burning in the ashtray next to him and took a long, leisurely puff. "This operation has been meticulously planned, down to every last detail. Even the timing of Tess's arrival was carefully monitored."

He grinned smugly as he continued to boast. "The two of you gave us a few moments of concern, but in the end, everything fell into place." He tapped the cigar on the edge of the ashtray, and the white ash dropped into the bottom. "It would seem that our diligence has paid off. Your good friend Dr. Bloom's programming has been successful. Tess will carry out her assignment."

"And if she fails?"

Flynn raised an eyebrow. "Did she look as though she might fail? Did she even glance at you with any degree of recognition or understanding of what you were trying to tell her?"

Ryan didn't answer. How could he, when deep in his heart he suspected that Flynn was right. Tess hadn't known who he was. She'd been totally taken over by whatever brainwashing techniques had been used on her. All the time that he had tried to help her, the seeds had already been sown, the deadly intentions simply waiting to be activated. Neither of them had suspected the truth behind her capture at the center.

"If for some reason she fails, then McCaffrey will take

over and do the deed. Tess will still be implicated, and McCaffrey will see that she is wiped out in the chaos that ensues. Starling will be dead before the evening is out."

"And what happens then? You step forward to take his place as Rone's running mate."

Flynn pulled the cigar out of his mouth and threw back his head, laughing with genuine appreciation. "How flattering that you think I'd even qualify for the position, Doctor."

"Hardly. I just can't understand any other reason for your involvement."

"We've had a much more suitable candidate ready to take over, and it's been a given that Starling would be off the ticket come fall. But it was critical to have him completely out of the voting public's mind before they stepped into the voting booths next November. The man has gotten entirely too popular for his own good."

"You're not afraid he'd simply become a martyr for the cause?"

"I think we've taken care of that possibility with some very carefully targeted mudslinging. It'll be released shortly after Starling's death. By the time the nation is done recovering from the fact that Vice President Starling was assassinated by the daughter of the nation's most beloved senator, we'll have planted enough evidence to suggest that Starling was involved in some highly questionable money schemes—in addition to a sordid affair with Tess Ross."

"What makes you think anyone will buy your smear campaign?"

"Oh, they'll buy it all right. No matter what the public says, they love a good scandal. The information released will be supported with ironclad evidence. In the end, it will be a miracle if the public even allows Starling to stay buried in Arlington." He crushed the end of the cigar in the center of the ashtray and stood up. "And now, you'll have to excuse me. I have a party to attend."

Ryan watched him cross the room, his brain racing, wildly trying to figure a way out of the mess he'd stepped into.

Flynn unlocked the door and stepped aside, waving one of the two men waiting outside into the room. Ryan slipped his hand into his pocket and touched his handkerchief, running his finger along the barrel of the plastic syringe he'd placed there earlier in the evening. It was loaded with a hefty dose of Thorazine. The syringe was his only weapon at this point.

The security detail at the entrance to the ballroom had been waiting for him, to ensure that he wouldn't make a scene in the middle of the hall. They had failed to pat him down and the metal detector hadn't picked up the presence of the syringe. Now he had to figure out a way to use it effectively.

"See that he stays here," Flynn instructed, reaching into the pocket of his uniform and pulling out a gun. "Wait until the uproar inside the ballroom erupts and then take care of him. I've planted enough evidence in the room to implicate him in the assassination plot." He glanced at Ryan, his expression slightly distracted as if his thoughts were already on the developing carnage about to occur two floors above. "Goodbye, Doctor. I could lie and say it had been a pleasure knowing you, but I won't insult your intelligence. You've inconvenienced me more than you'll ever know over these past few days. It will be good to see the last of you."

He stepped into the hall and nodded at the other man to accompany him. He closed the door with an ominous finality. Ryan turned to face the man advancing across the floor toward him. He slipped his hand into his pocket, preparing to take down whatever stood in his way of getting to Tess in time.

Chapter Fifteen

Ryan slipped out of the room and locked the door behind him. He hung a Do Not Disturb sign on the knob and then gave the hall a quick check. Empty. He ran for the elevator.

Behind him, the guard slumbered peacefully. Ryan figured he'd sleep until the morning. One less to worry about. He had no idea how many others waited for him two floors up.

He pressed the up button and the elevator doors slid open a few seconds later. The interior was crammed with a group of women. From the sound of the laughter and chatter, it was obvious that they were revved up for an evening of fun. The smell of perfume and alcohol drifted out into the hallway.

"Come on in and join the fun!" a sultry voice called from the back of the crush.

For a second, Ryan considered waiting for the next car. He didn't want to involve the women in whatever awaited him upstairs, but a woman in a slinky beaded dress and an abundance of flaming red hair grabbed his arm and yanked him into the elevator. He bumped up against her low-cut, well-endowed chest and murmured a polite apology.

She laughed and slid one rounded hip against his upper thigh. "Don't worry. We don't bite." She laughed, something low and wicked. "Not so it hurts anyway."

The group of all women laughed and the voice in the back added, "We're on a fast car to the top. Hang on."

"Guess everyone's in full party mode, huh?" Ryan said, forcing a false sense of amusement into his own voice.

"You've got it, honey," another woman said, breathing out enough fumes to make Ryan sure he could blow a Blood Alcohol Level above the legal limit all on his own.

"Out with the old and in with the new, is my motto," the redhead said. "That goes for my politicians, as well as my men."

The women all laughed again.

"You look as though you're in for a fun evening," Ryan said. "Mind if I tag along?"

"We'd be delighted, handsome," the redhead said, pressing in closer and giving the blond woman on his other side a sharp look of disapproval. The blonde ignored her friend's attempt to lay claim and leaned in closer.

Ryan slipped a hand around both their waists and grinned. He'd found his cover. His way in. As the elevator door slid open, he patted his jacket and affected a look of distress.

"What wrong?" the redhead asked, a red-lacquered, one-inch nail coming up to gently lift his chin.

"I seem to have lost my invitation."

Her well-manicured hand slipped quickly into the front of his suit jacket to check the inside pocket. Her touch lingered, sliding out to caress his ribs and down along the inside edge of his cummerbund. "Nope, definitely there," she purred in his ear. "The kind of invitation I prefer anyway."

Ryan turned a little to the left, disengaging himself from her roving hand before it got any lower. He covered his rejection with a gentle smile.

Disappointment flashed in her green eyes—eyes that seemed somewhat dull and lifeless compared to another pair of green eyes Ryan had grown to love, a pair of eyes he was desperate to see again.

"Guess I'm out of luck as far as getting into the celebration," he said with a sigh.

The blonde, smiling with secret amusement at her friend's obvious strikeout, patted his other arm. "Don't worry. We'll get you through." She glanced over her shoulder toward the rear of the car. "Right, ladies?"

A chorus of feminine voices shouted their agreement. They had a mission and they weren't about to fail.

The redhead shrugged, but before she could say anything, the elevator door opened and the women surged forward, pulling him with them on a crested wave of perfume and hair spray. As they started down the hall, they surrounded him, calling to each other as they headed for the security checkpoint.

In the middle of the group, Ryan studied the doorway leading to the terrace. He noted that the men manning the station were no longer Secret Service men, and the marine guard detail was also gone.

In their place stood two rent-a-cop guards, looking slightly harassed and overwhelmed. Apparently Flynn wasn't taking any chances. He'd effectively eliminated a possible roadblock to the planned assassination. Ryan couldn't help but wonder what excuse he'd used to get the other men to vacate their post.

The women pushed forward, surrounding the guards with their chatter and gaiety. Several of the women flirted outrageously, reaching out to drape their arms around the men and distracting them with flattery, flashes of long, bare limbs beneath elegant gowns and whispered invitations to sneak away and join them for a drink.

The two men didn't know what hit them. They craned their necks trying to take everything in, their expressions softening.

Two of the women stepped through the barrier, and as one of them passed Ryan, she slipped him her invitation, covering it with a quick peck on the flustered guard's cheek.

Ryan stepped up behind her and breezily waved the invitation at the guard who was watching the woman saunter away. She paused at the doorway to the terrace to flash the guard a final grin and a wave. The distracted fellow ran the metal detector over Ryan, not even bothering to check the invitation. He waved him through with barely another glance.

Ryan moved through the standing, cheering crowd. The noise was deafening, pressing down on him and making it seem impossible that he'd ever find Tess among them.

He strained to see over the heads of the people in front and alongside him. No one he recognized. Just a sea of excited faces, the glitter and gleam of the women's jewelry almost blinding in its brilliance.

Overhead, the lights had been dimmed, a single spotlight focused on the center of the dais. Jacob Starling had moved up to the podium, his ruggedly handsome face beaming out at the crowd. A large American flag, the stripes and stars waving in a breeze, had been projected onto a huge video screen behind him.

A woman Ryan recognized as the vice president's wife moved up to stand a step behind her husband. Her carefully coifed hair and elegant gown spoke of wealth and years of breeding. She stared in the direction of her husband, her expression an example of wifely adoration. A smile touched her lips.

Starling glanced over his shoulder at her, as if he had noticed for the first time that she'd moved up to join him at the podium. He shot her a look of appreciation. And as the TV camera projecting their image onto dual screens on either side of the dais moved in for the close-up, not a single person in the audience missed him mouthing the words, *I love you.*

The crowd went wild.

Mrs. Starling mouthed the words back to him and the crowd cheered even louder. This was American royalty at its best.

When Starling turned back to the audience, his confidence and ease with being on the stage in front of such a huge crowd was evident. These were his people. His most ardent supporters. He was in his element.

He leaned forward, his lips almost touching the microphone, and his deep voice boomed out over the terrace. "I don't think coming home has ever felt as good as it does tonight. At this moment. At this time. And in this very place."

Another wild cheer went up from the audience.

"—And I can't think of a better group of people to be in front of than all of you."

The cheers got louder.

Starling smiled broadly, and the power of that famous smile seemed blinding in the glare of the spotlight. Lights danced and glowed about the back of his head, giving off a visible halo effect.

Ryan couldn't help but think that the effect was an omen. A sign of what was to come.

He pushed through the crowd in front of him, weaving in and out of the people, trying to find Tess. Mrs. Starling had told her to sit with them up on the dais, but Ryan hadn't seen her anywhere in the row of people sitting behind the long table draped with red, white and blue banners.

Starling held out his arms as if to embrace the crowd and a light breeze drifted across the terrace. "How is everyone this fine evening?"

The audience erupted into a joyful chorus of responses. Their shouts were positive and playful, and Starling's image on the screens grinned wildly, his charming and handsome appeal engaging.

Ryan could almost understand the ultraright's fear of the man. He would be unstoppable. Unbeatable. A greyhound running effortlessly for the ultimate prize—the total support and dedication of the American people.

Starling launched into a speech about the past three years. He talked of his frustration, his disillusionment with the current administration's policies and his disappointment at not being able to make a difference.

Around Ryan, the crowd quieted, listening to their vice president's tale of woe. Their murmurs of agreement spoke of their sympathy for their crown prince's predicament.

Ryan knew the vice president was positioning himself for his announcement. And from the sizzle of excitement electrifying the room, the crowd knew the big moment was coming, too. Tension, thick and heavy, hung over the terrace. If the announcement wasn't made soon, the room would implode all on its own.

Ryan pushed his way through a tight group of people. Few people were sitting at tables. Most stood, craning to see the figure standing on the dais.

Ahead of him, near the front of the room, the group shifted and parted for a brief second. Ryan caught a flash of red and a glimpse of white-blond hair.

Tess!

But before he could move, the crowd shifted again and the red vanished. He slipped between a cluster of people ignoring their sharp glances of disapproval and murmured comments of annoyance. He pressed on.

He reached the spot a few seconds later, but there was no sign of her. The ball of anxiety in the pit of his stomach tightened. He needed to find her. Now.

Above him, Starling had swung into a rousing speech of no one being left behind. Of all citizens having a place at the table as they moved comfortably into the new millennium.

He searched the crowd and found Flynn, standing off to the side of the room. His posture was relaxed. Confident. But then he spied Ryan and he stiffened. He turned and gestured curtly to two men standing beside him. The two men's attention immediately focused on Ryan.

They started across the floor toward him, but they were as hampered by the unruly audience as he was. The crowd had whipped itself into a frenzy. People were yelling and stomping their feet. More than a few shrill whistles ripped through the air.

The noise on the terrace had reached a crescendo, almost crushing in its intensity. The sound pounded against Ryan's eardrums, sending his blood rushing like wildfire through his veins.

In front of him, a man shouted something and then stepped back. In the space of that single second, he saw Tess again.

She stood about thirty yards from him, a sea of bodies separating them. She didn't see him. Her head was tilted back to watch Starling and the video screens. She was close enough to the dais that the glow from the spotlight bathed her face in its warm glow. Her beauty was breathtaking.

But it was who stood behind her that sent panic through Ryan.

Towering over her, his body pressed close to hers, stood Ian McCaffrey. His hand lay on Tess's shoulder, his tanned fingers standing out in stark contrast to the ivory whiteness of her skin.

He leaned forward to press his mouth to the curve of her ear. Ryan felt his stomach tighten with dread.

Tess's stare was fixed and vacant. She seemed to have no reaction to McCaffrey's whispering. But as Ryan watched, she opened her clutch purse and stuck her hand inside.

Icy shards of fear raced through Ryan's veins. Oh God, he needed to get to her. Needed to stop her before she was forced to do something she'd regret for the rest of her life. Something that would surely destroy her.

She withdrew her hand from her purse, and the glow from the light glittered on something metallic in her hands. Ryan knew what she held—a gun.

She lifted the weapon with two hands and the crowd around her pressed in, oblivious to what was happening. The roar of voices built, the clapping and stomping of feet became unbearable.

Starling's own voice, amplified by the microphone, was barely audible above the yelling. The crowd had gone wild with excitement.

Ryan stood on tiptoes and cupped his hands. "Tess!"

She froze, the gun dropping to her side, hidden in the folds of her dress.

Across the floor, McCaffrey raised his eyes to met Ryan's. Anger flashed within the depth of his eyes like summer lightning gone berserk. His message was clear. Interference from Ryan would not be tolerated.

He spoke urgently in Tess's ear, and Ryan somehow knew that McCaffrey was using a word or key phrase to trigger something in Tess, to force her to respond to his commands. The roar of the crowd got louder, pressing in on them. Ryan struggled, pawing his way through the sea of bodies, trying to get to her.

Tess's gaze roved over the crowd as if searching for him. Her eyes were confused. Dazed. But they were no longer vacant.

She was fighting, trying to get out from beneath the conditioning of the seductive pull.

He could only hope that his yelling to her had triggered

something. Some memory. Some feeling. Something to interrupt the flow of evil feed into her brain.

McCaffrey straightened, seeming to realize that he'd lost his command over her. She was ignoring him, distracted by the crowd. He reached inside his own jacket and pulled out his own weapon.

Fear chewed at Ryan's stomach. His time was almost up. He had to reach her. If McCaffrey shot the vice president, Tess would go down with him. The Secret Service would be all over the two of them in a matter of seconds, and if McCaffrey was as suicidal in his approach as Ryan figured him to be, there would be no survivors. Tess would die in the same hail of bullets as McCaffrey.

He plowed through the crowd, pushing and shoving people aside. Angry shouts and taunts surrounded him, but he ignored them.

Tess turned and saw him.

Relief ripped through him, almost paralyzing him with its intensity. He could tell that something about his appearance had broken through to her.

She either remembered something or remembered him. He didn't know which and he didn't care. All that mattered was she had reacted. Somehow he needed to get to her, to pull her away to safety.

He was almost there, an arm's length away when the sound of a gunshot exploded in the warm evening air.

The crowd went silent for a second, moving restlessly, unsure what they'd heard. Ryan tried again to push his way through, but the bodies were packed in too tight.

From somewhere up front, a woman screamed, "A gun! She's got a gun!"

Another shot crackled over the heads of the crowd and they went berserk. Everyone tried to turn and run for the patio doors at once.

Ryan found himself pushed backward with the swell of

the crowd. He lost his footing and lost sight of Tess. An overweight woman elbowed him in the chin and stampeded around him. Ryan ducked under the arm of a couple attempting to run arm in arm.

Over the heads of the crowd, Ryan saw Starling drop below the top of the podium. Whether he was shot or simply getting out of the line of fire was unknown.

A swarm of Secret Service men rushed to shield him. People scrambled off the platform like frightened geese, their arms flapping for balance as they jumped, their faces twisted with fear. The red, white and blue banner attached to the table tore and fluttered to the floor. But no one noticed, they ran right over it.

Desperate, Ryan pushed his way through the crowd surging toward him, determined to find Tess. To save her.

He found her stretched out on her back a few yards away, her arms flung out from her side. The gun lay next to her.

Her hair had spilled from its elegant upsweep and lay fanned across her face, hiding her behind a pale veil. His heart pounding, Ryan knelt beside her and gently brushed the hair out of her eyes. Her eyes were closed, her face turned away.

It was then that he noticed the wet patch darkening the red of her dress, a sinister patch of black spreading along her entire left side. He could barely breathe as reality hit him.

She'd been hit.

As he bent to touch her, someone rounded him from behind, knocking him sideways. He fell to his knees, his palms skidding on the smooth tiles.

"Facedown on the floor," a voice ordered.

Ryan glanced up. Five or six men in suits and guns drawn surrounded him.

"She's hurt. Let me help. I'm a doctor—"

From behind, someone jammed a foot into his shoulder

and sent Ryan face first onto the floor. His cheek hit hard and for a moment his world tilted crazily.

"You don't need to do anything, buddy. Just stay down and stay quiet." The agent's foot stayed firmly wedged against his shoulder, pressing him to the floor.

Ignoring the command, determined to reach Tess, Ryan snaked a hand across the tiles to her. Nothing anyone said or did would stop him from getting to her. He had to know. He had to see if she was still alive.

He pressed his fingers to the side of her neck. Nothing. He wiggled forward a millimeter more, disregarding the increased pressure of the foot on his back. He moved his fingers along the warm skin of her neck, searching for a sign, any sign of life.

His own pulse pounded in his ears.

But he felt nothing. No flutter. No movement.

The man standing over him ground his foot into his back, emphasizing that he meant for him to stop moving. But Ryan crawled another fraction of an inch forward, trying one final time.

He needed to believe that he wasn't too late. That she hadn't already slipped away from him before he could reach her. Before he could tell her that she had beaten Flynn. Before he could tell her he loved her.

And then, beneath the tips of his fingers, he felt a faint fluttering beat. A relief so sharp and so painful Ryan thought he might die from the ecstasy of it rushed through him.

She was alive.

Her eyes opened, and he stared into the familiar green of her gaze. She smiled, a slight, one-sided lift of her mouth. "I didn't think you'd get here in time," she whispered, her voice raspy, barely above a whisper. "I kept thinking, what will I do without Ryan around to rescue me?"

He slid his hand up the side of her neck to gently stroke

the soft paleness of her cheek. "You'll never know because I plan on being here for a long time to come."

He lifted his head toward the group standing around them. "Get an ambulance," he shouted. "She needs medical attention now!"

No one moved, their eyes as hot and dangerous as molten steel just poured from the mold.

"Then let me help her. I'm a doctor." No movement. Another foot had joined the first to keep him pinned to the floor. "At least let me stop the bleeding."

His answer came when someone pulled his arms behind his back and a pair of handcuffs were snapped onto his wrists. Ryan bucked, trying to pull away, but they yanked him away from Tess and stood him on his feet.

"You won't be helping her or anyone else," one of the agents said. "If I was you, I'd be more concerned about my own hide."

Ryan twisted his body and tried shoulder-butting one of the men, but they immediately converged on him, subduing him.

"Don't fight them, Ryan," Tess said. "Just do as they say." Her voice had slipped a few notches as her strength seemed to seep away with each word spoken.

As he watched helplessly, her eyes closed and she drifted off. "Let me help her," he begged, no longer fighting. "She'll bleed out."

One of the men bent down and pressed a tablecloth from a nearby table against her side in a futile effort to stop the bleeding.

"Get out of my way," someone ordered from across the terrace.

Ryan looked up to see another man break through the crowd and stride toward them. He was about fifty-seven or fifty-eight, and upon reaching them, he immediately crouched down next to Tess, his big shoulders hunching a bit as he leaned forward to tenderly brush her hair back. His fingers trailed across her forehead in a touch very similar to a caress.

"Paramedics are on their way up, sir," the agent, who was applying pressure to the wound, said anxiously.

The older man nodded, never lifting his head.

His face, a map etched deep with the lessons of life, softened as he whipped off his jacket and gently lifted Tess's head to tuck it under. The revolver clipped to a holster nestled in the small of his back told Ryan he was an agent. The way the other agents deferred to him told him the man was probably in charge.

Across the terrace, the crowd parted like obedient lemmings and two paramedics burst through. Their heavy packs bobbed against their hips as they ran up.

The older man stood up, seeming to sense that he was only in the way. One of the paramedics took over from the younger agent, who was applying pressure.

His attention turned to the men holding Ryan. "Get him over to the hospital. I'm going in the ambulance. I'll question him there."

"Forget it. I'm going in the ambulance, too." Ryan tried to shake off the two men holding him.

The older agent's gaze, grave and infinitely weary, ticked over to meet Ryan's. Unlike a moment ago when he'd paused to stroke Tess's face and his sadness seemed overwhelming, nothing in his face revealed what he was thinking. "You'll go where I say you go, Donovan. I don't have time for you right now. Tess is my main concern."

He turned away.

Ryan didn't care how the man knew his name, but the fact that he seemed concerned about Tess calmed him some. He strained to see past the senior agent and over the heads of the two paramedics. One was hooking her up to a heart monitor and the other one was starting an IV. They'd already slapped on a pressure bandage. The reassuring beat of her heart playing out across the monitor's screen helped Ryan believe that she'd make it to the hospital.

"At least let me go with her to the hospital to make sure she's okay. Then I'll answer any questions you have."

For a moment he thought he saw a flicker of compassion in the old guy's eyes, but it was gone as soon as it registered. He turned away, pointedly ignoring him and blocking his view of Tess.

"Get him out of here," he ordered.

The two agents guarding him stepped up and pulled him after them. No amount of protesting had any effect. Ryan was forced off the terrace, forced to leave Tess's side.

Chapter Sixteen

"Tess. Wake up, Tess."

Tess pulled herself up out of the wet, clinging darkness and stretched to reach the voice calling to her. Everything hurt. Even her eyelashes hurt when she opened her eyes.

Ouch. She squinted a bit from the light overhead. Too bright. They were like phosphorous flares going off in her face. She closed her eyes again and then opened them slowly.

Still painful, but bearable.

A face appeared directly over her.

She smiled. Casper. Ken Casper. His battle-toughened face was deeply grooved with worry lines, deeper even than she remembered. He fumbled for her hand, wrapping a big, sandpapery hand around hers.

"Hey, ghost of mine," she whispered.

"You're in the hospital, sweetie. They're going to have to operate soon, but the doc says you're going to be fine."

"Where's Ryan?" The faintness of her voice scared her, sounding as if it came from somewhere outside of her.

"He's on his way. I came in the ambulance with you and sent him in a car with some of my staff."

She tried frowning and wasn't sure it worked. "I thought you were a romantic, Casper. Don't you know that you're supposed to let the handsome hunk ride with the beautiful woman. The old guy takes the cab?''

He laughed. ''I'll remember that for next time, sweet-heart.''

''The vice president?''

''He's fine. Not a scratch on him.'' He stroked the back of her hand. ''He's going to get some mileage out of this politically.''

''Still the same old cynical Casper,'' she rasped, her throat dry and scratchy. ''McCaffrey?''

A cloud shadowed Casper's face. ''He gave us the slip in the panic that ensued. But we're pretty sure he was the one who got off the shots. He dropped the gun beside you, so we'll run the ballistics and make sure. We'll catch up to him at some point.''

''What about Flynn?''

''He's in custody and singing like a bird, telling us all about the center and the Patriot's Foundation of Family Values. We'll be rounding up that crazy bunch for the next six months. But for now, the immediate threat is over.''

Tess nodded, and a great sense of peace settled over her. They'd won.

''We wouldn't have figured it out without you, Tess.''

Casper rubbed her hand, and then leaned down to smooth her hair back off her forehead. His touch was warm, but Tess couldn't help but wish the hand enclosing hers was Ryan's. She desperately needed to feel the heat of his skin and the sound of his voice.

She started to drift, and she tightened her hold on Casper's hand. Oh, God, she needed to hang on. She needed to be awake when Ryan arrived.

''It's okay, Tess. He'll be here soon,'' Casper said, reading her mind.

She pulled on his hand, coaxing him closer. ''Tell

Ryan—'' She sucked in another breath. "Tell him when he gets here that I need him."

It didn't matter anymore if he couldn't say it back to her. Even if he was still stuck on the whole concept of her being his patient and he couldn't love her the way she wanted. Nothing mattered to Tess except that she tell Ryan how much she needed him.

"You can tell him yourself. Just hang on, sweetie."

But Tess couldn't hang on. She fell over the edge and dropped into nothingness, spinning around and embracing the darkness. And as she slipped away, her hand falling from Casper's, she thought, *Please, God, let Ryan be here when I wake up, because I don't think I can get through one more day without him by my side.*

THEY TOOK OFF the handcuffs and pushed Ryan into a room on the second floor of the hospital. He didn't know the name of the hospital but he knew it was only a short ride from the hotel. Apparently the head agent had made arrangements for his arrival, because when the car pulled up front, two other agents met them at the door and escorted him upstairs.

Ryan surveyed the room. Small with no windows. The furniture had a definite institutional flavor. He paced, unable to settle. The agent with him took a seat by the door, his attention on a magazine. He pointedly ignored Ryan's questions.

By the time the door opened, Ryan was sure he'd worn a hole in the carpet. The senior agent walked in and nodded his head at the other agent, dismissing him.

He turned to Ryan. "I'm Supervising Special Agent Ken Casper of the United States Secret Service."

Ryan ignored the introduction. "Where's Tess? I demand to see her *now*."

"You're not in a position to demand anything, Doctor."

But then the man's face softened. "Besides, she's in surgery and no one can see her until she's out."

Ryan's heart slammed against his chest. He'd figured the wound was serious, but he couldn't deny he had hoped it was superficial. "How bad is it?"

"They couldn't tell me anything. But her surgeon will notify us when he's done." Casper motioned to the couch. "Sit down. I know you have a lot of questions, and I'll answer as many of them as I can."

Still on guard, Ryan stayed on his feet. "How do you know Tess?"

Casper sank down onto the edge of one of the chairs, stretching his long legs out in front of him with a deep grunt.

"I've known Tess since she was a toddler. I was good friends with her dad." The sadness Ryan had noted in the man's face when he leaned over Tess flickered across the agent's face again. "I was assigned to her father during his years as U.S. senator."

Realization hit Ryan. "Casper! You're the ghost that watches over her, aren't you."

He nodded. "When she was little, she called me Casper the Friendly Ghost." He shifted in the chair, trying to get more comfortable. "I got close with the family. When her dad died in the crash years later, I tried to help, but times changed and her mom needed to get on with her life. We kind of drifted apart. The last time I saw her was at her mother's funeral. That is, until—"

His voice drifted off and for a long moment the man stared into space, his gaze turned haunted, as if he was seeing their last meeting play out in front of his eyes and what he saw shot him through with terrible guilt.

"Until what?" Ryan prompted.

Casper's eyes flickered back into the present and he hunched over, his elbows coming to rest on his thighs. "Until she came to me a little over eight months ago to tell me that she thought her stepfather was up to his eyeballs in some kind of plot to hurt the vice president.''

"Which it turns out he was," Ryan said dryly. "So, you decided to use her to learn more."

"She insisted. And as much as I didn't want to, we knew that she was the only one who could get close. She wasn't supposed to go deep. We just wanted as much superficial information as she could gather—preliminary stuff that my own agents could use to infiltrate the foundation. We have a file yea thick—" he spread his hands a foot apart "—on that damn organization. But no one could get a handle on them. Mainly because infiltrating it was next to impossible."

"But not for Tess?"

"No, unfortunately not for Tess." He had rolled up the sleeves of his dress shirt and, for a minute, he fiddled with a button on the cuff. He lifted his head. "I think her stepfather took a certain delight in using her. In subjecting her to his brainwashing techniques. It would have been his ultimate revenge against her father. Flynn despised Senator Ross, saw him as the epitome of everything he hated. Blamed him for the weakening of the American military."

"Why would he take a chance using Tess?" Ryan asked.

"A maniac's ego perhaps. Who knows?" Casper shrugged. "Flynn knew how close Tess was to the vice president. He knew that of all the people he had to choose from, Tess was the one person who would never be questioned. Never be denied access to him. She was above reproach."

"So why put her life at such risk?"

Casper sighed. "Because we never thought he'd go this far. Tess had explicit instructions to stay on the periphery of the organization. To just get a feel for things and then report back to us. We never thought he was going to recruit her like he did."

"So when she disappeared, why didn't you go in after her? Get her out before they messed with her head?"

"We tried." He sat back, his massive arms lifting up to drape over the back edge of the couch. "But we weren't sure where he had her stashed. He's a cagey old bird—no one in Washington plays poker with Thomas Flynn without a few extra cards tucked up their sleeve."

"Sounds like you ended up playing without any extras up *your* sleeve."

Casper nodded

Ryan glanced up at the clock. Forty-five minutes and still no word.

"She's going to be fine, son." Casper fished around in his pocket for some change and then walked over to the soda machine. He stuck the coins in the slot and they jingled merrily on their way down to the collection box. He pressed one of the panels and a cola dropped into the bin below. "Want one?"

Ryan shook his head.

The tab on the can popped under Casper's thumb and the carbonation hissed in the quiet room. "When I finally discovered where they had her stashed, I sent in one of my best agents. He was killed by one of their operatives when he and Tess drove through the fencing at the center. She managed to slip away." His eyes met Ryan's. "She was lucky when she met up with you. I'm positive that she survived because Flynn was too spooked to just yank her away from you. He was determined to convince you that she was insane and belonged in an institution. He was too invested in her programming at that point to allow her to get away from him."

"Why didn't you just go in and shut the whole operation down? This is America—torture and brainwashing experimentation aren't supposed to happen here."

"Don't be naive, Ryan. None of that experimentation was

ever sanctioned by the United States government. And I wanted her out of there alive. Once she was with you and the two of you were on the run, we were able to swoop in and shut the center down. But Flynn was smart. He covered his tracks. We had no idea what he had planned.''

''What about the brainwashing she's been through? Do your experts have any thoughts on that?''

Casper sighed. ''I have a team of doctors in the wings willing to help her through this.'' He glanced up at Ryan. ''Although the head of the team mentioned that you've obviously already made headway in that department. Said you've somehow managed to interrupt the programming that Bloom implanted.''

The door to the waiting room opened and a young man in green scrubs stepped inside. ''Which of you is Ms. Ross's husband?''

Before Casper could speak, Ryan stepped forward. ''I am. How is she.''

The surgeon stepped forward and shook his hand. ''I'm Michael Keely, I worked on Tess.''

''Ryan Donovan.''

The surgeon's gaze swung over to Casper, his question unspoken.

Ryan quickly introduced Casper. ''Ken Casper. An old family friend. How is she?''

''She's doing well. She's currently resting in I.C.U. She's kind of groggy, but that's to be expected.'' He rubbed the back of his neck and moved his head from side to side, as if releasing tension from his shoulders. ''I had to remove her spleen, and I had to do some minor repairs in the surrounding area. But other than that she's recovering nicely.''

''Can I see her now?''

Keely nodded but held up five fingers. ''Five minutes. No more. She needs her rest and you look like you could use a shower and a few hours of sleep, too.''

Ryan indicated he would agree to the conditions with a quick nod of his head. He'd have agreed to anything as long as it meant he'd get to see her, to hold her again. He glanced at Casper, checking to make sure he was free to go to Tess.

Casper waved him out of the room.

RYAN HAD BEEN in enough Intensive Care Units in his lifetime to know what every beep, bell and flashing light meant. And like most physicians, an I.C.U. held no great mystery. He recognized them as places were life and death struggles were played out, no different than the ones played out on psychiatric units.

But no amount of training could have prepared him for the dread of knowing that someone he loved was on the other side of those familiar doors. Suddenly it wasn't just *any* I.C.U. It was the place entrusted to care for the most important person in his life.

Tess's room was the last one on the end of the huge horseshoe-shaped hall. The sliding-glass door leading to her private room was open, but the curtain was pulled. The low, steady beep of the heart monitor filtered out to him, and the simple act of hearing her heart beat with life sent relief through him.

He pushed aside the curtain and stepped inside. The sight of Tess on the bed was like an emotional punch to his midsection. She lay with her eyes closed, her lashes an inky fringe across pale cheeks. Her lips and skin were the color of ivory, almost blending with the starched whiteness of the sheets. Someone had pulled her hair back from her face, making her appear even younger and more defenseless. Seeing her that way tugged at his heart and made him feel even more protective.

A nurse stood on the other side of the bed, adjusting the IV. She glanced up and then reached down to lightly touch Tess's shoulder. "You have a visitor," she said.

Tess's eyes fluttered open and she turned her head. The breath he'd been taking stalled in the back of his throat, stunned into submission by the startling clarity in her eyes. And at that moment, Ryan knew it would always be like this. For the rest of their lives, he'd walk into a room and find himself brought to his knees by her incredible beauty.

He swallowed hard. What would he have done if she hadn't made it? If he'd been left behind, never to see or touch her again? He knew deep inside what would have happened. He would have died a little each day he was alone.

"It's about time you got here. I'd about given up on you." Her lips stretched into a slow, teasing smile, but he didn't miss the fatigue, the pain in her eyes.

"Hey, there, beautiful, you're the one who ditched me. Last time I saw you, you were leaving the reception with two E.M.T. flunkies."

Her grin widened slightly and she reached out a hand. "Do I detect a touch of medical snobbery in your voice, Doctor?"

Ryan laced his fingers through hers, soaking in the coolness of her skin and willing his own body's warmth to seep into hers. Her grip was weak, but he hung on, sure he'd never be able to let go again. "No, not snobbery. Just plain old-fashioned jealousy."

"I didn't think they were going to let you in."

He leaned down and pressed his lips to hers, hoping that the kiss would disguise the trembling in his voice. "Wild horses couldn't have kept me out." He leaned closer and whispered in her ear. "Besides, I lied and told them that I was your husband." He pulled back and grinned at her.

Her smile, so sweet and poignant that it made Ryan's heart ache with need, widened, and she reached up to touch his cheek. "That's a pretty big commitment. Sure you can handle it?"

He covered her hand with his own. "I've never been so sure of anything in my life." He turned his head and kissed the center of her palm. "Besides, I don't plan on ever letting you out of my sight."

Her smile faltered and her lids drifted closed for a brief second. Ryan pulled back, worried he was tiring her too much. But she hung on, tightening her grasp.

She reopened her eyes. "Did you know that it was your voice that rescued me? That kept me from shooting?"

"I hoped that was the case, but I wasn't sure."

"I heard you through all that noise and yelling and hung on. I cleared everything out of my head until all I could hear was your voice and your words."

He stroked several strands of hair back from her face, loving the soft feel of her skin beneath his fingers. Had he ever loved anyone as much as he loved her? Ryan didn't think it was possible.

Tess pulled his hand closer and rested her cheek against it. "Remember that day we met, and I told you I didn't need you? That I didn't need a doctor?"

He nodded.

"Well, I was wrong. I need you. And I won't ever make that mistake again."

Ryan's chest tightened, and he sat on the edge of her bed, slipping an arm beneath her and gently lifting her to him. Tess pressed her ear to Ryan's chest and felt the reassuring beat of his strong heart.

"I love you, Tess," he said. "And I want to marry you."

Tess blinked, seeing his face through a shimmer of tears. "I love you, too, Ryan Donovan."

It didn't matter that they were surrounded by hospital white and beeping monitors. For Tess it was more romantic than candlelight and soft music. He loved her. He wanted to marry her.

"And yes, I'll marry you," she whispered over the lump in her throat.

The nurse tiptoed to the door, shut off the light and let the curtain fall into place, leaving them alone and in each other's arms.

*   *   *   *   *

In September 2004 watch for
MIDNIGHT ISLAND SANCTUARY
by Susan Peterson, the newest installment in
Harlequin Intrigue's in-line series, ECLIPSE. *You*
won't want to miss this bone-chilling gothic tale!

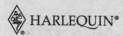

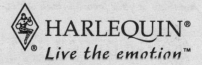

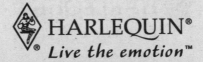

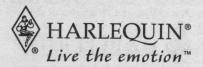

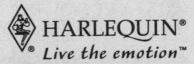

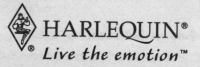

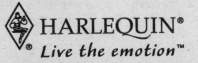